For my Best Friend:

Taylor Swift, bad TV,
Making me laugh, annoying me.
Giving me stubbornness to succeed,
Encouraging me to read.

Proof-reading my work (however long),
Helping me realise when I am wrong.
Proving there's no limit to what I can do,
Mum. I wouldn't be here without you.

PROLOGUE

9th October 1945

Dear Angeline,

I am unsure why it takes writing your name for me to feel content. I wonder if perhaps you are facing the same unrest that I am. Are you? Are you happy in London?

Autumn is here. The leaves are turning all shades of brown now, I can see my breath in the mornings and the apples in the orchard are ready for picking. The horses are doing splendid, I have added extra insulation in the stables to keep them warm during autumn and winter. I think they miss Florence grooming them every day. I don't have time.

There is a lot for me to do on the farm. Mother tries to help where she can, but I can tell she aches when she lifts something. Isn't aging terrible? A few soldiers have returned home, and we were hoping they would be able to assist us, but a lot of them are injured. Armless and legless. Sometimes both.

The patch of grass in the courtyard where the boys used to play football has all grown back now. Mother is usually protective of the grass on our land but even she looks disappointed. There is no evidence of the boys left behind.

I think she liked having boys in the house. The reality that she doesn't have a son anymore seems to have hit her now you have all left. Just like the fact I have to accept I no longer have a brother. Or a father. I think about them a lot more now that you are gone.

Peggy or Florence would know what to do with us. My mother and I, that is. They would sit us down and tell us we need to start communicating again, but we were never particularly good at that. It isn't that we don't talk, we do, it's just limited to things like: 'Isn't it nice we don't have to stick cardboard on the windows anymore?' 'Could you go and get some food from Henry's?' 'It's getting cold again, isn't it?'

We don't talk about the family that we've lost, not just James and father but you, the boys, Florence and the land girls. It isn't that we're strangers now, I know we aren't strangers. But you aren't here, and it doesn't feel like home anymore.

It's a ghost town here, Angie. I want it back. I want you all back.

It's like you're everywhere around the house. It's like you died, too. It hurts to think about it. It reminds me of the day you left. Your cheeks were stained with tears, and I held onto you, wondering if a hug could last forever.

I hope being back in London is good for you and you can see all of your friends. I pray your father returned safely and that Peter got to give him a big cuddle, just as he told me he would over and over again.

You and I know there are things ~~I wish I could say I need to~~ left unsaid. Writing it down is evidence ~~of what we~~ and I do not want somebody to find this letter. Goodness, it feels like you are back on the farm and Scary Mary is lurking in every corner trying to catch us out. But I kept you safe then and, even with you miles away from me, I will continue to do the same.

I miss it, I miss you.
Dorothea

21st October 1945

Dear Dorothea,

Your words have reduced me to a puddle of tears; I apologise if that was not your intention. I hope you know how much I wish I could have stayed with you. Leaving was the last thing in the world I wanted to do. I still feel your arms around me, so I like to think our hug will last forever. But I can also smell the smoke coming from the train, everything about the day I left is so vivid. And I hate it.

We miss you so much. Charles cries a lot and I have to hold him and try not to cry too. I always fail. On reflection, he left home aged four and came back as a seven-year-old, so it's not surprising that he doesn't remember much about London. Wales was his home for almost half of his life. As for the older boys, they seem happy enough, but I think they miss the grass to play on. I had never noticed how much London lacks greenery.

Some places here are almost unrecognisable. It seems a lot greyer now and there's lots of rubble on the streets. The air feels thick in my lungs, and I wonder if that's due to the bombing and the ash or the fact I'm used to breathing Welsh air.

I'm sorry to hear about the farm becoming so empty. I presume Florence and the land girls left soon after we'd gone home?

I always thought you were the heart of the place, but I suppose we were all the heart of it; that little family we made. I understand that you mourn not being a sister anymore, but you have the boys. You will always have

5

them no matter how far apart you are. You have me as well. God knows I need the reminder that I still have you because I don't have many friends here anymore.

It feels a lot like a ghost town here as well, even in the city centre. My father's returned safely aside from a broken arm, thank you for asking. It's been tense. Rebuilding relationships is tough.

Last Sunday, I asked him something I didn't think I'd ever ask. I didn't think it was what I wanted until I met you. I asked him if I could look into applying to university to study English. Mother thinks I want to apply so I can become a teacher because apparently, that's a 'woman's' job. It's nothing to do with jobs now. It's about me. I want to study English because I love reading and I'd also like to get better at writing. I'll be doing a lot of it since it's our only form of communication, for now.

Thank you for keeping the unspoken matters private, a busy household does mean your letters could end up in the wrong hands. I'm thankful it's only you and your mother in your home because I need to ~~let, I have to~~ tell you.

I miss your eyes. They were always so tentative. I miss the smell of hay and the grass in your hair, those dark waves that framed your face. That face that I held and kissed. I'm tracing your writing with my fingertips, all the swirly letters. It reminds me you weren't a dream.

I love you more than words can say. Perhaps I will find a way to describe it at university. I will look through countless dictionaries in search of the perfect words to explain how you ~~made~~ make me feel. Then I'll start earning money myself and I'll come back to you. I'll come back home. Can't you picture it? Try. Try to picture it and don't let it go.

Yours, always,
Angeline

CHAPTER ONE

Dorothea

In late November, the unforgiving wind would make her tears sting like needles as they trickled down her cheeks. Stubborn as she was, Thea remained outside trying to get used to the feeling, crying was a common occurrence, so she'd have to endure the pain. Sometimes there didn't have to be a reason, it just built up like a balloon being pumped with air until it suddenly popped. During the first months since she'd lost the Carters, Thea didn't let herself cry at all. She wondered whether that was why she did so much now.

She found herself on her father's old tractor, not putting it to use but rather using it as a bench, a sanctuary, a safe place. Thea wished there was a place like this that could contain her screams. Screams that she imagined were too loud to be let out.

Thea stuffed her hands in the pockets of the coat she wore, a thick material that no longer smelt like her father. She'd worn most of his clothes until they lost his scent; she planned on doing the same with James'. It seemed a waste, their clothes collecting dust and at least if they were worn, they'd be put to use, giving Thea a few days where she could feel close to them again. The way her mother's gaze lingered on the items made Thea feel somewhat guilty, but she never said anything. Her mother didn't say much nowadays.

She closed her eyes as her fingertips brushed over the contents of the pocket, the letters from Angeline that she folded three or four times just so she could keep them near her for the entire day. It wasn't just for sentiment, it was for safety. It was a miracle, in Thea's opinion, that they'd managed to hide for so long. Part of her contemplated whether it would have hurt less if they'd been split apart before the war was over, but it was ridiculous to think like that. They had been ever so lucky and 1944 had been the best year of her life. Because a life with Angeline was impossible, they'd never live in that domesticity again and Thea knew deep down, in the bottom of her heart, that Angeline would forget her.

Pulling out the last letter Angeline had sent her, Thea traced her graceful writing, closing her eyes at the idea of Angeline writing with Thea on her mind. She wondered whether her face would be as focused as it was when she played piano. Thea brought the paper to her lips with the whisper of a kiss.

"You'd like her," Thea spoke, voice booming in the quietness of the night.

She imagined her father leaning against the tractor, listening intently.

"You wouldn't be angry at me for it," Thea didn't know whether she believed what she was saying but she needed to hear it either way. "She was... You would understand if I could just tell you."

He didn't respond. Of course, he didn't. The lump in her throat felt bigger, felt painful.

"Listen to yourself," Thea spat. "You sound like a looney talking to yourself, talking to the dead."

The word felt like acid in her throat.

"You're *dead!*" She shouted.

There was no response other than the echo of her own voice bouncing against surfaces and coming back to her. She could no longer imagine her father before her, in his dirty old work shirt and his flat cap. He didn't die in the clothes he loved and neither did James. They died in a uniform, a representation of death and Britain. Stupid Britain...except he'd died in Italy, James in France. They were beautiful countries and perhaps they'd taken their last breaths during an April shower, maybe the rain made them feel like they were home again. She needed to know. She needed to stand there, on the ground where they'd died. Thea needed to hug her brother, to wrap her arms around her father's neck and sob uncontrollably.

"Why can't you just come back?"

Her words got caught in her throat. Thea knew what would have happened if they'd returned, if they'd found out about her, about Angeline, about everything. Mary had reminded her often enough; they'd weep and mourn the loss of a daughter and a sister. They'd lost her to sin, to the devil, that's what Mary had said. Now Angeline wasn't there the guilt remained at the forefront of her mind, eating her up. After everything Mary had said, all the kisses she'd shared with Angeline felt like a stab to her heart.

Thea was bleeding out.

*

"Where does this go?"

The stubby farmer with red hair was waving a rake in Thea's face.

"Well, it's not tack now, is it?" she groaned, wondering whether all men were that stupid.

"What's tack?" the man asked.

Thea pinched the bridge of her nose.

"Horsing equipment," she said, gesturing to the fact they were cleaning out the stables. "Shouldn't you know that?"

"Nah," Tom, if Thea remembered correctly, said as he whacked Short Stubby Red head on the back playfully. "Big Bill here just goes with the flow."

Thea felt rage in the pit of her stomach, she'd been trying to get them to sort out the back room of the stables for the past forty-five minutes and they'd barely got a thing done.

"Listen, if you boys would rather work on the fields, I will happily get on with this myself." She turned away, muttering under her breath, "God knows I'd get it done faster."

The pair scoffed, making no effort to disguise the fact they were laughing at her. The land girls, not even Mary, would ever mock her like that.

"Is there a problem?" Thea folded her arms, narrowing her eyes.

"You know for a girl, you've got one hell of an attitude," Tom remarked.

Thea nearly burst out laughing, turning away to hook up some saddles. She didn't register Tom moving up behind her until she felt warm breath on her neck, nearly jumping out of her skin.

"Seems like you need somebody to sort you out, huh?" Tom spoke lowly with his thick accent, tone suggestive.

Thea had frozen, she couldn't move from that spot. Never in her entire life had she ever experienced someone invade her personal space like that. Perhaps her father had kept her hidden from these types of men, but she was a woman now and she had to learn to deal with it herself.

"Please get away from me," she ordered, internally cursing the way her voice wavered.

Tom took a step back, holding his hands up innocently. Bill was smirking beside him like he'd done something to be proud of.

"Just saying, you're all wound up like a coiled spring," Tom continued.

"I'm just fine," Thea spat, trying to get around both Bill and Tom.

"He's only offering something nice, sweetheart," Bill replied.

Thea left as quickly as she could without breaking into a run.

It wasn't that she wasn't aware that things like that went on, Angeline had told her plenty of stories of men being too forceful. But out on the farm, miles away from Angeline or Peggy and without her father or brother, Thea had nobody to protect her. She had never needed protecting before and it wasn't like Tom had done anything too drastic. It just hurt to feel alone. Thea knew her mother would tell her to stick her chin up and get on with it, take it as a compliment. But Thea did not like being breathed on.

She headed back to the cottage, stopping when she saw her mother sitting at the kitchen table with her hair pinned up and her lips painted red. Her mouth was moving slowly as she breathed out words to herself, as if talking to yourself was a normal practice.

"I don't like the new ones you've employed," Thea cleared her throat, snapping her mother out of her daze.

It took her a moment to come back into the room.

"The new ones?"

"Tom and Bill," Thea leant against the kitchen counter.

Her mother hummed in acknowledgement.

"I didn't exactly have any other choice," her mother admitted. "We only had a few applicants as it was, and they insisted they had experience."

"Oh yeah, what experience was that?" Thea scoffed.

Her mother stared into space for a short while and then went over to the sink to rinse her hands. Her actions were pointless, they were just something to do. When the Carters had still been at the farm, there was always a plate in the sink to wash and dry but Thea hardly ate, and her mother only used a few dishes a day. It was just another reminder of how empty the cottage was.

"They didn't specify," her mother ducked her head.

Thea stared at the back of her mother's head in frustration.

"You didn't ask to see any paperwork?" Thea demanded.

"No..." she trailed off, turning off the tap.

"They could be criminals!" Thea raised her voice. "Heck, who knows if Bill and Tom are even their real names!"

"I saw paperwork Thea!" her mother shouted, turning to face her. "Just not about their work experience."

Thea folded her arms, chin tilted up in disapproval.

"I don't like them," Thea repeated.

"When will you realise not everything goes your way," her mother snapped. "Your father isn't here to make it all better and I will have no part in treating you like a child."

Thea kept her chin upright, taking the blow to her chest.

"He didn't treat me like a child."

Her mother's face softened, not quite enough to be kind, not with all the harsh lines around her eyes.

"He did. Because he wanted you to stay his girl forever."

Her mother dried her hands on the tea towel beside the stove.

Thea lowered her head, swallowing the lump caught in her throat.

"Well, at least I'll always be his girl now, considering he won't see me grow up," Thea faced away from her mother. "I'll be with the horses."

"Dorothea..." her mother caught her forearm before she could leave. "What did the men do?"

She looked at her mother's blue eyes, glossy with tears as they were almost all of the time now.

She had enough on her plate, some jokey nonsense some immature men sent Thea's way shouldn't have to be a concern of her mother's.

"Nothing," she cleared her throat. "On reflection, I was being silly. The men were just teasing."

Her mother sighed heavily, loosening her grip on Thea's arm. She grinned and forced a smile that mirrored the one Thea usually plastered on her own face.

"Men will be men. It makes it so much more wonderful when you find *him*."

Thea bit her cheek.

"And makes it so much harder when you lose them," Thea remarked.

"Don't be so disheartened," her mother said. "Just because I lost your father doesn't mean you'd lose your partner. Is that why you... Dorothea! You can't avoid marriage just because—"

"No! That isn't why. I just... I need time to grieve."

For once her mother didn't press her about the uncomfortable subject. Thea felt guilty when she used her father and brother's death to avoid romantic involvement. But Thea just couldn't bring herself to even begin talking to a man— she was a terrible liar as it was. Sure, there'd be men that were too focused on their own desire to realise that Thea wasn't happy, but how could she live like that?

So, if Thea had to use her grief to avoid marriage, she would.

Her mother didn't need to know that when that excuse ended, she'd still be avoiding it forever. Because in Thea's fantasies, in an impossible world; she didn't need a man to be whole. She had Angeline.

CHAPTER TWO

<u>Angeline</u>

With the final benediction said, Angeline let out a heavy sigh of relief. Her throat was a little sore from all the singing. Glancing over at the congregation, she could see her father sitting on the front pews that were reserved for the richer families. He checked his pocket watch before looking at Angeline expectantly. Singing in the choir had always been a huge part of Angeline's life in London before the war and even now as she bordered on the age of nineteen, she still sang every weekend with her chatty childhood best friend, Charity Smith.

"I could physically feel your father getting more anxious as the service went on," Charity whispered with a giggle as they took off the robes in one of the back rooms of the church, replacing them with their coats.

Angeline wore her light-blue short coat and Charity wore her wrap trench coat. Charity's was prettier, with a fancy brooch, Angeline found herself growing a little jealous of Charity's clothes sometimes.

"He's so angry at the moment. It's like walking on eggshells with him," Angie sighed, pouting as she gestured to Charity. "That's a beautiful brooch."

"Oh, this?" Charity looked down at it with her nose crinkled. "It's older than Reverend Johnson."

Angeline laughed half-heartedly as they hung up their cassocks and went to meet their families.

"Angeline!" she paled a little at her father's booming voice.

"When your father's face isn't as red as a tomato and you haven't got a busy day ahead of you, we should go shopping," Charity smiled as they approached the front of the church.

"That sounds lovely," Angie ducked her head as she approached her parents and brothers, Charity finding her own.

"You take forever, gossiping like old—" her father began.

"Robert," Angie's mother cut in, though cautiously. "It's good that Angeline is talking to her friends again."

Since returning to London, Angeline had found it hard to adapt to the new way things were. Friends hadn't been at the top of her priority list but, eventually, she'd rekindled her friendship with Charity. Ultimately, she'd needed as a distraction from... everything.

"Right. Very well then," her father turned away.

William gave Angie a sympathetic look, to which she responded with a smile. It wasn't that she'd expected her father to be all sunshine and rainbows

18

when he returned from war; she'd certainly anticipated he'd be different. Just not quite to this extent. He was angry even at the best of times, especially with Angie.

With Peter practically stepping on their father's ankles, Charles holding onto their mother's hand, Michael walking ahead and William beside Angie, the Carters headed back home.

"You sang pretty as always, Angie," Charles turned his head to flash her a grin.

Charles seemed to smile at every chance he got now he'd started losing his teeth. It always made something in Angie's gut twist; it was nothing but a reminder of how much he'd grown up.

"Thank you," Angie managed. "Mother, did you see Charity's pretty coat?"

"The one with the belt?" she asked.

"Yes, it's lovely," Angie sighed. "I'd love a coat like that."

Her father shot her an angry glance.

"I've just paid for your first term at university. You're not getting a silly coat," he snapped.

"I-I know!" Angie stuttered with wide eyes. "But I-I will pay you back for university. It's a loan."

"I'm fully aware of what the document says, Angeline," he spat.

"Well then stop making me feel guilty about it!"

Her mother's face paled significantly, and they stopped on the pavement. Her father faced Angie, a stern finger pointed in her face.

"We've talked about this attitude, Angeline. I will complain about the loan as much as I like, until you pay it back. And money wouldn't be an issue if you just got married."

Angeline stared at him for a moment, his serious expression didn't falter. Angie burst out laughing.

"You still think people marry for money?" she chuckled.

He grabbed her wrist firmly silencing her.

"That's all marriage is," he said, his voice no longer laced with anger or impatience.

He knew he was in control.

Her mother's eyes were darting around, checking nobody was watching. Her father was admired now, a person of interest to the rich. The Carters were climbing back up the social ladder, and it appeared that their reputation was more important to her mother than Angie being unfairly shouted at.

"Father, I'm only eighteen."

"I got married for the first time at twenty," he snapped before clearing his throat and standing up straight. "So, let's view it as a condition. You can go to university as planned if you start to consider... other options."

Angie stared at him, tears brewing in her eyes.

"F-fine."

"Wonderful," her father smiled as he checked his watch again. Angie wanted to smash it with a hammer. "Ah, it's almost eleven."

"What time are the Clark's arriving?" her mother asked timidly.

Her own mother hadn't even defended her, Angie thought with a deep sadness. Neither had her brothers, but that was to be expected. The thing with the boys was no matter how poorly their father behaved, they always had an instinctive desire to impress him and follow his orders.

"Two," her father said. "I'd like you to meet their son, Angeline. I think you'll like him very much."

Angie had to duck her head, so her father didn't see her scowl. Evidently, when her father wanted her to 'consider options', he didn't mean she could explore the possibilities herself, he meant that he would choose for her.

Angie couldn't stop frowning, so she kept her head low, watching the streets of London as they walked home. Some buildings were still being re-built and there was excess rubble scattered on streets in poorer areas. Approaching their own street, Angie acknowledged how it had been mostly removed of debris and the houses that had needed fixing had been fixed already. The streets of the working class remained filthy. It made her sick to the stomach.

"What are we wearing for lunch, father?" William asked as they reached the house.

"Oh, I almost forgot to mention, you boys will be going out whilst we have lunch."

The door was opened by Maria, one of the only maids Angie knew from before the war. The other few were newly employed, thanks to her father's army pension.

Michael turned his nose up at the prospect of missing lunch with the Clarks. Angie thought she would give anything to swap places with him.

"But there are macaroons and teacakes!" he whined.

"We'll save you some, darling," Angie's mother promised.

"Yes, we will." Angie's father faced Maria as she took their coats, "Take Angeline upstairs to dress properly."

Angie furrowed her brow and looked down at her dress. It was one of her favourites, cream with buttons down the centre.

"I'm in my Sunday best," Angie protested.

Her father didn't even acknowledge her talking, Angie tried to glance at her mother with pleading eyes, but she'd turned her back on her.

"Come with me, Miss," Maria smiled.

Maria had beautiful dark features and deep brown eyes. Recently, her face had been the only one that seemed to show her an expression of kindness.

"I bet you're excited," Maria said as they headed upstairs.

Angie nearly laughed.

"Not really."

"Oh, but I've heard he's ever so handsome!" Maria said as she opened Angie's wardrobe.

"Who's handsome?"

"George, I think his name is," Maria held up a navy-blue dress, looked at Angie and shook her head before hanging it back up again.

"I have no interest in talking to somebody to help my father with business."

Maria inspected her with a sympathetic expression before taking out a deep red dress and closing the wardrobe.

"It's just what happens, I suppose," Maria shrugged.

"But I thought... with letting me go to university that perhaps he'd let me have some independence," Angie sighed.

Maria handed her some horribly scratchy-looking undergarments.

"I am not wearing those."

"They're in season! Brand new! You're rather stubborn nowadays, love. I remember a little girl who was always on her best behaviour."

Angie took the items grudgingly, as well as the dress, slipping behind her room divider to get changed.

"You're right. I wasn't like this... before," Angie agreed.

"And what changed?" Maria asked from the other side of the folding screen.

Angie froze before slipping on the red dress. She closed her eyes tightly and could almost feel a hand on her bare shoulder, a kiss behind her ear. *Thea.*

"Angeline?" Maria called when she'd be quiet for a while.

Angie came out from behind the screen, turning around for Maria to do up the buttons of her dress.

"I'm not sure. I suppose I'm stubborn because I know my worth," Angie lied.

"Well," Maria said, "there isn't anything wrong with being stubborn."

"We're women. Of course, there's something wrong with being stubborn," Angie laughed.

Maria opened her mouth to respond but no words seemed to come.

"What do you know about the Clarks then?" Angie asked reluctantly.

Maria did her make-up and told her everything she knew about the wealthy family that were coming for lunch. Angie dreaded the typical, boring conversations they were to have. She knew it was, according to society, time for her to meet a man.

Charity and Angie often went to get milkshakes at the local café. Charity would tell her all about the boys she'd been seeing, seemingly a new one every week. It didn't sound entirely unpleasant, being taken to see films at the cinema and going to dance halls. But there was a part that Angie dreaded, and Charity revelled in, holding hands, touching, *kissing*. She was too scared to find out whether it would live up to…

Don't think about it, pretend it didn't happen.

"Now, don't you look pretty as a peach!" Maria gasped excitedly when she'd finished, bringing Angie back to the present.

She looked at her reflection; pink lips, cheeks appearing soft with powder that hid her freckles, eyes dark with mascara.

"Thank you."

Angie ducked her head, she couldn't look. It was all so different, so wrong. This wasn't what Angie wanted and yet she couldn't open her mouth and say *no. No, father. I don't want to meet a man because I love somebody else.* Somebody she couldn't be with, somebody who was miles away, somebody that wasn't from a rich family, somebody that was a girl.

"I think you're ready!" Maria squealed excitedly.

No. No, I'm not. Angie wanted to scream until her lungs stung and she'd deafened everybody in London.

"Yes," Angie met her own eyes in the mirror. "Yes, I am."

CHAPTER THREE

Dorothea

The walk to the village dragged nowadays. The cobblestone streets seemed endless, and each step made her ache. It wasn't that Thea was physically exhausted, her body was used to hours of manual labour a day. It seemed that her emotional state was what was tiring her.

The streets were swamped. Despite the war casualties, there appeared to be even more people than before. Thea loved the tranquillity of Wales, but now it was disrupted. She stormed through town with a scowl on her face. Fredrick from the butchers waved, as did the baker's wife. Thea didn't smile or wave back. Nobody questioned her abruptness, and that was how she preferred it. At first, once everyone realised that James and Arthur Miller had not returned from war, she'd been overwhelmed with best wishes and sympathy. The fake smiles she forced had drained her.

There was only one person whose comfort Thea actually appreciated after the Carters had returned to the city.

Thea's brother loved women. But she knew his love for most of them didn't go any deeper than an appreciation for their bodies. Judy Tucker had been an exception. She was a pretty girl; shoulder-length, blonde hair, piercing blue eyes, and a dimple on her right cheek. One thing that differentiated her from the many women James courted, was that she wasn't just for fun. Thea could see it in the way James had spoken about her and from the sparkle of pride in his eyes when he'd introduced her to their parents. James loved Judy. Well, James *had* loved her.

Thea liked her, which was also different. Thea usually hated the women her brother spoke to, or he wouldn't be talking to them long enough for Thea to meet them. A lot of the time Thea already knew them, because they were the girls that had teased Thea relentlessly in school, though she'd never said a thing to James. But Judy wasn't like those girls. She was polite, family-orientated, and rather timid.

Thea met up with Judy on Saturdays, outside the old, abandoned church with ivy crawling up the old sandstone bricks. Thea always spotted her in the distance before she approached her; with her head hung low as she held a black umbrella above her head, looking like she'd just come from a funeral.

"Hello," Thea called, grabbing her attention.

Judy looked up, smiling ever so slightly as Thea approached her. Thea wondered whether it took heroic effort for her to smile nowadays as well.

Judy made a polite comment about the poor weather, provoking Thea to look up at the sky, clouded with grey. It felt like everything was dark these days, so she'd barely noticed the dimness.

There was always a slight awkwardness between them; two people hurting, trying to comfort each other, two people forced to be friends due to circumstances. It wasn't that Thea didn't like Judy, she just didn't actively *seek* friends.

Judy took down her umbrella. Thea thought she used it like a shield, so people wouldn't try and talk to her as she passed through town, rather than a method of keeping the rain off her. It was barely spitting anyway.

"How's your mother?" Judy asked as they began walking past the old church, on a path headed through some fields.

"Well, you know her," Thea managed a smile.

"I wish I knew her better," Judy admitted, "James only invited me around a couple of times. That's probably why Mrs Miller doesn't take me seriously."

Thea pouted.

"I suppose my mother didn't know how close you two were," Thea said. "James was very precious of you. He's always been like that; finds something good and doesn't want to share it."

Judy looked down, fiddling with her bare ring finger on her left hand. Thea swallowed.

"He was like that," Judy sighed. "He went on about how much he wanted to marry me."

Thea understood her brother's motive, the instinct to make what you love yours, forever. Despite not understanding marriage until recently, Thea understood why people wanted the sacrament so desperately.

She would have married Angie if she could have.

"He loved you," Thea told her as they came up to a field of sheep.

Judy lowered her hand, holding her head up with a teary smile as she watched the sheep wander around the field carelessly, freely. It was difficult to not feel jealous of them. Of course, they had a deadly fate, but they didn't have to live their lives in fear, oblivious to their impending doom.

"So much lost," Judy whispered.

Thea ached to hug the poor girl, who was shivering, but not from the cold. Judy wiped her eyes and shook her head.

"I'm being so selfish, goodness," Judy said. "I'm here crying over your brother, as if you haven't lost him too. And your father! Oh, I'm so sorry..."

"No," Thea watched her with a sincere stare. "It's a different kind of love, Judy. You were going steady for almost a year."

I fell in love within a month, Thea ached to say, *I know how you feel.*

Judy folded her arms around herself. She looked so small in her dress and coat, like a child swamped in adult clothes and adult feelings.

"You seem to understand it better than my own family does," Judy bit her bottom lip. "My mother tells me I'm being selfish and that I'm lucky my father returned and that I should stop pining for some boy."

Thea nodded in understanding, leaning against a fence.

"I can't even bring myself to see my friends," Judy practically whimpered.

"That's alright," Thea smiled sympathetically, "just take your time and—"

"You could come with me!" Judy interrupted. "We could meet my friends together. Oh, Dorothea, I'd feel so much more relaxed if you were there with me."

Thea's eyes widened as she hadn't anticipated *that*.

"Okay," Thea blurted out. *Why?! Why did she say that?!*

"Thank you!"

Judy hugged her unexpectedly and nearly knocked her off her feet. Thea realised it was the first hug she'd had in months. She went limp.

"Great!" Judy said, leaning out. "How's next Tuesday?"

"Fine," Thea replied without thinking.

She was terrified because Thea couldn't *do* friends, Thea didn't *have* friends.

"We're going to see a film, I think," Judy continued, appearing visibly brighter as they started walking back into the village.

"Sounds exciting," Thea said.

Her palms were sweating, her heart was racing. But perhaps making Judy feel better would send her on the way to feeling brighter too. That's what she hoped, anyway. All Thea seemed to do was hope.

*

Clothes. Thea scanned her wardrobe, frowning at the dull colours, all greys and greens and browns. *What did normal women wear?* She didn't own a dress or a skirt, and it soon dawned on her that she'd have to ask her mother. Which, considering the lack of conversations between them, wasn't ideal. She'd hoped she could sneak out to the cinema without her mother questioning it, but that now seemed impossible.

"Mother!" Thea called from upstairs.

There was no response.

"MOTHER!"

"Goodness, Dorothea!" Her mother shouted back before the sound of footsteps could be heard from Thea's bedroom.

"I need help," Thea mumbled as her mother opened the door.

"Sorry?"

Unsure whether her mother had actually heard her, or whether she just wanted to hear Thea say the words again, she repeated grumpily, "I need help."

"You're going to have to elaborate," her mother said.

Thea held her arms out at the wardrobe in an awkward gesture. Twenty years old and she was asking her mother about what to wear.

"I'm going out this evening."

Her mother's face was a picture; eyebrows raised halfway up her forehead, mouth gaping like a goldfish.

"Can you just... can you help me?"

She stared at her from the doorway, her hands falling limp by her sides, eyes glossy with tears as she nodded.

"Of course," she croaked.

"Great."

Her mother turned away, heading to her bedroom. Thea didn't know whether to feel offended at the fact her mother knew she'd have no clothes suitable for going out in, or whether to feel happy that she'd saved Thea the embarrassment of asking to borrow one of her mother's dresses.

"Where are you going?" her mother asked.

Thea had anticipated questions.

"To the cinema with Judy and her friends," Thea replied.

Her mother looked like she'd cry again and Thea nearly groaned.

"I have a few dresses from when I was younger," her mother said as Thea came into her bedroom.

She glanced at her father's side of the bed with an ache in her chest. Her mother pulled out a pink dress with an open collar and a frilly-looking red one, briefly distracting her from the heartache. Thea scrunched her nose up in disgust as her mother laid them out on the bed.

"These were my absolute favourite," she said with a dreamy smile. "Wouldn't fit a leg in them now."

Thea rocked on her heels as her mother faced the wardrobe again, Thea hearing her unhook an item with a short gasp. She pulled out a familiar sky-blue dress. Thea held her breath as she recalled where she knew it from, the photograph of the Miller family. Thea and her father in their dungarees, James with his floppy mop of curly brown hair, and her mother in the centre in that very same blue dress.

"Your father's favourite."

Thea glanced at it, hand touching the material on instinct.

"I'll wear it," Thea blurted.

"Are you sure? I have—"

"Yes," Thea interrupted, "I like this one."

Thea took the hanger from her mother, nearly tripping over her feet as she stumbled to her bedroom, clumsily closing the door, and slipping it on. After a while of trying to fasten the buttons by herself, her mother spoke up from behind the wood of her door.

"Need any help?" she asked.

Thea muttered a response and her mother looked like she was about to cry *again*. Thea shot her a warning glance.

"There," her mother whispered.

Thea looked down at the unfamiliar item, the way it felt too light against her legs and tight around her waist. But after a wriggle around, and a tug of the sleeves, Thea relaxed.

"Oh, you look so beautiful," her mother rambled, "I'll just put a little makeup on your eyes, maybe your lips and—"

Thea wasn't listening to her mother, too busy staring at her reflection as she swallowed.

"I look like you."

Her mother managed a weak smile, instantly changing the conversation.

"I bet Angeline would revel in this," her mother chuckled. "All those times she asked you to wear a dress..."

And suddenly any positive emotion Thea felt left the room.

"Angeline isn't here anymore."

"Yes but—"

"If you want to do my make-up we better hurry up, I have to leave soon," Thea snapped.

Her mother didn't say any more on the matter as Thea followed her to the dressing table, where she sat on the stool as her mother got to work.

It didn't take long, her mother insisted that she didn't need much. Looking in the mirror, Thea could barely recognise her reflection; red lips, cheeks shaped with powder that hid her pale skin, eyes dark with eyeshadow. It all felt so different, so unfamiliar. But she couldn't just say no to Judy now she'd promised her.

"I think you're ready," her mother smiled.

No. No, I'm not.

"Yeah, I am."

CHAPTER FOUR

Angeline

Maria escorted Angeline downstairs into the dining room, where she could scowl at the endless array of shiny silver cutlery. The lunch wasn't anything special. Rationing was slowly easing over time, but still very prevalent. Not that Angie minded; she was thankful for plain foods. Anything too flavourful left her feeling rather ill.

"Your father wants you to sit here," Maria cleared her throat, gesturing to a chair on the opposite side of the table to Angie's usual spot.

"I don't even get to choose where I sit?"

Maria managed an awkward smile, rubbing her forearm. Angie sat where she was asked with a huff.

"Chin up, Angeline," her mother raised her eyebrows from the doorway.

This was nothing like the mother Angie knew before the war. Did this version of her mother even care about her feelings at all? She entered the room behind her father. He'd changed into a dinner coat and her mother into a long blue dress.

"A bit too much make-up, don't you think Maria?" her father shot her an irritated glance.

It took Angie a moment to realise he was talking about her, like she was a doll or a model in a magazine. Like she wasn't even in the room.

"I-I'm sorry, Sir," Maria stuttered.

"I can take it off," Angie suggested, trying to grab an opportunity to leave the room and compose herself, or just escape the lunch altogether.

"Leave it. Just sit up straight," her father demanded as the doorbell rang and Maria rushed to the front door.

Angie looked over as the Clarks entered, starting with a plump older man linking arms with a woman with dazzling features hidden by the joyless expression on her face. They were clearly the mother and father of this pathetic man her father wanted her to meet. He entered the room after his parents began greeting Angie's father.

The man looked older than Angie, and quite clearly took after his mother in terms of his good looks. His face was chiselled; cheekbones high and soft chestnut curls atop his head, but he had a pair of grey eyes that were lifeless. They seemed to contrast with his attractiveness. Angie could already tell he was a lost soul; brainwashed by a world of snobbery.

"...I'd like you to meet my daughter Angeline," her father said.

She was unsure of whether to stay sitting, so she just forced a smile, her cheeks aching with it.

"Well, aren't you a beauty?" the plump man said with an unsettling grin.

"I do believe it is I, who is of an appropriate age to compliment Miss Carter, father," the grey-eyed man laughed.

Angie's father laughed along with him, and Angie just stared at them in utter bewilderment.

Grey-eyes held his hand out to Angie.

"I'm George Clark," he introduced as Angie gave him her hand for him to kiss, just like she'd been taught to.

Angie prayed he wouldn't feel her sweaty hands as she grew more anxious. Thankfully, he let go without any question. The plump man and his wife sat down near the head of the table and George sat down opposite Angie, his lifeless eyes watching her like a hawk.

There was some awkward clattering as they all helped themselves to food, Angie content with just a few sandwiches.

"Terrible weather today," Angie's mother commented.

It took everything within Angie to stop herself from rolling her eyes.

"Yes, thankfully the rain didn't start until after we got home from church. Angeline is in the choir, you know?"

And so, the conversations began, the pointless chit-chat as lifeless as George Clark's eyes. Angie found herself staring into space as she ate her food, thinking of absolutely nothing because if she let herself think, she'd imagine herself back in Wales. She'd imagine herself cheerful again and she couldn't do that now, it would just remind her how far from reach happiness was.

"So, you were evacuated," George commented, Angie staring at him as she tried to remember what he'd just said.

"Sorry?"

"During the war, your father said you were evacuated with your brothers."

"Yes, to Wales," Angie mumbled.

She could almost hear her father in the back of her mind telling her to speak up, sit up straight, smile.

"I am not a fan of the Welsh, I must say," George's father said. "Their reluctance to advance is most unpleasant. It makes business difficult. And, well, they all speak some kind of gibberish."

There was a chuckle from Angie's father.

"I was worried when the children came back," her father grinned, "I thought I wouldn't be able to understand them."

The laughter continued and Angie pinched herself under the table.

"They mostly spoke English," Angie spat, unable to bite her tongue.

The laughter stopped. Angie would have been content if everyone at the table wasn't suddenly staring at her.

"Angeline gets defensive," her father cleared his throat. "She's still adjusting, she got attached more so than the boys."

Again, he spoke as if she wasn't even there.

"They were my family for years," Angie argued.

Her father's displeased expression became one of ferocious anger.

"And yet your brothers are just fine and you're still feeling sorry for yourself."

"They aren't fine!" Angeline cried, shoving her chair back with a terrible squeak across the floor. "Charles comes into my bed every single night and he cries. God, at least when we were there it felt like home. Thea—They cared what I wanted!"

Angeline didn't want to see the expressions on their faces, not that she could see through her tears anyway. She stumbled out of the room hearing her father's footsteps behind her as she ran, fumbling for the front door keys. She tried to unlock it but was stopped by her father's tight grip on her wrist, she dropped the keys.

"That's *enough* of this!" he hissed.

Angie sobbed, falling limp against the wood of the door. He grabbed her face with cold hands.

"Please don't make me go back in there, father, I *can't* do this," she cried.

He lowered his hands slowly, letting a deep breath out of his nose.

"We need to get you help, Angeline," he said. "This is not healthy."

She looked down at herself through teary eyes, her dress wrinkled from the fight.

"I'm not ready."

He watched her with a look Angie couldn't quite decipher.

"I'll ask the Clarks to go home," her father uttered with finality. "I want to see you in my office once they've left."

Angie nearly cried with relief as she scrambled to retreat to her bedroom. She lifted up her mattress and searched under her bed to find the letters. *The* letters. Usually, Angie tried to stop herself from looking at them, it was too risky in such a busy house. But she needed reassurance.

The letters weren't recent because Thea hadn't written in a while; Angie wouldn't allow herself to question why.

She tried to imagine herself at the farm, back *home,* as she read Thea's words with great difficulty, cheeks burning with red hot tears. Angie slumped on the stool by her dressing table mirror, following the words with her finger. Growing more frustrated at the blurry letters, she snapped her eyes up to look at her wobbly reflection.

Her face was stained with dark makeup, her lips still painted red. Along with her rich red dress, she thought she'd become everything that Thea had hated about her at the start. She was privileged, a simple path chosen by her parents. She was living a lie.

"I'm sorry," she sobbed.

The Angeline Carter from six months ago was gone without Thea.

Hearing the front door close downstairs, Angie shot up, fumbling to put her letters away. Anticipating a booming voice, the silence became eerie and the mutters from downstairs sent a shiver down her spine.

Part of her imagined Thea would be proud of how she'd stood up to her father, but another part thought Thea would have seen her as weak. She only had to hang on for a few more months and do what her father said, then she would be able to escape it all.

"Angeline?" Somebody spoke at last.

Not her father but Maria's timid voice from the landing. Angie didn't respond.

"Your father is waiting for you in his office."

Angie clenched her fists and stood up from the floor, where she'd found herself after putting all the letters back.

"Miss Angeline?"

Angie opened the door, tilted her chin up.

"I don't need you to escort me," she spat in a manner she had never once spoken to the maids before, especially not Maria.

She rushed down the stairs, turning the golden doorknob of her father's office without knocking. He was sat, all tall and mighty in his chair, hands folded across his lap as the fire in the corner of his office crackled. Angie sat on the chair opposite him, counting the abundance of paperwork spread across his desk.

The silence spread out across a few minutes.

"You didn't tell me about Wales," her father finally said.

Angie kept her gaze down.

"I told you everything you wanted to hear. I told you they were generous, I told you we were safe."

"And yet it seems there's far more to know than just that."

Angie felt her shoulders tense up.

"Angeline, who is Thea?" her father continued.

At that moment, Angie was convinced she'd cry, laugh, or both.

"Dorothea was the daughter of the farmer whose farm we stayed at," Angie explained with a wavering voice. "She's my friend, I write letters to her."

Her father hummed in acknowledgment, tracing his finger up and down a whiskey glass, Angie hadn't been aware he had. It wasn't uncommon for her father to drink during afternoons. Especially after he came home.

"You mentioned her in your little... outburst, just before."

Had she? Angie couldn't even remember. She'd just let her frustration out, and yet didn't feel any better. Sometimes consequences were not worth getting something off your chest.

"Well, we were very close. We were all very close. I miss her, that's all."

Her father chewed the inside of his cheek, a habit when he was thinking. Angie braced herself, pinching the skin of her wrist under the table.

"I think the issue you have is something simple," he stood up, taking a sip of his whiskey. "Denial."

"Denial?"

"You clearly cannot move on." Her father elaborated, "The war is over, Angeline."

Angie stopped pinching herself. Her father had no right to sit there, all high and mighty in his leather chair, telling her she couldn't move on. If anybody was trying to move on it was her; planning to start university rather than moping around and letting her life unravel before her very eyes with no input.

A part of Angie was still holding onto Wales, but at least she wasn't holding on to the life before the war, like her father. It was foolish for her to think he'd come back a changed man, thankful for food, warmth and a roof above his head. In reality, he'd returned more ambitious and more power-hungry, driven by money just as he had been before.

Angie *was* ready to move on, just not by marrying.

"I promise you, father," Angie knew it was pointless arguing, so she'd make a compromise. "When I return, after my studies, I'll be different."

His eyes narrowed. Angie could see the flames from the fire flickering in his eyes. He was issuing a warning.

"I hope so, for your sake."

CHAPTER FIVE

Dorothea

They were all playing a game with her. Judy was trying to tease her. Thea was almost certain that was the case. She was waiting outside the cinema and Judy wasn't there. Granted, Thea had left half an hour early and time did pass slower when she was dreading something. But Thea was convinced she'd been there for at least an hour. Unsure of whether she was happy she didn't have to socialise or be distraught because she'd been lied to. Thea leaned away from the wall she'd rested on, prepared to leave.

"Hey, Dorothea!"

She stiffened before rubbing her sweaty hands on her dress skirt. Well, her mother's dress. Thea turned.

She stammered back a greeting.

Judy was smiling, arms linked with two other women. So, they'd met up before coming to meet Thea. That was fine, they were friends who Judy hadn't spoken to for a while. It was understandable that Judy had wanted to prevent any awkwardness before going to the cinema with Thea. That was fair, kind even. So why did it make Thea terrified? Was Judy preparing them for Thea's terrible social skills?

The woman on Judy's right arm was watching her intently, the other woman was eyeing her curiously but being more subtle about it.

"This is Eileen," Judy introduced as she unlinked their arms, she then gestured to the other woman, "and Lizzie."

Thea grinned as she looked between the two, unsure of what else to say.

"You're right, Judy," Eileen, said, "she looks just like James."

Thea rubbed the back of her neck. James was handsome, so it was surely a compliment. Or was she implying she looked like a man?

"You don't mind going for a walk, do you? We're too early for the cinema yet." Judy changed the subject, clearly sensing Thea's discomfort.

They were early? Thea had to hide her surprise; she thought she'd been waiting for ages.

"A walk sounds nice," Thea said.

Following Judy and the girls further into the town, Thea nearly tripped over her own feet. Her mother had insisted the only appropriate shoes to wear with a dress were pumps or heels (heels was *never* going to happen). Thea wasn't used to wearing anything so thin and delicate.

"So, how have you been since it ended?" Eileen asked.

Lizzie was quite secluded, but Thea could feel eyes on her occasionally. She didn't want to question it.

"I've dealt with it," Thea shrugged.

The silence continued.

"Sorry, how have you been?" Thea blurted out.

Eileen laughed.

"I wasn't asking you so you'd ask me," she said. "I'm just trying to get to know you, Judy hasn't said much."

"I said a bit!" Judy protested.

Thea wasn't offended. If her and Judy didn't have James' death to bring them together, they wouldn't have been friends in the first place. They were friends because Judy wanted a way to stay connected to him, and it would've been what James would've wanted. But she hadn't known her brother all that well. Thea kept her eyes on the pavement as they walked through the town, trying to think of something interesting about herself she could say but came up short.

"It's alright, Judy," Thea assured her. "There isn't much to say anyway."

Lizzie looked back at Thea with an inspecting gaze and Thea's eyes locked on hers, narrowing in question. Lizzie turned away.

"You work on a farm, Dorothea!" Judy laughed, "Surely there's a lot to say!"

"I do chores, I tell some idiot men what to do, I eat, I sleep," Thea murmured.

"Take away the chores and that's an ideal life!" Eileen cackled.

Thea managed a smile, thinking of invasive Tom and his evil sidekick.

"What do you do, Eileen?" Thea asked.

It seemed she'd been waiting for that as she turned to Thea and flashed her left hand; Thea caught sight of the sparkling metal around her ring finger.

"Eileen doesn't need to do anything!" Judy scoffed. "Caught herself a rich one!"

Eileen gestured to her dress, Thea didn't really appreciate fashion, but she knew an expensive item when she saw one.

"You think I got this second-hand from *Molly's*?" she smirked.

Molly's was a shop in the local village, where Thea got most of her clothes from when she bought new ones, which was a rare occurrence. Thea liked *Molly's*.

"It's too colourful," Lizzie finally spoke.

Thea hadn't anticipated her voice to be so soft.

"Colour is in!" Eileen argued, "You're just old-fashioned."

"I'm younger than you."

Eileen mimed zipping her mouth shut.

They walked into the cinema with Thea tagging behind, feeling slightly more at ease than she had when she'd woken that morning, when she was too anxious to eat anything in fear of it coming back up again.

"So, do you like romance films, Doroth—?"

Before Eileen could finish speaking, she interrupted, "No."

"Right," Eileen said with wide eyes.

47

Judy eyed her suspiciously as they approached the cinema. Judy held the door open for everyone and then tagged behind with Thea.

"You know... you talk with me all the time about James," Judy said quietly, "If you need to talk about any men that you—"

"You misinterpreted what I said," Thea replied, "it's just my preference in film."

Judy nodded, joining the queue behind Lizzie to buy her ticket. With their tickets and two large boxes of popcorn purchased, they went into the screen. Judy sat beside Eileen, leaving Thea to sit beside Silent Lizzie on the back row. Thea looked down at the box of popcorn for them to share and placed it between them, clumsily knocking half onto Lizzie and some onto the floor.

Thea apologised, cheeks burning.

Lizzie looked down at the popcorn on her lap and then stared at Thea.

"I... you can have the rest." Thea handed her the red and white striped box.

She didn't say anything until the opening titles appeared on the screen with loud music playing.

"I don't like popcorn," she said, almost inaudibly.

"That's alright," Thea rubbed the back of her neck as Lizzie flicked the popcorn off her lap.

With Lizzie's eyes cast downwards, Thea could see her long dark lashes that brushed the tops of her cheekbones. She had some stray hair loose across her face, which should have looked messy but actually rather suited her. She didn't look all that frightening until her emerald eyes snapped up to meet Thea's.

"You realise you paid to watch a film, not stare at me?"

Thea's stomach plummeted and she cast her gaze to the screen.

"I know," Thea whispered, inaudible over the music coming from the speakers.

Thea would call herself a hypocrite if her confidence hadn't entirely melted away, because about twenty minutes into the film Lizzie was staring at Thea, as opposed to the screen. But Lizzie was scowling.

The tension between them was clear as day, Thea just didn't know *why* it was there. Eileen and Judy were friendly, and Thea hadn't had any issues with them so far. It seemed Lizzie was being deliberately difficult for some unknown reason.

The film had a slow start and Thea couldn't really concentrate on the storyline. It was something about a husband coming home to his wife after the war, which was undoubtedly why Judy had been crying on Eileen's shoulder since the film had started. Her sobs had subsided now, but she'd dab her eyes every now and then.

Thea felt too uncomfortable after a while, from Lizzie's judgemental staring and all the kissing that was happening on the screen. She stood up from the red chair, whispering to Judy and Eileen in the row in front that she was just going to the toilet. Judy nodded with a sniff and Thea made her way down the steps carefully, she'd had enough embarrassingly clumsy accidents already that day.

The bathroom smelt strongly of disinfectant and looked as if it had been barely used, along with the practically empty cinema. Thea concluded that people hadn't quite gotten used to the concept of post-war life. Of course, moving on from such a terrible time and getting back to life as normal was easier said than done.

As Thea came out of the cubicle to wash her hands, the bathroom door swung open. Lizzie was standing in the doorway in her dull yellow dress, hands clenched by her sides. Thea chewed the side of her mouth as Lizzie approached her.

"Your brother wasn't anything special," Lizzie finally said, breaking the dam.

Thea stared with wide eyes.

"I-I'm sorry?"

"Don't pretend you didn't hear me."

"Why are you bringing James up?" Thea asked as she dried her hands. "I don't even know you... I don't—"

"He broke Judy's heart, more times than I can count," Lizzie said. "She just remembers all the good stuff."

"I know... James was like that at the start. He changed. He loved Judy."

"Yeah, well he told me he loved me too."

Thea's eyes widened further, mouth parting. Lizzie was pretty, strawberry blond hair and a confident stance which James had always liked before Judy. It shouldn't have surprised Thea that they'd had a fling.

"I'm sorry," Thea ducked her head. "He broke a lot of girls' hearts when he chose Judy."

Lizzie let out a scoff.

"You think he *chose* Judy?" Lizzie raised a brow. "I wish he had. But he didn't. And I... and I knew they were together and I still... we still..."

"He cheated on Judy?"

"Yes," Lizzie's harsh expression hadn't faltered, she had no sympathy for Thea.

"No... he loved her," Thea stammered, "He changed. He was good... he was... he died a good man. A hero."

Lizzie's mouth twitched into a frown, and she shook her head.

"He broke my heart. And Judy is the only one that gets the excuses. She was grieving so she didn't meet up with her friends for months whilst I still had to. You think I was ready?"

"No..."

"Now I know you aren't your brother, and you can't take back what he did," Lizzie concluded. "But you deserve to know the truth, don't you think?"

Thea nodded, she knew she should be angry, but Lizzie didn't seem to be telling Thea for sympathy, she seemed like the type of person that would despise sympathy. She told Thea so she knew the truth.

"Thank you," Thea said.

Lizzie's eyes widened in surprise, and she watched Thea suspiciously.

"I was expecting you to hate me."

"Do you want me to?" Thea asked.

"No," Lizzie bit on her bottom lip. "Maybe. Perhaps I deserve to be hated."

"You aren't a bad friend, Lizzie."

"How did you know I was thinking that?"

"I just... I think we're more similar than you think," Thea shrugged.

Lizzie stared at her. This close, Thea could see the freckles that dusted her cheeks.

"Eileen was right," Lizzie whispered after a while. "You look just like him."

Thea managed a weak smile and through her squinted blurry eyesight; Thea couldn't help but think that Lizzie looked sort of beautiful. That she could look just like...

"We should get back to watching the film," Lizzie finally said.

Thea nodded, following Lizzie back to screen six where she could sit in silence and beat herself up for her thoughts. Her strange, wrong, twisted thoughts.

CHAPTER SIX

Angeline

Charity Smith was waiting outside the Carter's house. Angie hadn't shown her face in public for five days. She wasn't a particularly social person anyway, not anymore, but she had never avoided Charity for this long since coming home. She was Angie's only friend in London and, right now, it felt like she was her only friend in the world.

"Alright, now I am certain something is wrong," Charity remarked as Angie jumped at her presence.

"Goodness, you scared the living daylights out of me!" Angie gasped, nearly smashing the empty glass milk bottles she was placing on the porch.

"Why are you doing chores?" Charity's eyes were calculating.

Angie rubbed her hands together with a self-conscious smile.

"It's not really a chore, I'm just trying to help out."

"You have maids."

"And four brothers that need attending to." Angie shrugged.

Charity slanted her mouth, tapping her foot against the ground as if she was bored or suspicious of all Angie's responses.

Angie noticed Charity was in another dress she was jealous of, long and blue with white stripes. Angie's father hadn't even wanted to pay her university fees, so there was no chance she'd be receiving new clothes. Her birthday was at the end of the month, but she didn't think she'd be getting any presents. Perhaps at Christmas, but that was over a month away.

"I'm taking you out," Charity declared.

"Oh," Angie frowned, backing away towards the front door, "I'd rather stay at home, it's a kind offer— really— it's just—"

Charity tilted her chin up stubbornly.

"I refuse to take no for an answer," she said. "Come on Angie, don't start fading away again."

Judging by Charity's expression, Angie wouldn't be getting away from her.

"I don't have much money, I could ask the cook to prepare a picnic," Angie suggested, visibly deflated at her defeat.

"Alright."

Charity looked a little disheartened as her plan had probably been shopping. Angie held the door open and gestured for Charity to come inside. She followed, eyes widening at the sound of footsteps rampaging towards her.

"CHARITY!" Charles beamed as he ran into an unexpected hug.

Charity, after getting over her initial shock, grinned and hugged him back.

"You're here!" Charles rambled, "We're always busy on Sundays so we never get to see you after church! It's ever so frustrating; Angeline's *always* grumpy so she never invites anybody over to the house and all of William's friends leave me out when they come over and Michael is *always* grounded so none of his friends come over and Peter—"

"That's enough, Charles. And stop hugging her, you're squeezing her brains out," Angie tutted, pulling her little brother away from her friend by his shoulders.

Angie decided she would have to talk to him later about the fact he thought she was always grumpy. Angie always tried her best to keep a smile on her face, especially around Charles. It made her heart sink to know she'd been unsuccessful.

"It's just lovely that you're here," Charles concluded as he fiddled with his hands.

"Well, it's lovely to see you," Charity tapped his freckled nose.

Before the war, Charity would spend many long summer evenings on the porch of the Carter house eating jam sandwiches and playing dolls with Angeline, occasionally running down onto the grass to play catch with Charles. He often got left out when their father took the older boys out to play cricket. He'd been so little at the time, so Angie was surprised he even remembered

Charity at all, especially since it seemed he'd forgotten most things about their time in London.

"Who's here?" A voice called from the living room.

William trailed into the hallway, followed by Peter and Michael who were both smiling.

"Charity, what a surprise to see you here," Peter said.

"It really is! Angie never invites anybody—"

"That's enough, Michael," Angie hissed, her cheeks burning red.

There was an awkward silence, a familiar feeling. Silences weren't rare, considering all that had changed. Communication almost had to be retaught for some people and relationships had to be built back up again. It wasn't quite as drastic in Charity's case, but it sometimes still felt like there was an elephant in the room.

War was the elephant.

"You must stay for dinner," Charles broke the silence after a short while.

"She doesn't have to do anything," Angie snapped. "We're having a picnic and I'll be skipping dinner."

Angie went to take Charity's wrist gently and head for the kitchen when a deep voice halted her.

"What is this about skipping dinner?" her father asked, closing his office door before striding down the hallway.

It was typical that Angie had managed to almost avoid her family for five days and, now that she wanted to be left alone with her friend, they had all decided to show up.

"Charity came over, I suggested going for a picnic."

Angie prayed nobody would notice how quiet her voice suddenly sounded.

"Well, I haven't seen Charity in a long while," her father checked his pocket watch. "Dinner will be ready in an hour or so, why don't you stay?"

Charity tensed, eyes shifting between Angie and her father.

"I suppose we could have a picnic another time," Charity said. "Late October isn't exactly an ideal time for one."

With that, her father grinned, catching Angie gaze for a second before heading to the kitchen to ensure there was enough food for an extra plate.

*

"I hear your father's business is going well, Charity," Angie's father said during dinner.

Of course, money was always at the forefront of her father's mind. Angie would have tuned out of the conversation if she wasn't so cautious about her brothers' making comments about her antisocial behaviour again. It wasn't that Charity would judge her, but she'd be concerned and ask questions about how Angie was doing.

Charity didn't deserve the burden of her secrets and she wouldn't understand as it was.

"Brilliant," Charity beamed. "It seems unfair that people like us are doing well for money, and yet we still have to ration."

Angie looked at the table of food. They weren't exactly in short supply, there was still enough for everybody to go to the bed with a full stomach.

"Well, it's all to do with how much the country can import and... well I won't bore you," her father smiled. "I understand your point."

There was a clattering of forks against bowls amongst the silence.

"Where's mother?" William asked after a short while.

Angie hadn't even noticed she wasn't beside her father at the table, she hardly said a word as of recently. The irrational part of her mind wondered whether it was because of Angie... if it was because she knew about Dorothea— but that was unrealistic. If Angie's mother knew what had happened in Wales, she would have told her father and Angie wouldn't be sat at the table. She would have been sent away to some insane asylum, or maybe prison.

"She wasn't feeling too well," her father cleared his throat.

"She's poorly?" Charles dropped his fork with a clatter on his plate, watching his father with worried eyes.

"Nothing bad, just a headache."

Everyone seemed overly jittery about illness and injuries; war had increased a fear of death.

"Send her my love," Charity said.

Angie's father nodded. He had a look in his eye that Angie couldn't understand.

The meal passed by achingly slowly, with bland conversation. Angie was shaking her leg under the table, which didn't seem to go unnoticed by William. They finished their meals, and the maids took their plates away, Maria giving Angie a brief smile.

Just as Charity was getting ready to leave, Angie's father raised a question.

"I suppose you're aware about Angeline's decision to go to university. She was accepted into the University of Edinburgh just last week."

Charity halted.

"I... I wasn't told that, no," she said.

Angeline felt fire shooting through her veins.

"I was going to tell you," she insisted.

"It's fine."

There was a moment of awkward silence and Angie was entirely grateful her brothers were in the other room, not there to make any comments. Angie only wished her father hadn't been there to bring university up. He turned away and went back to his office, smug, like he had the world right in the palm of his hand.

"Sometimes I wonder whether you only talk to me because we were friends before all this," Charity admitted, wrapping her arms around herself. "I'm the only one that puts any effort into our friendship."

"Charity, no—"

"They changed you," Charity continued. "I don't know who they are, or what they did. But the people you stayed with in Wales, they don't live normal lives like you and I."

Angie clenched her fists.

"This isn't about her. Them," Angie corrected. "This isn't about them."

Charity watched her with a blank expression.

"The Angeline I knew didn't want to go to university," Charity said. "She wanted to settle down with a nice—"

"You sound *just* like my father!" Angie snapped.

Charity jumped, as if she was genuinely unsure what Angie would do next. As if she had considered the possibility that her childhood best friend would hurt her.

Charity sighed, composing herself.

"I came here today because I care, Angeline," Charity said. "All of my other friends think you've lost the plot. I didn't think they were actually right."

"You think I'm crazy because I want to go to university?" Angie laughed. "That's just—"

"This isn't about that!" Charity pinched the bridge of her nose. "This is about you staring into space when people talk to you. It's about the way you ignore me for weeks. The way you haven't said a thing about what happened in Wales. The way I look at you and I

60

don't see the smallest *hint* of the Angeline I knew before the war."

Angie let out a weak laugh, shaking her head.

"I'm not the Angeline you knew before," she spat. "So, get over it or just leave me the hell alone."

Charity backed away from her with an expression of disbelief as she fumbled for the door handle. She slammed it shut as she left, and Angie clenched her eyes shut.

All she saw was church choirs, her old friends, fresh lemonade, daisy chains, pigtails, ribbons, dolls, and Charity. All she saw was how far from reach it all was now.

And she cried.

CHAPTER SEVEN

Dorothea

Much to Thea's surprise, her outing with Judy, Eileen and Lizzie had been the first of many. Her usual Saturday walks with Judy usually turned into a walk with Eileen as well. Granted, Eileen would be the one talking the most, but it didn't matter to Thea in the slightest. It felt as though a weight had lifted off her shoulders, with the uncertainty of what to say, gone. If an outsider saw Eileen, Judy, and Thea on Saturdays, they wouldn't suspect two of them were grieving.

Lizzie didn't show up very often. When she did, she wouldn't stay long and her gaze was always fixed on the ground, like she'd turn to stone if she made eye contact with anybody. Thea didn't like it when Lizzie left.

From their conversation at the cinema, Thea assumed Lizzie had nobody to talk to at home about James and her feelings. Thea knew exactly how it felt to keep a secret, especially one that meant a hefty load of guilt would be sat on your shoulders.

When Lizzie did occasionally make an appearance, Thea noticed her lips always twitched into a frown and she clenched her fists so tight that Thea had been sure there were marks on her palm from where her nails had been.

It wasn't like there would be any benefits if Lizzie told Judy that James had been cheating on her. Judy had only just started smiling again and wearing clothes that weren't black. Telling Judy that her dead boyfriend had an affair with her best friend wouldn't do anybody any favours. Such scenarios made Thea wish she was as rich and careless as Eileen, winking at the men in the streets and flaunting her new dresses, entirely carefree.

Thea didn't have such luck, given her abundance of concerns in the world, which were mostly about preparing the farm for the frosty winter approaching. Getting men to cooperate with orders when a twenty-year-old female was giving them out, was not an easy thing to do.

"Tom, it's just a quick check of the pipes," Thea snapped when the man was complaining that she hadn't shared the workload out 'evenly'.

They were in the backroom of the stables, where Thea could get the equipment for Tom. But the man's dark brows pulled together.

"Yeah, and all Joshua has to do is move some pigs!" Tom argued.

Joshua was the new boy; he'd only just turned sixteen and seemed like he was the only person on the farm who actually did as Thea told him. He blushed and ducked his head.

"Between checking pipes and moving pigs less than half a mile, I know which I'd choose," Bill perked up.

"And which one is that?" Thea asked.

"Pigs."

Thea glared at Bill and pressed her lips together in a tight line.

"I give the orders around here, and you'd be listening to me if I was a man," Thea hissed. "Tom, you are checking the pipes."

There was a moment of silence before a vicious scoff pierced the air.

"Playing that card, are we?" Tom laughed.

Thea clenched her fists, nostrils flaring.

"Why'd you give Joshua easier jobs?" Bill cut in.

"He's sixteen!" Thea snapped.

Not to mention the fact his job wasn't easier in the slightest. Joshua didn't bother hanging around to listen to them argue. He slipped away to do his tasks. His feet crunching against the gravel outside was the only sound.

Tom edged closer to Thea. She didn't feel safe this early in the morning, when her mother was still asleep in bed, and she was standing alone in the backroom of a stable with Bill and Tom.

"Your morals aren't in the right place," Tom said to Thea.

"My morals?" Thea raised a brow, holding back the temptation to tell Tom she didn't think he even knew what the word morals meant.

"Yeah, the way you live, isn't it?" Tom's thin, cracked lips pulled into that unsettling smirk.

"Morals are more what one considers right or wrong," Thea was unsure what he was getting at.

"Someone swallowed a dictionary," Bill scoffed.

Tom's gaze didn't leave Thea's face.

"What I mean is that you aren't like a normal dame," Tom shrugged. "It's pretty weird how you want to be a man."

"*Excuse me?*"

"I told you once before," Tom stepped closer, right into her personal space, "you need someone to straighten you out, all you have to do is say the word."

Thea tilted her chin up, hissing through clenched teeth.

"You get away from me, or I'll sock you in the jaw."

She could see Bill in the corner of her eye, closing the stable door. Fear coursed through her veins.

"Will you? Will you *really*?" Tom asked in a venomous tone.

Before Thea could say another word, he'd got his hands on her, shoving her jacket down off her shoulders.

Suddenly, the touching abruptly stopped and there was the rustling of paper as Tom searched in the front pocket of her father's old jacket.

"Are these the letters you meant, Bill?"

Letters? Letters... *Letters!*

"You get off them!" Thea screamed and flung herself at Tom who was unfolding them, she could see Angeline's beautiful writing all swirly and perfect and for *her* eyes only.

She scratched at Tom, trying to get them out of his hands but he just laughed, and she could tell just how easy it was for him to pull them right out of her grasp. Bill grabbed her by her shoulders and held her still as she tried to scramble from his grasp, having no choice but to watch Tom read.

"Your words have reduced me to a puddle of tears," Tom began.

Thea cried out, thrashing against Bill as he tried to hold her still.

"I still feel your arms around me—"

"Stop it!" Thea sobbed, limbs aching with exhaustion from struggling.

But she didn't stop fighting.

"Sounds like we were right," Bill laughed from behind her. "I caught you reading them. Tell us, was he rich?"

Thea tried to hit him, but Bill grabbed her wrist.

Thea didn't believe in God. Even if he was real, Thea imagined that he wouldn't have much sympathy for her. She silently prayed for a miracle anyway, a miracle where Tom didn't get to the bottom of the page and see the name signed at the end.

"Alright," Thea whined desperately, "you made a point! You've embarrassed me, I'll let you choose your jobs from now on, or whatever you want just please, *please* give them back!"

Tom's eyes widened and Thea's heart plummeted right into the depths of the earth as she squeezed her eyes shut, anticipating his reaction when he saw who the letter was from.

"I miss the smell of hay and the grass in your hair... That face I held and kissed. What a poet he is! No wonder you—"

"What in God's name is going on in here?"

Thea's eyes snapped up to the door to see Lizzie.

Lizzie.

Thea hadn't seen her in weeks and to see her standing there was almost too shocking for Thea to feel any sense of relief.

That was until Lizzie flung herself at Bill, slapping him hard across the face. The man yelped, backing away from Thea as Tom dropped the letters abruptly and scuttled out of the stable. Lizzie brushed her dress down and looked down at Thea, who was scrambling around on the floor in a hurried rush to fold all of Angeline's letters up.

Thea's eyes welled with tears at the sight of Tom's grubby fingertip marks all over Angeline's words.

"Dorothea, you need to tell your mother."

Lizzie was talking but Thea didn't process a word she said.

"No, no..." Thea whined, hugging the paper tightly to her chest.

"Dorothea."

Suddenly, there was a hand on her shoulder, bringing her crashing back down to earth. Through teary eyes, Thea looked at Lizzie with her heart-shaped face and concerned, sued brows.

"They took them off me," Thea sobbed, folding up the letters into a tight square.

Lizzie looked down at where her hands were clasping the letters.

"Are they from your father?"

"No... not father..." Thea wiped her nose and sniffed, flopping limply against the wooden wall of the backroom.

"No?" Lizzie shuffled to sit beside Thea, her hands on her knees as she listened to Thea intently, prepared to soak up every word as though she cared. Maybe she did.

"My friend," Thea whispered finally.

"A boy?"

"I don't want to talk about it."

There was a beat of silence and suddenly Thea tilted her head in confusion.

"Why are you here?" she asked.

Lizzie's mouth fell open and then she closed it, then opened it again.

"I was thinking about what you said, I guess," Lizzie managed.

Thea looked at a spot on the ground she tugged her jacket back on, putting the letters back where they belonged.

"And what exactly was that?" Thea frowned. "We both know that you and I hardly speak on those Saturday walks."

"Not then," Lizzie said, "at the cinema."

"That doesn't—"

"That doesn't really narrow it down much," Lizzie finished Thea's sentence, tucking a piece of hair behind her ear, and swallowing before clasping her hands together.

"You said we're more similar than we think..." Lizzie said. "I think that's right... that you were right. So, we should definitely try."

"Try..." Thea pressed her to continue, raising a brow, her face feeling slightly stiff from the drying tears.

"Try to be friends," Lizzie concluded.

Her eyes were on the ground as they always were. If Thea had been in the mood for confrontation, she would have questioned Lizzie. *If you really wanted to get to know me, you wouldn't ignore me every time we're out with the girls,* Thea thought. And yet she was sat there biting back a smile.

Lizzie didn't strike Thea as a person who really liked having friends. Quite frankly, Thea was honoured.

"Not that I like you or anything, I just think you need a bodyguard from the evil men."

Thea let out a laugh, throwing her head back.

"Slapping men is my strong suit, I slapped your brother often enough," Lizzie chuckled but Thea didn't miss the fleeting look of sadness in her eyes.

"I think... I think I'd like that very much, Lizzie," Thea smiled down at her.

Lizzie didn't look up from the ground. But she was smiling too.

"And it might be nice to talk about something other than Eileen's fiancé," Lizzie said.

"Ah, so, this is entirely for your benefit," Thea sighed.

"Oh, absolutely," Lizzie's nose crinkled as she laughed.

Thea's heart felt lighter in her chest. She was overwhelmed to the point of shaking, but Lizzie was a comforting presence beside her. For the first time in months, Thea felt that there was a possibility of finding joy in her life without Angeline. But, suddenly the letters in her pocket felt as heavy as stones.

And she ached again.

CHAPTER EIGHT

<u>Angeline</u>

She sat with her legs dangling out of the window. Her bare feet were knocking together. The flickering lights in the sleeping city of London served as an aching reminder.

Back in her happy place, when the sun went down, the only light was that of the ghostly moon, which reflected in Thea's blue eyes like the ripples of lake water. There were no clear lakes in the city and the moon was hidden behind a thick layer of fog from the factories nearby. And Angie was alone.

The latter didn't bother Angie too much anymore. Company from her family was more a thing she dreaded than longed for. Her brothers didn't seem at all interested in their big sister; they'd called her 'grumpy' enough for her to get the message. Her father hadn't changed, which was part of the problem. But her mother had.

She had a face like stone, and she currently felt more like a stranger than her mother. Angie wondered whether that was how Charity felt about her, whether she saw Angie as a stranger now.

She'd gradually come to terms with all the change, it was inevitable after all. It didn't have to be something to fear. She'd start university as a new person in the spring term. Spring was for new life. It was about time Angie experienced a new beginning. It was about time she listened to her father and stopped dwelling on the past. Dwelling on a time when nightfall meant kissing under the blanket of darkness. When darkness meant love, because the stars and the moon kept all her secrets for her. For them.

"Thea!" Angie squealed from the edge of the lake.

Thea was drenched head to toe after jumping in. Her overalls were heavy with water and her dark locks stuck to her face as she strolled towards Angie. Angie laughed breathlessly and backed away from Thea so she wouldn't get her dress wet.

"You're going to catch a cold." Angie pressed her lips together, pulling a very serious face.

"It's one of the hottest days of the year."

Thea took a bold step closer to Angie.

This close, Angie could see her wet lashes and the water droplets that trickled down her cheeks, her nose, her lips.

"Well, it's night-time now."

"I'm aware," Thea brought a hand up Angie's arm, cold fingers caressing her skin as she trailed up to her shoulder. "My favourite time in the world."

Thea dropped her hand and Angie wanted to grab it and put it back. Her skin felt like it was burning with the desire to be touched.

Thea pouted, looking down at herself. Angie looked around at their field, their sanctuary, just to check they were alone. She was met with nothing but the night, the rustle of a calm breeze that warmed her skin. Thea's lower lip was trembling, but Angie didn't think she was cold.

"I've heard night swimming is better with minimal clothing," Angie said.

Thea hesitated.

This was new. Awkward. Thea's eyes had widened in shock.

"Or not, just joking," Angie laughed under her breath, a deep crimson blush crawling up her skin as she internally cursed herself for making the suggestion.

"No, I mean... I..." Thea stammered.

Angie squeezed her eyes shut and covered her face with her hands as she tried to block out the world. Part of her hoped God would choose this time to escort her to Hell. Angie hadn't considered the thought that Thea wasn't attracted to her like that. But they'd kissed. Was it possible to only kiss and not want anything else?

"Please forget I said anything."

"Angie."

"No," Angie mumbled into her hands.

Thea laughed. At the sweet sound, Angie dropped her hands and focused her eyes on a wild violet that was hidden amongst the grass.

Thea's fingertips were trailing up her arm again and Angie watched her hand. Noticing Thea's now bare arm, she followed it back to its source. A lot more of Thea was exposed than previously.

Now, she stood in her undergarments.

Oh, Jesus Christ, Angie was going to Hell.

Her skin looked paler now there was more of it revealed, but not in a sickly way. Thea was like snow, almost translucent. Her arms were toned, and her collarbone was as prominent as her cheekbones and jaw. Drowning in thick and heavy clothes most of the time, Angie had never had a chance to realise how feminine Thea's body was. Her waist was thin, and Angie thought she looked slightly too slim, because she could see a hint of her ribcage. She subconsciously thought about her own body and the undeniable fact that she carried a little more weight than Thea.

For a brief second, Angie considered running to the guesthouse to find Florence and cry about how much she longed to look thinner. Another option was to just sob at Thea and apologise profusely for the fact she wasn't as beautiful as other women. But, neither of those options seemed acceptable, because Thea was glowing. Angie was positive she was genuinely glowing.

And how could Angie walk away from that?

"Say something," Thea whispered, the sound jolting Angie out of her trance.

Angie hadn't registered the tears in her eyes until she felt them falling down her cheeks. Thea's eyes burned with concern and her mouth went slack. Angie considered blurting out all her concerns. But she settled for the easy option, the other worry that was always in the back of their minds anyway.

"Why is it wrong to love you?"

Thea reached out for Angie and lowered her head to press chaste kisses to Angie's forehead, her hands cupping the back of her neck as she pulled her close.

"The night keeps our secrets for us, Angie, nobody is going to know. Don't worry."

"I don't want it to just be some secret."

"It's not to me. It's everything to me."

Angie wrapped her arms around Thea's neck. Her feet lifted off the ground and she leaned against the brunette on her tippy toes.

Angie wasn't sure how long the embrace had lasted. She didn't care as long as the moon was still high in the sky. Angie brushed her lips against Thea's ear.

"Take me in the lake," Angie whispered softly.

"Angie," Thea leaned back, mouth slanted.

"I'm alright. I swear."

"We have time. It doesn't have to be now," Thea said.

"We don't know how long we have."

Angie originally had it in her head that the summer would last forever, but the days now blurred together in a haze of happiness, and all Angie could focus on was the present.

Angie ended the conversation by pressing their lips together, despite the fact her neck was aching from leaning up to Thea. As if reading her mind, Thea hooked *her hands under Angie's thighs and pulled her up, so they were level. Angie wrapped her legs around Thea's waist, and she held Angie as if she were as light as a feather. Thea smiled into the kiss and walked down the slanting ground, edging into the lake. When the water reached Angie, she gasped.*

"Cold?"

Angie shook her head, unable to form words as she moved in for another kiss. Thea stopped her, tilting Angie's head to the side so she could press kisses to her neck. Angie let out another gasp as Thea brought them deeper into the water of the lake. She could feel Thea's hands, finding their way to the buttons of her dress that was now half under the water.

Angie didn't mind, it was just a stupid dress.

Thea stopped kissing and met Angie's eyes, searching with careful intent.

"Is this alright?"

Angie let out a short laugh. She could hear her own heart beating, her eyes were burning with unshed tears. But there wasn't time to hold back, to be self-conscious.

"Yes."

Angie opened her eyes and stared out over the rooftops of London. She wished it was possible to go back in time and stop herself feeling so anxious.

It was the first and last time it happened.

The war ended shortly after, and Angie returned to London. They had barely spoken about it. It played on her mind. Was Thea disgusted by the sight of Angie's body? Was that the reason why she hadn't sent a letter in such a long time? Perhaps, if they'd spoken about it, it wouldn't play on Angie's mind as much. Perhaps then, she'd be able to look back fondly at the memory.

But it was one instance, and Angie tried to remind herself that it didn't sum up their relationship.

Angie hoped Thea still thought of her, just like she'd promised. Thea was convinced Angie would move on and make new friends, but the concept made her feel sick to the stomach.

She tried to dismiss the thought as she closed her window with practiced ease, tugging gently at the blinds before slipping under her sheets. Her bed was too soft, she thought she'd sink right into the mattress and suffocate. The beds at the farm had essentially been camp beds but Angie didn't find herself sleeping in her bed very often. Dozing in a grass field had been uncomfortable at first, but it seemed Angie had grown used to it. So, she'd have to get used to this again too.

Tired of thinking, and with sleep over-coming her, Angie's eyes fluttered closed.

CHAPTER NINE

Dorothea

Her hands had gone numb. It tended to happen when she'd been out for hours in the cold. She struggled to unlock the front door, never mind undoing her shoelaces. Just as she was about to stand on the heel of her shoe and kick them off without the hassle of untying them, her mother clicked her tongue from the hallway.

"You'll ruin your shoes if you keep doing that."

Thea just smiled.

It was frustrating, but at least her mother's complaining hadn't melted away like all of her other traits had since she'd been grieving.

Noticing her smile, her mother's brows pulled together.

"You're in a good mood," her mother said with a slanted mouth as if the words didn't taste right.

Thea hated it when people pointed things like that out, but she couldn't bring herself to care because her mother wasn't wrong. She had felt happier over the past few weeks.

Anticipating Christmas, Thea had suspected she'd be lonely at the thought of not only a Christmas without her father and brother, but one without the Carters too. But Thea didn't feel alone in the slightest.

Hearing the padding of feet approaching her, she felt her mother sit beside her with another tut. Without a word she started to untie Thea's laces, something she hadn't done since Thea was a little girl.

"Who do I have to thank for you feeling so chirpy?" her mother asked as she pulled her right shoe off.

"Judy and her friends, I guess," Thea rested her elbows on her knees, her chin in her hands.

Her mother's face was a picture, the wrinkles by her eyes crinkling and her mouth twitching into a smile. She looked so unbelievably proud. Thea hadn't seen that expression directed at her before and she wasn't sure whether that fact made her angry or overwhelmed.

Thea's left shoe was pulled off and her mother's smile had not faltered.

"Is there a reason you've come in so early?" her mother asked.

The reminder of what was happening in the evening made Thea's stomach erupt with butterflies. Not the good kind; the kind that made you feel sick with anxiety. They felt more like moths than butterflies. Maybe wasps.

"Party," Thea managed to croak out.

Her mother's eyes flickered with sudden concern. Thea stood up from the porch step and turned away so her mother couldn't comment on the look of panic on Thea's face.

"A party?"

"I can do it," Thea interrupted, stopping at the bottom step before she ran upstairs to escape the conversation. "I'm twenty years old."

"Whose party?"

"Judy's cousin," Thea replied. "It's a Christmas party."

She wiped her sweaty hands on her thighs before storming upstairs in her usual manner. She rushed around her bedroom, flinging her wardrobe open and scanning it for clothes that were suitable for a party. But, of course, there was none. Briefly spotting her own reflection in the mirror, she groaned at the sight. She was covered head to toe in mud and was dressed like a *boy*.

Thea shouted for her mother.

"I'll find you a dress," she replied, Thea could hear the smile in her voice.

Thea was finally acting as her mother had always wanted. Despite the anxiety Thea initially felt when she met new people, she was growing used to socialising. Meeting new people was nowhere near as scary as Thea had originally thought, and she'd found that she didn't mind the company after all.

Plus, she had a true friend now, even if Lizzie had insisted, she only spent time with Thea to protect her from Tom and Bill. Thea also had Judy and Eileen, but it felt less forced with Lizzie, since they'd both discovered they had quite a lot in common.

After walking with Eileen and Judy, Lizzie came by on Saturdays and kept her company whilst she did her chores. Tom and Bill avoided Thea whenever Lizzie was there, scuttling off like a field mouse when Thea started her father's old tractor. After Thea had mastered a glare that resembled Lizzie's, they didn't even bother her during the week, and they'd finally started to get on with their work.

Tom didn't bring up the incident again, undoubtedly fearful Thea would tell her mother about his invasion of Thea's privacy. Thea wondered what Tom thought about her now. Perhaps he suspected she had a soft spot for her long-lost 'boyfriend' from London. At least, she prayed he still thought the letters were from a boy.

Lizzie didn't bring up the letters again either. Thea found that, as time went on and she spent more Saturdays with Lizzie, Thea didn't think about the letters much herself either. After all, she was rather busy. She had new people to meet and a party to go to.

*

Thea regretted every decision she had ever made that led up to this moment. The moth-wasps in her stomach were back, making her insides twist and making her certain she was about to throw up on the dress. Not only would the stain and stench be embarrassing, but she genuinely liked the dress. It was cream with an open collar and a belt around the waist and had buttons

81

slightly off-centre. Thea wasn't exactly curvy, but she had a slim waist that she knew girls longed for. It was just a shame she was also too tall and lanky.

Thea couldn't help but feel like she was a sheep about to encounter a pack of wolves as her knuckle hovered over the wood of the door.

Was this even the right house? Thea looked at her palm where she'd written the address, the ink had smudged from her nervous sweating, and she couldn't read the house number correctly. That combined with the overwhelming feeling of dizziness and blurry eyesight made it impossible to focus.

"Are you going to knock?"

A voice came from behind her, and she jumped out of her skin.

Face flushing, she spun around.

"No...I mean yes! Yes, I am! Is this the r-right—?"

"Jesus Christ," the guy muttered breathlessly, looking Thea up and down.

"No, Dorothea," she joked awkwardly.

The man, with dark skin and deep brown eyes laughed. He was looking at Thea like he was greeting an old friend.

"You look just like him," he said taking a step closer to her as if to inspect her. "Your jokes are just as bad too."

Of course, people here knew James. Thea should have prepared herself for that.

They shook hands.

"I'm Sammy, James and I went bowling together."

Thea caught sight of the scars that crawled their way up his hand and arm. It looked like he'd been seriously injured from some kind of fire. It took a moment for the penny to drop.

"Thank you for your service," Thea remarked, hoping she'd guessed correctly.

Sammy withdrew his hand.

"He deserved to come home," he said, eyes sincere.

Thea hoped he couldn't tell that she was contemplating the truth of that statement, considering all the hurt he'd caused Lizzie and the hurt he would cause Judy if she knew about the affair. She knew he wasn't a bad person, and he certainly didn't deserve death, but Thea was beginning to question whether she really knew her brother at all. But all the same, Sammy's sympathy felt more personal knowing he had experienced war first hand for himself, and it was nice to hear something other than 'I'm sorry for your loss.' This felt genuine.

"We should probably..." Sammy gestured to the door.

Thea nodded and knocked on the door, the sound made her bubble with anxiety once again. The door was opened by a woman with wide-set eyes and thick blond hair. She'd clearly spent slightly too long doing her makeup, her face caked in powder.

"Don't you look all pretty?" Sammy flirted at her from behind Thea, stepping past her to kiss the woman's cheek.

"Enough of that," the woman giggled, batting her eyelashes before whacking Sammy gently on the chest and turning to Thea. "Hello, lovely."

Was this the point where she introduced herself? Thea opened her dry mouth to speak but no words came out. The woman was raising a brow.

"I– Judy," Thea managed.

"Oh! You're Judy's friend! She did tell me to look out for an anxious woman, though she said you'd be wearing something more... masculine."

Thea's cheeks burned.

"I normally wear trousers or overalls," Thea stammered, "I work on the farm. It's more practical, s-so..."

"Well, I think you look just fine in a dress," she smiled. "Judy!"

"Yes!" a voice slurred from inside.

It sounded like Judy alright, just slightly jollier. Tired? Thea couldn't put a finger on it. Until Judy swayed into view, holding onto the doorframe to keep herself upright.

"Dorothea! Dorothy? D?" Judy mumbled, "How on Earth do you shorten a name like that?"

She had lipstick smudged across her mouth, her dress was wrinkled, and her eye lids looked heavy as she struggled to keep her eyes open. She was undeniably drunk, the woman who had answered the door was laughing at her.

"I must apologise for the state of my cousin," the woman laughed.

This woman was her cousin, and she was just letting Judy humiliate herself. Is this what normally happened at parties? Thea wondered. She didn't suspect it was normal to have consumed so much alcohol one could barely stand before all the guests had arrived.

"You look lovely in this dress!" Judy reached out for Thea, tugging her inside and squeezing her cheeks before planting a sloppy kiss on her forehead.

It wasn't uncommon for friends to do that, but Thea and Judy weren't that close and rarely showed affection. Thea's eyes widened and she tried to squirm away, but Judy wrapped an arm around her shoulders.

"Let's get you a nice drink," Judy slurred.

Thea was preparing for the worst night of her life as she was dragged into the kitchen. It was brightly coloured, rather jarring, with patterned red curtains and empty bottles of wine scattered across the counter tops. Other than someone getting some ice out of the freezer, the kitchen was empty, and it sounded like people had gathered in the room next door. Thea hoped the quiet room would ease her into the party atmosphere. But it was hard to relax with Judy, placing her hands on Thea's shoulders and shoving her into a chair with a bottle of beer whilst searching around for the bottle opener, still swaying, and holding onto the counter to keep herself upright. Thea's heart ached. She hadn't seen many

85

people drinking this much alcohol in her lifetime, only her mother who would pour herself an extra glass of wine when she was feeling sad.

"Judy," Thea said, her voice laced with concern.

"Dorothea," Judy mimicked, opening Thea's bottle with a drunken smile.

"Was this party a good idea?" Thea asked.

Judy sat on the kitchen chair opposite her, placing a hand on Thea's shoulder.

"You'll be fine! Trust me. You look so nice and I'm sure people will want to talk to you and—"

"I meant was the party a good idea for *you*," Thea interrupted.

Judy pulled her hand back, retreating into herself with hunched shoulders and an audible swallow.

"Why, what a silly thing to say," Judy said.

Thea tried to meet those sad blue eyes, but she was hiding behind a curtain of blonde hair.

"I'm sorry." Thea placed the bottle on the kitchen table. "It's only that alcohol isn't good for those who are grieving."

A strange noise came from Judy; Thea thought it may have been a cry until she looked up to see the woman biting her lip to suppress a grin.

"Grieving, what a funny thing," was all Judy said.

She stood, taking Thea's discarded bottle on the table before making her way to the door.

"I'd rather be with somebody who won't shame me for having a bit of *fun*," Judy snapped.

Thea watched as she stumbled into the room next door, hearing a cheer when she entered the room. Looking at an unopened brown bottle on the countertop, Thea narrowed her eyes, taking it as a challenge as she popped it open and took a big gulp.

Thea could have fun too.

*

It smelt like summer. Perhaps that connotation was too kind; it smelt like sweat, bodies, ale, and sickly-sweet perfume. The anxiety Thea had felt previously had evaporated into nothing but a small tugging in her chest, one she decided to ignore for as long as she could.

"So, you got any other siblings?"

Thea was conversing with a man on the sofa in the living room. She'd met the dark-haired fellow at the door earlier in the evening but couldn't remember his name, only that he knew James.

Everybody seemed to know James.

"I don't have any now, do I?" Thea snorted.

The taste of her estimated-seventh beer was unpleasant; overly bitter with a hint of a flavour Thea thought tasted very much like out-of-date fruit. The flavour wasn't half as bad as the bubbles that tickled the back of her throat, making her wince after every gulp. Yet, it was wonderful. Not the drink itself but the feeling. The bubbles made her float away and for once, Thea didn't feel like she had to float back down to earth. She could just hover above the world and watch the evening play out like a film.

The man beside her was pulling a weird face, his lips twisted, and his brow furrowed, as if there weren't any words in the English language he could say in response to Thea's depressing statement.

"No," Thea cleared her throat, sitting up in an attempt to compose herself. "I don't have any other siblings. Just Judy, who I suppose, had my brother returned, may have been my sister-in-law."

The man's face finally returned to a somewhat normal state.

"They really were sweet on each other, weren't they?"

The noise of the party came to Thea's attention as she pondered that fact. The sound of singing, Christmas music playing faintly in the background and flirtatious young men and women laughing at jokes Thea wouldn't find funny. She tried to come up with a response for the man but came up short. Could James really have been 'sweet' on Judy if he'd been cheating?

"Yeah."

Thea stumbled to her feet, suddenly far more aware of where she was.

The warm, floaty feeling was suddenly replaced with a desperate desire to escape as she looked around at all the bodies; Judy with a tatty Christmas hat on, giggling at a bloke with blond hair, Judy's cousin dancing with her cakey make-up that had stained the collar of her dress, all these... *people*... these people she didn't relate to. And all these strangers, an ocean of unknown faces. Who even was this man she was talking to?

"If you'll excuse me..."

CHAPTER TEN

<u>Dorothea</u>

Thea stumbled her way to the door, bumping up against some people that didn't even turn to see who was barging past them. They just drank from their bottles and glasses and laughed and laughed. *What was so funny?!*

The bottle Thea clutched almost slipped from her grasp as she fumbled with the front door, throwing herself outside into the winter air. She stumbled down the porch steps, lungs stinging at the sudden change of air temperature. Thea couldn't breathe or—

"Why is it I always find you during a crisis?"

A voice! Somebody was finally noticing her; she wasn't just another face in the crowd. Thea would have let out a sob if she hadn't seen who it was.

Lizzie was standing at the bottom of the driveway with her white skirt flowing in the wind, her strawberry blond locks framing her face, a thick coat wrapped around her. Thea slumped against the bottom step, searching desperately for her voice because she was not prepared to humiliate herself.

"B-because I'm always having a crisis," Thea replied, wishing her words hadn't been so shaky.

Lizzie let out a gentle laugh, as if she was afraid too much noise would startle Thea. Thea saw how her eyes were glazed with concern as she approached her, kneeling to her like she was a child that had fallen and grazed their knee.

"You look terrible."

Thea ducked her head self-consciously, fiddling with the dress material.

"Yeah... I know. I-I don't like it either... it... my mother. Yeah... my mother forced me to wear it," Thea lied.

Lizzie scoffed.

"No, the dress is fine. I meant..." Lizzie placed a hand on Thea's forehead, brushing her hair back and studying her face.

If Thea wasn't cold and struggling to move, she definitely would have flinched away from Lizzie's patronising actions.

"W-what you don't l-like it when I got make-up on?" Thea sniffed, flapping her hands around drunkenly. "Don't I look like James as much now?"

Lizzie took her hand away with a scowl.

"What in God's name do you mean by that?"

Thea froze. The truth was she didn't mind, Thea knew Lizzie only spent time with her because she reminded her of James. If she'd wanted company, she'd be better off with Eileen or Judy, so the only explanation for Lizzie liking her had to be her similarity to James.

"First thing you said to me..." Thea rambled. "Well, the first *nice* thing you said to me was 'you look like him.' That's all I get. Nobody wants to know Dorothea, it's always 'Miller? As in James Miller? You're his sister! Woah! He was a great man. He deserved to come home.' And that would all be fine if he was a good person, but he isn't— wasn't."

Lizzie's eyebrows pulled together as she digested Thea's rant. Thea let out a frustrated groan, resting her head in her hands.

"You talk a load of rubbish when you're drunk."

Thea laughed into her hands, then mumbled,

"Not that drunk."

Lizzie watched her, no longer concerned but now slightly offended, judging by the way she'd folded her arms.

"You think that's it? That I'm friends with you because of *him*?" Lizzie asked.

Thea looked up, eyes searching for something in Lizzie's expression that she could understand. Thea felt as if she understood nothing about Lizzie.

"I like you, you're my friend," Lizzie told her. "James is... I've moved on."

The outside chill seemed suddenly warmer, either because Thea now felt assured or because she was verging on hyperthermia. She pondered on what Lizzie had said, taking quite a while to process her thoughts, which was new. Thea's thoughts usually raced around her head. Moving on was a strange concept when relationships made a person. Interactions with others were what made a person who they were. So how could somebody ever truly move on?

Angeline. The name came to Thea's mind out of nowhere, after weeks of silence and what felt like peace. Thea had practically forgotten those sun-kissed cheeks, golden hair, and golden specks in her eyes and golden... golden everything.

"Dorothea, hey," there was a hand on her arm. "You went away for a moment then."

Thea looked at Lizzie through teary eyes.

"I...forgot what we were talking about."

"You're drunker than I thought," Lizzie laughed. Surprisingly, it wasn't intimidating. "Let's get you home."

Thea went where Lizzie led her, her gentle hand on her arm pulling her up, then wrapping around her waist to help her stumble down the old, cobbled streets back to the farm.

"Y-you just got there..." Thea said after a long while. "The party... you should go back."

"I'm not leaving you like this," Lizzie replied, her breath warm against Thea's cheek. "Plus, it won't be any fun without Eileen."

Thea squinted, processing the name.

"Oh! Eileen wasn't there... where was she?"

"She's got a fever and a sore throat," Lizzie said. "Normally I wouldn't believe her, but this is Eileen, she'd

93

have to be very unwell to miss a party, especially a Christmas party."

Thea slurred, "Didn't notice she wasn't there."

Lizzie laughed; it was almost familiar how soft it was.

"Don't tell her that. Though, I'm guessing you didn't realise I wasn't there either."

Thea bit her lip as she thought about it, thinking too much made it hard to stay upright. Her knees buckled in slightly and the arm around Thea's waist tightened.

"I did think about you earlier, before I was drunk," Thea admitted. "I was looking forward to seeing you, but then I started drinking... loads of people and noise...had to leave."

Lizzie was watching Thea, something she tended to do a lot. Undoubtedly sympathy, or looking for similarities to James, or disgust. With a sudden wave of drunken confidence, Thea looked right back at her. Lizzie's eyes were wide with surprise for a moment but then they narrowed, studying Thea's expression.

"I hope your mother's asleep," Lizzie said, snapping her eyes down and continuing to stumble down the path to the cottage with Thea pressed against her.

"She sleeps a lot."

"Ah. You don't?"

"I'm in bed a lot, but I rarely sleep."

Lizzie's eyes widened; cheeks tinted with a blush that was visible even in the darkness.

"Who's the fella?"

Thea had to hold back a wheeze of laughter, except in her drunken state she failed to hold it back.

"I mean I lay awake, I can't sleep," Thea laughed. "No men involved."

Thea had never had much luck with men in general, not that she was looking for any. She had her fair share of decent family men in her life with her father and James, though she hesitated to include him. All of Thea's grandparents had passed away, her father's brother didn't keep in touch and Thea wouldn't be surprised if he had died at war. And then her mother was an only child, so no uncles from her side.

Men that weren't family tended to be overbearing and vile.

"I suppose avoiding them isn't a bad thing," Lizzie uttered, concentrating on the task of opening the gate to the farm.

Thea tried to stand up straight without support, trying to act sober as she fumbled with the lock. It was a weak attempt, she slumped against the fence and bit back a wave of nausea.

Thea gagged into her elbow.

Lizzie manoeuvred Thea over to a bush and looked away.

"If you're going to be sick," Lizzie gagged. "Please do it into a bush and don't get it on your clothes because I cannot stand the smell."

Thea batted Lizzie's hands away, swaying without the support.

"It was just a bit of nausea. I'm not going to vomit," Thea said.

Lizzie responded with a curt nod, any colour had left her cheeks and Thea had to suppress a laugh because this confident, stubborn, self-assured woman's worst fear was vomit.

For some reason, that reminded her of Angeline.

Thea didn't bother with the lock in the dark and swung her legs over the fence, stumbling onto the floor. That had never happened before. It took a moment to see the dress she wore had got caught on the wood of the fence, a big tear creeping up the skirt. Lizzie's mouth fell open and she leaped over the fence with an ease that had taken months for Angeline to master.

Thea didn't want to question why she'd started comparing Lizzie to Angeline.

Lizzie gasped when she noticed the tear on the dress and the mud that had splattered Thea's dress and cardigan. "Your clothes!"

"Your clothes," Angie had laughed breathlessly.

"What about them?" Thea teased.

"You..." Angie pressed her lips as she pulled a very serious face. "You're going to catch a cold."

Thea froze, scrambling to her feet as the memory came back. It felt like somebody had stabbed her in the chest.

The lake, the kisses, the secrets.

"I don't want it to just be some secret."

"It's not to me. It's everything to me."

96

Overwhelmed by the sudden emotion, Thea glared at Lizzie, her drunken mind deciding that it was Lizzie's fault she was suddenly reminded of Angeline. Beautiful Angeline, who Thea was forgetting when she'd promised she wouldn't, she'd *promised.*

"Don't you—" Thea slurred and pointed accusingly. "You aren't her! You don't get to say her words you don't get to…"

"What?" Lizzie's face fell and she held her hands up, as if she was afraid Thea would pounce at her like a wild dog.

"You're not *her*!" Thea shouted, though she sounded choked up as tears threatened to spill.

"Hey…" Lizzie's voice came back gently. She took a step closer to Thea. "Listen, you're drunk and confused. I'm just here to get you home safe, 'kay?"

Thea unclenched her fists, shoulders lowering. What was she doing? It wasn't Lizzie's fault Thea was suddenly reminded of Angeline; it wasn't Lizzie's fault that Thea hadn't thought of Angie in so long.

"Christ," Thea rubbed her hands across her face, sobbing into them. "I'm such a bloody mess."

She heard the sound of footsteps edging closer and felt a hand on her shoulder. Thea dropped her hands, looking at the wobbling image of Lizzie through her teary eyes. Lizzie held her arms out and Thea flung herself into them, hugging her tight.

*

A creamy light filtered through Thea's blinds. The curtains hadn't been pulled over, so the unfamiliar brightness must have woken her up, along with her unbearably dry mouth which she acknowledged as she smacked her chapped lips together. The previous night's events didn't come all at once but filtered into her mind gradually in fragments of voices and images. She thought of Lizzie's wide, concerned eyes, people talking about James, beer bottles and sickly smells of perfume. Yet the name that ghosted her lips was Angeline's.

Thea hadn't thought of her in so long, why she suddenly came to mind was beyond her knowledge. Because it wasn't as if Angeline had miraculously turned up, it wasn't as if Angeline would ever show up again. And yet Thea tortured herself for coming so close to forgetting her.

There was a rustle of sheets, a gentle sigh. Thea had her eyes closed, trying to overcome her impending headache. She was aware enough to know that she herself had not let out a sigh or moved an inch. Thea dared to open her eyes slightly, unsure what she was expecting but it certainly hadn't been Lizzie Thomas at the foot of her bed, a scratchy old blanket thrown across her sleeping form. In the calmness of the morning, Thea didn't jump up in confusion but instead opened her eyes fully to gaze at her strawberry-blonde hair that was fanned out across her forehead and the pillow she lay on. Her lips were parted, eyes only lightly closed which gave Thea the inclination that she wasn't a deep sleeper, just like Angeline. She rested on her small hands; her freckled right cheek slightly mushed against them.

The sight was suddenly painfully familiar.

Angeline's parted pink lips and rosy cheeks, when Thea was able to lie so close to her, she'd feel her warm breath tickling her nose and it would smell like the apple pie they'd had for dessert that evening. Back when Thea was allowed to press a kiss to her forehead, gentle in the hope that it wouldn't wake her girl. But she was a light sleeper. Her hazel eyes would snap open and focus on Thea before they crinkled as she smiled up at her.

"I can hear you thinking."

Thea hadn't realised she'd closed her eyes as she'd recalled the memory, but she sat up straight and looked anywhere but at Lizzie as she roused from the bottom of her bed. Thea didn't know how to find words, the questions she needed to ask. She rubbed her eyes, eyelids feeling heavy with makeup from the night before that she had not yet removed.

"I'm just a bit confused," Thea said.

Lizzie said nothing as she sat on the bed, teeth chattering now she wasn't under the blanket, still wearing her long white skirt and blouse from the night before.

"You don't have to go," Thea said.

Lizzie looked over at Thea with a gentle smile before standing and opening the blinds. Thea winced at the brighter light. Lizzie put her hand up against the cool glass of the window, Thea noticing the blanket of white on the Welsh hills that had caught her attention.

Thea regretted standing so abruptly as her headache decided to make itself very known. She hissed in pain as she stumbled to the window. Thea couldn't deny how much she loved snow, a childhood excitement that never seemed to fade. The pair stood, watching the snowfall for what must have been a long time. The fields were white with it and the sky was a warm grey. They let it pass, letting Thea gather her thoughts.

"I'm sorry about last night," Thea muttered.

She couldn't remember all of it, but the thoughts of her ripping her dress, hunching over with nausea, crying. It was enough to assume it hadn't been the greatest Christmas party in existence. Not to mention the fact Lizzie hadn't even gone to the party but helped Thea stumble all the way home and *stayed.*

"You didn't do anything wrong," Lizzie lowered her hand from the glass, wrapping her arms around herself.

Thea had to bite back the urge to find her a jumper to keep her warm.

"I ruined what might have been a nice night."

Lizzie scoffed.

"How would you have a nice night with so much to worry about? I don't even know how you stand each day, let alone a party."

Thea furrowed her brow, lips parting. *What had she said last night to make Lizzie think she was so hard-done-by?*

"I'm fine," Thea replied, still focused on the falling snowflakes.

"Well then you aren't human."

"So, what am I? An alien?"

Thea remembered Peter explaining his space comics to her, it didn't appeal to her but the way his eyes lit up at the thought of superheroes, monsters and aliens was precious. Thea tended to think of the boys more often than she did Angeline, because her friendship with the boys wasn't a sin in the eyes of society. Her relationship with Angeline had been doomed to end badly from the start.

Whenever Thea was in a vulnerable state, it was Angeline her mind went to, but this felt different. So many things about Lizzie made her remember the years with the Carters; the summers by the lake with Angeline who had violets in her hair, winters spent by the window as they watched the silent snow fall outside.

Lizzie's laugh brought her back to reality.

"I just mean you've suffered so much. Your father and brother passing, a whole farm to run by yourself, those idiot workers and—"

"And?" Thea pressed.

"And... losing whoever those letters were from."

Thea swallowed audibly; she hadn't brought up the letters since the incident with Tom had happened.

"You've lost a lot too," Thea said, diverting the conversation.

"That's just it, I haven't. Every Saturday I come and see you and I get everything that's bothering me off my chest and you just... you *listen*," Lizzie rambled. "Even though you have so much going on, you never say anything and I didn't even know how much you'd suffered until you were drunk. If that doesn't make me a terrible friend, I don't know what does."

Thea looked behind her at the bed as she remembered last night, stumbling into it with makeup and tears running down her face. Lizzie taking her shoes off for her and making sure she was safe all night, uncomfortably wrapped in a scratchy old blanket at the bottom of Thea's bed.

"Lizzie, you stayed. You stayed and that's enough."

Lizzie dug her teeth into her bottom lip. Thea could practically hear the cogs in her brain turning.

"You kept saying stupid things about me only being friends with you because of James," Lizzie mumbled.

"I was drunk."

"Drunk words are a sober person's thoughts."

Thea stepped away from the window, dizzy from standing for so long with a deadly headache. She perched on the edge of her bed, taking a deep breath in through the nose and resting her head in her hands, licking her lips as if it would stop her mouth feeling so dry. She was certain she'd never drink again after this hangover.

"I don't trust people easily, I'm sorry," Thea began. "I always think when people talk to me that there's always a reason behind it, I never think it's because they like me. I suppose growing up with my family as my only companions had its perks at the time, but now I'm just this mixed-up, awkward, twenty-year-old who can't make friends."

Thea heard Lizzie's feet approach the bed as she sat beside her.

"I do hate to break it to you, but you made friends with me," Lizzie said.

"Then you're crazy to accept."

"As an alien you have no right to call me crazy," Lizzie replied sternly.

Thea sat upright, a smile still gracing her lips as she looked at Lizzie's round, glossy eyes. Filled with affection and a gentle concern, Thea hadn't thought the Lizzie she had first met at the cinema was even capable of.

They both stayed facing the window, the individual flakes of snow building up on the rooftop where Thea spent so many summer nights. Summer nights that she needed to try and forget.

"You said something stupid last night, too," Thea thought out-loud.

A crease formed between Lizzie's brows.

"I didn't have anything to drink."

"You said you'd moved on from James," Thea elaborated. "But that's ridiculous, nobody ever moves on from a person. Relationships with people make us who we are."

"I meant I wasn't in love with him anymore," Lizzie murmured, cheeks reddening at the subject.

"With all due respect, Lizzie, if you don't love somebody forever, I don't think you ever truly loved them in the first place," Thea said.

"And you think he deserved my love after what he did to me?"

A flash of the aggressive old Lizzie made Thea's heart sink.

"I just mean that—"

"I really don't see why you think you're qualified to talk about love," Lizzie interrupted. "I bet you've never even slept with a man."

The tone of Lizzie's voice was almost venomous, the uncomfortable tension rising did nothing to help Thea's hangover. But Lizzie's face fell after saying that, lips parting and eyes softening. Lizzie wasn't wrong, so it didn't bother Thea. But part of her wondered whether it was that obvious, not that people would judge her for it, they'd just think she was waiting to get married.

"Oh, Dorothea I... God I'm sorry," Lizzie groaned. "I'm trying to be a better friend and I go and say stuff like that."

"It didn't offend me."

Lizzie seemed completely at war with herself, twirling a piece of strawberry blonde hair around her finger with her eyes darting everywhere. Thea didn't know how to break the tension, so she stood up and shuffled over to the bedroom mirror, retrieving a cloth to clean away her spoiled makeup. In the reflection of the mirror, she saw Lizzie watching her.

"You're right, perhaps I never loved James." Lizzie was quiet for a moment, watching Thea clean her face in the mirror. "Did you love the man, the man who sent you those letters?"

Thea froze, lowering the wipe from her face with her heart in her mouth. Feeling caught out, like an elephant standing in a room with mice, Thea racked her brain for an idea on how to end the conversation as quickly as possible.

"Yes," Thea blurted out.

Clearly her mind didn't have the energy to come up with a logical plan to approach the subject.

"How did you know?" Lizzie asked.

"When they played piano."

When she laughed, when she smiled, when she walked, when she talked, when she breathed, Thea thought to herself, looking at her own glossy eyes in her reflection.

Lizzie let out a hum of surprise. Thea should have thought before she spoke, falling in love with a man because they played piano was far too... poetic. She should have said something like 'when he said he wanted to marry me' or... or... why did people love men?

Thankfully, Lizzie's questions ended there, and she started folding up the blanket she'd slept under, shaking the duvet as she began to make the bed. Thea spun around, going to help because she may have been raised on a farm, but she had her manners. She was just picky about when she used them.

They silently tucked in the sheets and puffed the pillows, Thea glancing at Lizzie every now and then, cursing herself whenever her freckles, long lashes and light hair reminded her painfully of somebody it shouldn't.

CHAPTER ELEVEN

<u>Angeline</u>

"Any post this morning, Maria?" Angie asked on a bleak morning as she headed downstairs for breakfast.

Christmas was a few weeks away and she hadn't received a letter from Thea since the end of November, and Angie had a lot she needed to get off her chest.

"Nothing that didn't go straight to your father's office, Angeline," Maria replied as she passed Angeline on the way upstairs to make the beds.

It went on like that for a while. Angie would ask if there was a letter for her, and Maria would shake her head and take the post straight to her father's office. Angie's father once spotted her searching through the post that had been discarded on his desk. To Angie's surprise, he didn't shout at her. He just looked down at his daughter, brow furrowed in a concern Angie was sure to be fake. She had turned away and retreated into the living room.

She watched snow falling outside the bay window, praying that, in the hustle and bustle of

Christmas, Thea had just forgotten to send a letter. It was the only likely explanation.

*

"Miss Angeline!" Maria called upstairs, "there's a letter here for you!"

It had been days since Angie had left her room for anything more than a meal or a walk. Her mother rarely left her room either, Angie didn't know what was wrong with her. Her father insisted that Angie came downstairs to eat her meals with the rest of the family, when her mother didn't have to, which hardly seemed fair.

Selfishly, Angie didn't care why her mother was moping around like Miss Havisham, because she hadn't stood up for Angie when she'd been forced to have all those awkward dinners with young men her father wanted her to marry. Angie held a grudge against the woman that had her mother's face but didn't talk and stared at walls. She wasn't the mother Angie had left behind.

But the second those words left Maria's lips; worries melted away like candle wax. Dwelling on her mother's self-induced solitude wasn't a priority.

Angie nearly slipped into the old grandfather clock in the hallway, stumbling over to Maria. She held her hands out like she was receiving mass. It was even more important than that, Angie thought sinfully. Looking at the letter with a raised brow, Angie tilted her head, because Thea never sent her letters in an envelope that large. Turning it around to view the front, she saw

108

her name plastered on the envelope. The logo in the corner laughed at her: the University of Edinburgh. This letter wasn't from Thea. All these weeks of waiting and when she did finally get a letter, it wasn't even from her.

Her vision blurred as the world around her span.

Charles must have followed Angie to see what all the fuss was about. Without a word, he looked up at his big sister with his round brown eyes and hugged her hard, face buried in her side. It seemed Charles always knew when she was on the verge of crying. As much as Angie appreciated the hug, that just pushed her over the edge. She knelt to wrap her arms around Charles, face pressed into his soft hair. She felt his small hands rubbing her back.

"Don't be sad," Charles whispered to her. "Why are you sad?"

Angie shook her head, wanting to tell him it was nothing serious, that she was fine. But her throat had closed up. In the rush to hug her brother back, Angie had dropped the letter on the ground. Maria picked it up.

"A letter from the University," Maria said, puzzled. "Surely this is just about starting in January."

Quite frankly, Angie didn't care what it was about.

"As if any of that matters," Angie hissed as she pulled away from Charles, who'd jumped at her tone of voice.

Another maid passed by to put some empty milk bottles on the porch, looking worriedly between the three of them. Angie clenched her fists together tightly and turned on her heels.

There had to be another reason why she hadn't got a letter from the farm. Angie had a deep aching in her bones, telling her that something terrible had happened. But she wondered whether that feeling was just the sense of betrayal. What scared her most was that she didn't know whether she'd rather accept that she'd been forgotten or accept that something terrible had happened to prevent a letter getting to her. Most of Angie's days had been spent reading the soothing words written for her by Thea, the ones hidden under her bed. She'd lost Charity as a friend but with Thea's letters Angie could shift to a reality where she was still on the farm, so it didn't seem to matter. At least she had Thea, even with all those miles between them.

At least, that was what she'd thought.

Unsure of where to go and what to do with herself, Angie climbed the stairs two at a time. At first, she'd presumed her feet would just take her to her bedroom, but they carried her past it, and up the next flight of stairs to her mother and father's room.

The top floor of the house always felt colder, especially in winter, but the chill that pricked at Angie's bare arms now was nothing short of freezing. It appeared darker too, she squinted her eyes to see. And, despite the fact her mother had rarely left this floor in months, it felt abandoned. A part of Angie wondered whether her mother was a ghost.

With great difficulty, she navigated the door to her parents' bedroom, wondering why on earth all the curtains were drawn when it was past midday. She twisted the doorknob, eyes scanning the bedroom in search of her mother.

The woman was sitting at her dresser, the curtains still closed, but there was enough light to see her expression in the mirror. Her mother stared at her reflection like it wasn't there, like she was looking out the window at a boring snowy scene. The mother Angie knew would never let herself look so terrible. Mascara was stained under her eyes, there was a smudge of lipstick on her chin and her blonde hair was a bird's nest atop her head. Angie's mother from before would never let herself go like this; she'd cover up mirrors rather than view herself looking so awful. What ever happened to her opinion about appearance being the most important thing a woman has? Who was this stranger sitting where her mother should be?

"Angeline, my darling," her mother croaked, like her voice hadn't been used in months. "Oh, how I've missed you."

Angie clenched her fists; nose twitching as she visibly cringed. *Missed her?* She spoke as if Angie had only just returned, as if there wasn't just a set of stairs between her bedroom and Angeline's.

The fact Angie had spoken so proudly of her mother back on the farm, the fact her mother had been the thing that she was most looking forward to about coming back to London, felt so humorous. Because this woman who stared at mirrors in her bedroom all day, was a stranger.

"My eldest and youngest children; the one who I've had for the longest and the one who's meant to need me the most, and they're the ones that never come to see me," her mother sighed.

Angie stuck her chin up defensively.

"Charles doesn't understand why you aren't just downstairs as normal," Angie argued, "and, quite frankly, neither do I."

Swaying side to side on her stool, her mother closed her eyes, as if dancing to music that wasn't even playing.

"William, Peter and Michael come up and see me."

Angie wondered whether her mother had even heard what she'd said, or if she was intentionally ignoring her daughter. Taking a step forward, Angie kicked a leg of the stool her mother sat upon, jolted out of her strange daze, only for her to gasp and look at Angie with wide, accusing eyes.

"Why are you hiding away up here?"

Her mother's round eyes were crinkled at the corners with old laugh lines, Angie couldn't remember the last time they'd been put to use.

"Because nobody needs me downstairs anymore," her mother stated, eyes flickering up to meet her daughter's. "You get to an age in your life when women just... lose value."

Angie felt rage bubbling up her throat.

"That's *it*?" Angie spat. "You just... this is all just because you feel sorry for yourself?"

She could laugh, it was so ridiculous.

"Charles is seven years old! He left this house when he was four! He hardly remembers you, and you could change that if you just spoke to him like a *normal* mother instead of wallowing in your own self-pity, up here like an old, widowed hag!" Angie roared, hand itching at her side to slap her mother right across her make-up-stained face.

Retreating into herself with a lowered head, her mother sat stiffly as the wind outside seemed to turn more violent, a cold draft tickling at Angie's ankles as it howled as loud as Angie's thoughts.

"I hear him crying," her mother whispered, voice wavering. "I don't go down to see him because I can hear you run across the landing to his bedroom. Tell me when Charles cries at night what is it he wants?"

Angie knew her mother wanted to admit that it was Angie he was pining for, but she wouldn't lie or give her mother the satisfaction.

"He wants to go home," Angie replied.

Her mother chuckled, racking out sobs between each laugh.

"Have you ever considered that maybe *I* want to go home too?" Her mother asked, Angeline frowning in confusion because her mother *was* home. "Don't look at me like that, Angeline, you're old enough to know home isn't a place. It's a feeling. It's love..."

113

Angie watched her mother's hazel eyes, which looked so much like her own, as they trailed up to catch Angie's gaze. Her expression was suddenly soft, vulnerable, and all Angie could see was herself. God, looking at her mother was like looking at her own reflection in a mirror. It made her stomach churn.

"Love?" Angie echoed. "You have your children and husband home. Safe. In what world are you lacking love?"

Angie had little to no sympathy for her mother, who was practically implying life had been better without her family. Angie had seen the pain, how much it took a person to stay sane when losing a loved one, and here was her mother saying she'd been better without them.

"I don't lack love from you and your brothers," her mother answered quickly, looking away.

So, this was about her father.

Angie could write novels about all the things she disliked about her father, but she wouldn't turn away from her family just to waste her days feeling sorry for herself.

"Marriages have blips," Angie argued. "That doesn't justify this."

Her mother stood up; her shoulders hunched with her finger pointed at Angie. Her mouth had twisted into a nasty scowl, eyes dark and exerting fury. As if realising the intensity of her expression, her mother's face fell, and a sob pierced the air. She covered her face with her hands before raking them through her hair, fiercely gripping at the strands.

"I'm sorry that you have to suffer in this world, Angeline. I'm sorry you don't get the privileges that your brothers and your father have. I can't bear to see you forced into an unhappy marriage. You have to be happy. You have to change the way it is. You have to get out. Don't lose value, don't let them take your value. Because you grow up and they take it from you. They will try to take it from you."

Her mother was pleading, lowering her hands from her hair in order to take Angie's. "But look at you, so young, so intelligent, so stubborn. You can stop them. You have to promise me that you'll try."

Speechless, Angie nodded. She thought of all the questions she had, but they came to mind all at once, too quickly to voice them. Her mother's breathing still sounded like harsh whimpers as she lowered herself back down onto her stool to stare at her reflection again. Angie had initially entered the room with the intention to discuss university; to admit that she was changing her mind, that she wasn't happy enough to focus on her studies for three years, that she didn't think she could leave her brothers with her mother acting so selfishly. But her mother turned and smiled weakly, visibly exhausted,

"I'll do better. I'll do better, for the boys."

And Angie knew what she had to do, for her own sake.

CHAPTER TWELVE

Dorothea

With aches in her limbs and a pang of hunger in her stomach, Thea trudged along the hallway and into the kitchen to finally sit down. The old wooden chair by the window creaked under her weight as she slouched against it, bending down to unfasten her laces. They'd been fastened far too tightly since Thea had put them on first thing in the morning, but there hadn't been an opportunity to take a moment to retie her laces *all* day. After kicking her boots off at the heels, she padded over to the sink in her sodden socks to fill the kettle with water, before turning on the stove and leaving it there to heat up. Stretching, her back clicked and she winced. A rest over Christmas couldn't come sooner.

The winter months were always the toughest, even Thea's father had sometimes complained about them. And her father had been nothing but hard-working.

Her mind was sprinkled with memories of him now the 25th drew nearer.

Thea welcomed them because they blocked out the memories she was trying desperately to forget.

Angie's giggles when Michael and Peter were running around on Christmas Eve, after stealing the stockings that had been hanging on the fireplace and sticking them on their heads. Their legs brushing secretly under the table as they drank warm milk and ate the traditional Christmas shortbread her mother always made. Thea could still taste it now. She'd never understand how flour, butter and sugar could taste so delicious.

Thea remembered snow speckled in the golden locks of Angie's hair, when she hid snorts of laughter behind her hands as Thea tried to catch snowflakes on her tongue.

It was hard trying to forget someone that you couldn't picture your life without.

She had to give herself some credit, the last letter Angeline had sent her was at the end of October and Thea hadn't replied— but that didn't mean she hadn't read it meticulously. This reminded her that she hadn't looked at it for a while, and it still remained folded in the pocket of her coat.

Before she went to retrieve it, the kettle whistled. Thea lifted it off the stove, hissing when some boiling water splashed onto the back of her hand. Scuttling back over to the sink, she ran it under cold water and examined the damage which was thankfully minimal.

She couldn't even make herself a cup of tea when thinking about Angeline. That thought combined with her stinging hand made her nose itch and eyes prick with tears. When her hand became too cold from running it under the icy water, she sat down on the old wooden chair and buried her head in her hands, her mug of tea getting cold, abandoned on the kitchen counter.

"Dorothea!"

Her mother's aggressive shout felt like it vibrated against the walls of the cottage, as the sound of her footsteps became louder. Thea didn't respond, concentrating on clearing her throat, sniffing and wiping away her tears. Because her mother could read Thea's emotions like an open book most of the time. Despite the fact Thea had to lie to her mother about her feelings a lot, she didn't *like* doing it in the slightest. She stood in the doorway of the kitchen, hands on her hips with her mouth hanging open.

"Not only have you trodden mud all along the hallway, but all over my kitchen too? I just mopped the floor!"

Thea ducked her head, busying herself as she picked up her muddy boots, brushing past her mother in the doorway to put them away. When she wandered back into the kitchen, she watched her mother wiping away the water she'd spilt on the countertop and pouring away Thea's failed mug of tea. After filling up the kettle and leaving it to heat up again, she carefully fetched the teapot from the cupboard beside the sink.

Thea found her eyes tracing over the floral design on it, waiting for her mother to speak again, to tell Thea to get the mop and clear up her mess.

"Stay and have tea with me," her mother said without turning.

It wasn't a question.

Without a valid reason to say no, Thea let out an audible sigh and she wandered into the dining room.

Thea acknowledged that it felt darker, as she sat on her chair. She stared at the empty seats, which were absent of her favourite evacuees from the city, absent of her half-asleep brother and laughing father. In this loneliness, Thea thought the room suddenly seemed so much larger. It was as if the four walls surrounding it had been stretched out, and the once average-sized table had been replaced with one for a giant. When the Carters had been there it felt like there'd been no room at all—

Thea pinched the palm of her hand again.

Her mother's presence was announced by placing a tray on the table, the pot of tea steaming. There was a small plate of shortbread too. Thea had forgotten how hungry she'd been, practically salivating at the sight. Her fingers went slack from where she'd been pinching her skin under the table, and she reached across and took a piece, eating it whole. With a familiar eyeroll and tut, her mother sat opposite Thea and poured their tea with a sigh.

"It's bizarre, how many people there are in the village now," her mother said.

"People feel safe here," Thea mumbled with her mouth full of biscuit. "I don't mind all that much, it's nice to see new faces."

Her mother had been bringing her teacup up to her lips but upon hearing what Thea had said, she lowered it.

"That doesn't sound like something you'd say at all."

Thea took a swig of tea before shrugging, her brows pulled together.

"Well, anyway, I bumped into Judy on the way to Henry's," her mother continued. "She told me to tell you she was sorry about the party? I admit, I can't remember exactly what she said. She rambled a lot. I do wish you'd tell me things, Dorothea."

Thea herself did not remember much about the party.

She remembered arriving and feeling out of place, seeking Judy as a familiar face because Lizzie and Eileen weren't there. Her hazy memories suggested there'd been some sort of disagreement with Judy; perhaps Thea had told her to stop drinking so much? But that didn't seem right. If it was, it was quite hypocritical considering Thea was so drunk she nearly threw up and had to get walked home and taken to bed by Lizzie Thomas.

Lizzie who hadn't judged her after the disastrous night and, much to Thea's surprise, still showed up the following Saturday with a smile on her face, to sit with Thea whilst she worked, despite how cold it was.

"I saw you sneaking someone out of the cottage the morning after the party as well," her mother blurted out. It seemed as if she'd spoken unintentionally, simply incapable of keeping the fact to herself. "So... we should discuss that."

Thea fiddled with her hands under the table, biting the inside of her cheek. It wasn't as if anything inappropriate had happened, or that her mother would even suspect it had. Thea was merely worried about her mother's response if she admitted that she'd been too drunk to stand.

"If you're sneaking men in the house, they could at least have to decency to—"

"What?! Oh my— No! That isn't what—" Thea's brain stopped working, her face on fire.

Her mother shook her head, watching Thea as if she could see right through her. Her back was straight, and her brows were raised with a knowing look. Thea thought the sight was almost humorous. Here was her mother thinking she knew exactly what was going on, when it couldn't be further from the truth.

She had a sip of tea, waiting for Thea to gather her thoughts and learn how to use words again.

"It was Lizzie," Thea managed. "I got drunk, and Lizzie had to walk me home."

"Where did she sleep?"

"On my bed."

"Where did you sleep?"

"I slept there too. She slept at the end of my bed." Thea laughed awkwardly, rubbing the back of her neck. "Honestly, mother, she's my friend. It's not that strange."

A silence stretched between them before her mother spoke again.

"Friends don't share beds."

Her tone was intimidating, almost vicious. It took her back...

"You don't sign a contract when you become friends with somebody, Dorothea."

Her mother had told her, back when Angeline had only been at the farm for a few weeks.

"You sign a contract when you get married."

Thea had argued.

"Yes, but that's different."

"How? Everybody says you're supposed to marry your best friend."

"This is all beside the point," her mother had said, *"anyway, the relationship a woman has with a man is very different to the relationship a woman has with another woman."*

"But what if your best friend is a girl?"

Thea couldn't forget the way her mother's eyes seemed to darken when she'd asked the question. Thea knew then that she'd never let her mother find out, that she'd do everything in her power to stop it.

"It was convenient," Thea elaborated. "You were asleep, and I didn't want to bother you."

"She could have slept in the spare room."

Gulping down the remainder of her tea, Thea ate another piece of shortbread and stood up. Arguing with her mother for no valid reason was a thing of the past and Thea didn't want to start it up again. It wasn't like sharing a room with a friend was something to argue over, perhaps if she'd been angry at Thea for drinking that would have been understandable.

"I'm not all that sure I know who you are anymore."

The words sent a shiver down Thea's spine. Or perhaps it was down to her mother's tone, so down-hearted, thoroughly exhausted. Leaning against the doorway of the dining room, Thea swallowed thickly around crumbly shortbread and met her mother's eyes.

"I'm not sure you want to know who I am."

Instead of scowling, tears fell down her mother's aged face. Those grey streaks in her hair stood out, the wrinkles on her face crinkling as she let out a sob of despair. She pressed a hand against her heart and wept. Even after the death of her father and James Thea had never seen her mother break down like this.

Her cries were unrestrained, raw emotion that pierced the air and made Thea's insides twist painfully. Her hands shook as she stumbled over to her, pulling the chair away from the table so she could kneel beside her mother. Thea took her cold hands, watching her fall apart.

"Mother... "Thea's voice broke.

Her eyes opened, looking down at Thea and suddenly she felt so young, so small. Suddenly, Thea was a little girl with dark-brown ringlets, short enough to look up and see her mother on her right and her father on her left. She'd hold both their hands as they wandered through the village as her father sang a song in Welsh. Back when she could cuddle up with her parents, beside her big brother, as they read a book together. When there was no war or battles, between countries or between families.

"I failed them," her mother whispered, resting both her hands on Thea's cheeks, which Thea now realised were damp with tears.

"Don't say that."

"I only had to do one thing, I just had to keep you safe, and I didn't."

"You kept me safe!" Thea placed her hands on top of her mother's. "I'm safe."

"For now."

"Wh—"

"What do you think happens when people find out?"

"Find out about what?" Thea dropped her hands, eyes searching.

"When people find out about what you are."

CHAPTER THIRTEEN

Angeline

The stench of paint tickled her nose from where she was; staring out the bay window at the front of the house, eyes fixed on the snowy world outside the fogged-up glass. She imagined the ghost of her past self, sixteen years old and leaving for Wales, looking back through that same window to see her grand piano centred in the middle of the room, when she'd wondered if she'd ever play it again. The thought had felt like a blow to her chest at the time, but now she was finally home to feel the smooth black and white keys beneath her fingers, her mind was... blank. Making music was the last thing in the world Angie wanted to do.

Squirts of craft paint and giggles occupied the other side of the room as William, Michael and Peter tried to teach Charles how to make paper chains. They had nothing but flimsy left-over newspapers and paint that Maria had found, which had been clumpy and mostly dried out.

It had been William's idea to try and make decorations. Angie imagined it was because it was Christmas Eve, so he wasn't allowed to meet his friends. Perhaps, it would put everyone in the festive mood that was currently non-existent. The only thing in the house suggesting it was even Christmas was the tree in the corner of the room, with sagging branches and an abundance of baubles in some areas and none in others. Under normal circumstances, Angie's mother would have decorated it to perfection. No clashing colours or tangled lights, no wonky star or half-eaten candy canes hanging from the miserable pine.

It had been days since Angie had gone upstairs to see her.

The uncertainty of what to say was too much to bear. Never mind the fact there was no way to help her or to make her feel valued again. Hopeless, Angie would watch through the crack of her bedroom door as her father ascended upstairs to the top floor every night. Upstairs, to her vulnerable, broken mother.

The difficult part about the whole situation was that Angie couldn't look her father in the eye. Her father was not entirely to blame for her mother's unhappiness, she'd married him after all. Her mother probably hadn't understood at the time that many marriages failed as time passed. Her mother had been so young when they'd got married. She was undoubtedly too blinded by the idea of love to reject him. Her mother was a victim of a society demanding nuclear families.

Angie's father called her into his office most days, to discuss student accommodation and all the information about university for when she started her first term in January (later than everybody else). The 'adjusting' excuse had given her a few extra months to make her decision.

In her father's office, Angie would sit on her hands resisting the urge to punch him as he spoke to her, well *at* her. Angie had never thrown a punch in her life, but the compulsion was eating her up. His voice was *so* irritating. It was like nails on a chalkboard, demanding attention.

"If you aren't going to play anything, come and help paint!" Michael called.

Angie spun around on her piano stool, eyeing the paper trimmings and paintbrushes making pots of water look like dirty dish water. Charles was lying on his stomach with his tongue out in concentration as he slapped paint onto strips of paper. William had taped some string from the mantelpiece to the other side of the room and was attaching the paper with pegs onto the makeshift washing line for them to dry before they made them into colourful paper chains.

Angie shuffled over to where her brothers sat.

She crossed her legs and Peter passed her some newspaper, instructing her to cut it up so he could paint the strips. They did this for a while and occasionally they'd share a Christmas memory but, other than that, the only noise was that of the crackling fire from the corner of the room. It was the brightest light they had on such a grey, snowy day.

"Thea would like this," William said.

Angie wasn't sure whether it was the interruption of the silence or the name that made her stop cutting.

"She liked it when we weren't arguing," Peter agreed with a smile.

"We argue a lot more now, don't we?" William sighed.

"She isn't here to split us apart," Michael said.

There was the soft melody of the boys laughing to distract Angie, who had her eyes narrowed as she tried to concentrate on cutting up the stupid newspaper rather than crying about Thea again. Suddenly, there was a warmth against her arm, where Charles was leaning against her. Looking down, she could see his red eyes and shiny cheeks.

"I'm here though," Angie said weakly, not because she was jealous of how much the boys cared for Thea, there had never been any competition there.

It was because she knew they'd never see Thea again. Angie was the best they had.

The boys didn't reply or continue with their crafts. Charles had turned his face into Angie's arm entirely, teary eyes dampening the beige cardigan Angie wore. Her hand found its way into his hair instinctively, combing gently through his blond hair that had darkened over the years.

William's hair had stayed light, but he'd changed the most; he was taller and, unlike Angie, had lost his childhood chubbiness. He was all lean now, which made sense considering he was coming up to fifteen— *fifteen years old.* Peter and Michael seemed to look more and more like Angie's father every day and if Charles had aged significantly Angie wouldn't dare acknowledge it. In her mind, he was (and always would be) her baby brother. The one she read to on a rickety train-ride to the countryside, the one who she always picked up whenever he fell over.

Charles shifted away from his older sister and, as if reading Angie's mind, shuffled over to the bookshelf beside the forlorn Christmas tree. Leaning up on his tippy toes, because being short was a family trait of the Carter's, he fetched a book from the third shelf and hugged it to his chest as he came back over to sit between Angie and Peter. The battered pages were distinctive; this book had travelled with them, survived a war with them.

It didn't appear as magnificent as it had once been, the green and red font had faded, the image of the lion didn't seem all that happy to be stuck on the front cover of the book, a victim of time. Charles placed it in Angie's lap, wiping his face before leaning against her again. William, Michael, and Charles had shuffled closer; no matter what age they were it didn't seem the pleasure of being read to would ever fade.

She began to read.

Time passed between them, and they let it go. After about seven chapters, William stood to check if the paper chains were dry before taking them all down and putting them in a pile. Angie closed the book over with the utmost gentleness and they wove together the red and green slips of paper into five chains. One was taped across the living room, hanging over the piano, one wrapped along the banister of the first flight of stairs, much to the frustration of the maids who huffed about how difficult it would make it for them to dust. The final three were hanging from doorways. Maria had almost walked into one, but she didn't tut and sigh, just smiled softly.

"It feels like Christmas now," Michael sighed contently once they'd finished, all lounging on the cushions which they'd thrown on the floor by the fire.

"Not without father and mother," Peter said.

"Yes, well, that won't be happening anytime soon," Michael shrugged. "Mother's too sick."

Sickness— *that's* what she'd told the boys? Angie felt frustrated, but of course the boys wouldn't understand the truth.

"Where's father then?" Angie pressed, wanting the boys to acknowledge the fact he had no excuse.

"Working," Peter replied defensively.

"Of course," Angie managed through a clenched jaw.

Charles was laying on his front, eyes on the fire so Angie couldn't see his expression from where she sat on a cushion behind him. He'd struggled the most,

130

settling back into life. He seemed to treat Angie as more of a parent than their mother or father, which was concerning considering she was moving up North in less than a month.

"I'll miss you," Angie blurted. "All of you, when I move away."

Charles tensed.

"We'll miss you too," William said.

"You won't be away for long," Charles proclaimed, confident and sure as he sat up. "You won't, you'll come right back."

"Charles, that's stupid."

"It's not!" He argued, scowling at Michael.

"She's going to move away for a long time," Peter said.

"Probably forever."

"Shut up, Michael!" Charles cried.

"Maybe if you weren't such a baby, you'd grow up and realise Angeline isn't your mother!" Michael snapped.

"I don't think that!"

Angie put a hand on Michael's shoulder, looking at him with raised eyebrows before raising a finger to her lips. It wasn't fair for Charles to be blamed for the fact he clung to Angie. It wasn't his fault that their mother wasn't there for him, and it wasn't his fault Angie was the closest Charles had to a mother.

"Michael isn't wrong, Angie," William mumbled. "Charles isn't a baby anymore and I think the fact you haven't acknowledged that yourself is part of the problem."

William suddenly looked so different to Angie, as if she were noticing how much he'd aged for the first time. He wasn't that little boy with polished shoes and cute jumpers that the maids dressed him in. He was mature, wise, not that he hadn't always been, but now he just seemed so much *older*. And he was there telling his eldest sibling how to act which, quite frankly, made Angie feel nauseous. Her mouth hung open.

"Just leave it," Peter muttered to William, like this was a matter they'd discussed before.

Angie saw red.

"Charles is the *one* thing that feels familiar to me. You've all changed so much. William, you used to be so polite and— Michael! I used to teach you piano, now you only have eyes for ball games and comics and... Peter... you used to love me! Now all you talk about is father and soldiers. Charles hasn't changed and he *needs* me. He's the only one that still needs me. You all don't, Thea doesn't. Go ahead and criticise me for holding onto Charles before he grows up and forgets about me *just* like everybody else does."

The sound of nothingness was deafening. The boys' faces paled as they ducked their heads guiltily. Charles looked like he wanted to collapse into Angie's arms and sob until the sun went down but was clenching his fists as he fought the temptation, refusing to seem needy. Angie rubbed her temples, picking up *The Wonderful Wizard of Oz* book off the floor and tucking it back on the third shelf where it belonged, a distraction until one of the boys spoke again.

"I'm sorry," William finally said.

Angie slumped down by the fireplace, hugging her legs as she watched the dying fire crackle. She rested her cheek on her knees, eyes burning.

"Everything's changed," she whispered to nobody in particular.

"It'll get better," Peter said, it sounded more like he was trying to convince himself.

Angie turned her head to face the boys, "I shouldn't have shouted, I'm sorry too."

"So much for not arguing," Michael chuckled.

"Well, I suppose you were right," Angie faced the fire again. "Thea isn't here to stop it."

CHAPTER FOURTEEN

Dorothea

Sprinting to Lizzie's had been the first rational thought Thea had as she stumbled away from her mother after she'd said those words:

"When people find out about what you are."

What. Like she'd been reduced to just a *thing*.

Running through the town and grabbing the first person she recognised by the collar of their shirt and demanding them tell her where Lizzie Thomas lived, must have caught people's attention. But Thea's secret was out. And the world was crumbling around her like mother's shortbread; the sweet flavour of it was still on her tongue. The man she asked, a man from the party whom Thea couldn't remember the name of, pointed to the street with cramped-together houses with one room up and one room down. That would explain why Lizzie had never invited Thea over, living in such a small space in comparison to Thea's vast farmland, she must have felt embarrassed.

In such a hurry, Thea forgot to say thank you—but there were more important things on her mind: how could she explain to Lizzie that her mother was suspicious of them? How could she beg Lizzie to tell her mother she was wrong? Lizzie would be repulsed at the idea, of course, and she wasn't the type to repress her emotions. Thea had heard stories of her slapping a guy who made a rude remark about her once. Thea believed it. So, perhaps Lizzie would get so angry at Thea's mother for thinking they were... involved like that. Perhaps she'd be so disgusted she'd come back to the cottage with Thea and curse and shout at Thea's mother for ever suggesting such a thing. Thea was certain that would be her reaction, and it would be perfect. Her mother would apologise profusely, and Thea would be safe to hide again. Because she couldn't bear the thought of her mother knowing, she just *couldn't*.

The knock on the wood of Lizzie's door scared Thea, even though she was the one who made the sound. It had felt so quiet on the run to her house, like the world had stopped to stare at Thea, the sky, the trees, the ground, all asking Thea what the hell she planned on doing now.

"Lizzie."

The name slipped from Thea's lips like a prayer as she knocked on the door again.

There was shuffling behind the door, some fumbling for a key. And then her face, peering through the gap she'd cracked open.

"Dorothea!" Lizzie opened the door fully, shaking her head at her as she took Thea's wrist and pulled her inside. "You must be freezing!"

The door clicked shut behind them and Thea looked down at herself wearing thin, cotton work trousers and a loose shirt. It seemed Thea's body hadn't processed it was December and she was wearing summer clothes, the adrenaline racing through her had blurred any sense or logic. The fact she'd ran to Lizzie's proved that.

Without another word, she was wrapping a blanket over Thea's shoulders. It was scratchy; similar to the one Lizzie wrapped herself in that night Thea got drunk. Holding onto her upper arms, Lizzie looked her in the eye.

"What's the matter?"

"Nothing much."

"Oh, is running like a loony to my house on Christmas Eve in nothing but a shirt and trousers going to be a yearly occurrence?"

Despite everything, Thea laughed. She laughed hard until she wasn't really laughing anymore, and she could taste salty tears as they fell down her cheeks.

"Jesus Christ, Miller."

Lizzie tried to meet her eyes again as she took her hands off Thea's arms and hovered, visibly unsure of what to do, or how to comfort her.

"Sorry," Thea sobbed, burying her face in her hands, the blanket slipping from her shoulders. "God—

136

I'm so sorry. It's Christmas of course, you must be busy and—"

"No, no, I'm not busy," Lizzie wrapped the blanket back around her, smiling nervously. "Just worried about you."

It suddenly felt colder now Thea was inside, or maybe it was nerves making her teeth chatter. Lizzie led Thea into the main room, the only room downstairs, sitting her down on a creaky rocking chair. Thea took in the tightly packed room; a fireplace, a table and chairs, a make-shift bed in the very corner. Lizzie was watching her as she looked around, a brow raised like she was waiting for Thea to insult it.

"If this is a problem—"

"No, it isn't."

Thea cut her off. She wasn't prepared to lie and say it was a nice house because it was cramped, unappealing and had darkened spots of mould on the white walls.

"Good. Because, really, it has everything we need until I move out," Lizzie rambled. "I sleep down here so my parents can have the upstairs room. But they stay at my Grandmother's a lot. They're there now, so I can sleep upstairs on the bed. It's not like I have any siblings and... and it's not normally this chilly, the heater broke but we have the fire and—"

"Lizzie," Thea interrupted, "I'm not here to judge you."

Strangely, it felt good to know that Lizzie had to experience this slight vulnerability. But it didn't last for long, and Thea couldn't help but feel patronised as Lizzie pulled up a chair from the dining table, dragging it over to sit beside her. Thea felt like a child who'd got in a fight at school, like Lizzie was her mother sitting down and coming close to find out every little detail of what had happened.

"What's going on?"

Thea didn't know how to start, not without crying some more. She pulled the blanket tightly around herself.

"Dorothea," Lizzie said, mirroring what Thea had said just moments ago, "I'm not here to judge you."

Lizzie still seemed slightly awkward beside her, something that Thea could relate to, because she herself had never been very good at comforting people. She had no idea what she'd do if Lizzie showed up on her doorstep sobbing.

"My mother saw you after the party. She saw you sneaking out the next morning." Thea shook her head, laughing to herself.

It was humorous that during all the time Thea had spent with Angeline, her mother hadn't suspected a thing. But after spotting Lizzie one time, her mother jumped to the conclusion there was something more going on, when there wasn't. Maybe a pathetic part of Thea wished there was, as a way for her to forget, to cope. But Lizzie wasn't like that. Lizzie loved James.

"Oh," Lizzie smiled along with Thea, clearly misinterpreting what Thea's laugh had meant. "So, she was angry you got so drunk I had to stay the night? Don't worry, that'll pass."

Lizzie's head was tilted, clearly questioning why on earth Thea was crying over the fact her mother found out about a drunken night she'd had at a party.

"It's not that." Thea pressed her lips together, closing her eyes.

"You know, you really aren't giving me much to go off here."

"She thinks something happened."

"What?"

"Something... between us," Thea gestured between them awkwardly.

"Like an argument?"

"No." Thea looked at Lizzie with pleading eyes, wishing she could just read her mind, so she didn't have to say it out loud. "Not like an argument like... like something really..."

"A bad argument?"

Fiddling with the corner of the blanket, Thea focused on the frayed edge trying to think of a way to say the words. Lizzie didn't move, her eyes still on Thea as she waited patiently for an explanation. Thea regretted the decision to come to Lizzie's when her mother was suspicious of them as it was, but it felt like Lizzie had been the only source of calmness over the past few months. Just seeing her took weight off Thea's shoulders. But how could she be so sure Lizzie could be trusted with this?

It was her only choice now.

"I'm not like you, Lizzie," Thea began. "I'm not like Judy or Eileen or any of the other girls in the village."

"I know, that's just why I like you."

Lizzie seemed surprised at her own words but, despite her awkward expression, she didn't take them back.

Thea rubbed her temples in frustration at the words that were stuck in her throat. The truth that was stuck in her throat.

"My mother thinks— that we— that—"

The stupid room was closing in around her. The smell of mould suddenly pungent, the tea and shortbread that Thea had eaten earlier threatening to come back up. Her tongue suddenly felt huge in her mouth, heart pounding so loud she was certain Lizzie could hear it.

But the familiar furrow of Lizzie's brow, the specks of yellow in her eyes, the softness of her jaw and the tenderness of her expression grounded Thea. It was absurd how Thea had thought of her as such a cold person at first. Now, Thea saw Lizzie for who she was; a brave, stubborn woman who'd been left heart broken. Of course, it took so long for her defensiveness to fade, it was all about breaking down the walls she put up to protect herself. Just like Thea did when she was younger; a mechanism to stop people from seeing her as vulnerable.

Thea wondered whether this was what James saw looking at Lizzie, all those months ago. Did she look at him with that warmth in her eyes? Did she look at him like this? She must have looked at James with this much care and more. And, *God*, did Thea want more. She wanted to be looked at like this forever. Thea wanted to feel loved again.

Without letting her mind process what she was doing, using every scrap of dignity she had left, Thea's hand cupped the back of Lizzie's neck, her fingers tangling into the strawberry-blond strands of her hair. Lizzie's lips parted, whatever she was about to say cut off by the press of Thea's lips to hers.

This was when Thea expected to get shoved away. Her shoulders were tense as she anticipated a forceful push against her, her spare hand gripping the arm of the rocking chair, feet planted firmly on the ground in case Lizzie pushed her so hard she fell off.

But the push didn't come.

Only a small gasp against her own lips, and then the feeling of Lizzie's hands, holding Thea's face so gently. The position should have been awkward, both of them almost slipping off their chairs, but Thea was too occupied to care. Any emotion that wasn't to do with how Lizzie was making her feel was forgotten.

It wasn't like anything Thea had felt before. The gentleness Thea had seen in Lizzie's expression seemed to have evaporated, only to be replaced with a fire of lust and want. Without separating their lips, Lizzie took her hands off Thea's cheeks, wrapping her fingers around Thea's wrists and pulling her up off the rocking chair that responded with a creak. There was a burning

141

in Thea's chest that made her lungs tighten and her heart hammer against her ribcage.

Suddenly, Thea was angry. Angry at the world that hated her so much for wanting this. Angry at her mother for knowing what was going on between her and Lizzie before anything had even happened. Angry at Lizzie for kissing her so hard, and angry at herself for kissing so hard back.

She was desperate. Thea was *so* desperate. The world had turned her into this hopeless person, she wanted to love slowly, softly, and yet this was what her love got reduced to. Thea didn't get the handholding, the dates, the slow burn. She just got needy, desperate acts in the dark. Angeline had been an illusion, a glimpse at a fantasy world. Thea was pathetic for even writing back in the first place, for holding onto her letters that she should have burnt. She'd held onto the hope Angeline provided like a lifeline; the glimpses of the love that she wanted but could never have. But Thea knew the truth now. Angeline was gone and this was the best Thea would get.

Stumbling against the nearest wall, only separating for short gasps of air, Thea's hands came to rest on Lizzie's neck. Thea could taste tears, but she didn't know whether they were Lizzie's or her own.

"This is bad," Lizzie rasped out.

"No, no. It's okay," Thea cupped her jaw.

A selfish part of her wished Lizzie hadn't gotten emotional and started to contemplate what she was doing.

142

It was easier, Thea had learned, to deal with the guilt afterwards. Lizzie kissed her clumsily again and Thea waited for when everything bad faded again.

And the world became nothing but lips and hands.

CHAPTER FIFTEEN

Dorothea

Their legs were tangled under a thin sheet that provided no warmth. Lizzie's face was pressed in the crook of Thea's neck. Earlier, Thea had felt her breath there, gasps muffled into Thea's skin. But when the haze of guilt came over them and all pleasure faded, neither of the women moved.

Lizzie's breathing had slowed, quietening as if she believed if she made no noise and she stayed very still, it would all be forgotten. But their warm bodies and lack of clothes told a different story.

Strangely, laying on Lizzie's makeshift bed (that was really nothing but sheets and pillows on a cold, hard floor) made Thea feel alive for a short while. Until reality made itself known as it always did, in heartache and fear.

Letting her fingers trail along Lizzie's back, the sharpness of her bones under thin skin was almost frightening. Thea hadn't lain with a body like this before. Angeline had skin that glowed with health, her body protected by softness in all the right places, from just the right amount of food throughout the years. Lizzie had skin like paper in comparison, Thea could feel her ribcage as she stroked up and down her sides. Living on the verge of poverty would do that to a person.

The heat from the fire had vanished as the flames died, leaving nothing but ashes and an uncomfortably bitter temperature in the downstairs room where they lay.

The loneliness of Lizzie's life was calling from every object in the room; the fireplace with no heat, the rickety wooden chairs, the mould festering on the walls, the scratchy sheets they lay upon.

Thea should have left.

She would have if Lizzie had not just settled. And if her soft breaths had not finally evened out. And the muscles in her back had not finally stopped being rigid with tension. But then, Thea thought, even if Lizzie was not keeping her here, would she really leave? Where would she go? Home wasn't an option; her mother would see the truth written all over her face. She'd seen it before Thea even made the move to press her lips to Lizzie's. There was simply nowhere else for Thea, no other home or safe place.

She started making a list in her head of all the people she knew.

Judy Tucker was the first person she crossed off. Thea hardly knew where she stood with her after seeing her so drunk at her cousin's party. Her mother had mentioned that Judy had passed on an apology, but even so, they were hardly close.

Eileen wasn't an option either. Thea didn't quite know where she was up to with her fiancée, but imagined they'd be moving in together soon and Thea couldn't intrude, especially on someone that she didn't know all that well.

That was it. They were the only people she knew. There was Lizzie, of course, but Thea had to get out of her way, the Millers had ruined her life enough.

This all felt like too much to be thinking about so early in the morning. She knew in her mind that she should rest, and yet her body rejected the idea entirely. Thea shifted her legs out from where they were intertwined with Lizzie's, carefully lifting her to rest on the pillow rather than against Thea's shoulder. Her nose twitched, lips parting as she resettled against the pillow. Her hair was a mess across her forehead and Thea knew she shouldn't, but she brushed it out of her eyes, tucked it behind her ear, and pressed a kiss to her temple before padding across the floor, picking up the trail of clothes she'd left and putting them on.

Thea found the scratchy blanket Lizzie had wrapped around her discarded by the front door and pulled it up over her shoulders, kneeling to the fire and shovelling in coal to get it going again. In the makeshift bed, Thea could hear the chattering of Lizzie's teeth as she slept. Once the fire was lit again, Thea went back over to Lizzie and tucked her in, bringing the thin sheets right up to her chin.

Paper wasn't difficult to find, there was only one cabinet in the downstairs room and there was a pen in the same drawer. Thea slouched by the fire, staring at the empty white pages. The idea had been festering in the back of her mind for a while, like a pile of perfect firewood that Thea hadn't given the match to light.

Until now.

She paced and thought whilst Lizzie slept and the fire flickered.

Thea had been too focused on finding somebody close by that could help her, but maybe that wasn't what she needed. Perhaps, somebody that *wasn't* close to home would be just what she needed. She finally settled, sat by the fire with crossed legs as she picked up the pen and chewed on the end of it. She left a space in the right-hand corner of the page; she'd have to find their addresses at some point but now she just needed to write. To beg.

Peggy, she wrote on the first sheet of paper. Her hand was shaky, the words slanted and messy but readable. *I have nowhere to go. I ~~am it's~~ know it's been a long time and that you may have forgotten me. I don't blame you; we have all tried to forget the life the war forced upon us. I know that you have a life in London, and I would be selfish to cause disruption. But ~~I must I need~~ I have to ask if there's any place I could stay. Somewhere cheap, a rented room, anything, just somewhere near you because I don't think I can do this alone. I cannot stay here any longer but I'm too scared to start a new life without an ounce of familiarity...*

Thea wrote on until her hand ached. But she didn't stop there.

Florence, she began, on the new sheet of paper. *You knew the truth about me, it seemed, before I even knew the truth about myself. You must remember that day we talked. You told me of your cousin, I cannot remember his name, but your cousin who loved another man. I don't know what happened to him, Florence, I don't know if his truth was exposed. But mine has been. My mother knows ~~I can't~~ ~~I need~~ ~~please~~ I can't stay here if my mother knows. It will only be so long before other people realise too.*

The morning light was seeping through the windows when she'd finished writing and both sides of the two sheets of paper were covered in pleas. Thea would send them as soon as she found the addresses of the two ex-Land Girls. They hadn't sent letters since they'd returned to the city. But life was busy, and Thea understood she was nothing but a reminder of their past on the farm, away from their families. She was part of the past that everybody was desperately trying to forget.

If, by some miracle, either of the ex-Land Girls were to accept and welcome Thea to stay in the city, she'd try and keep out of their lives. She'd use them as a crutch until she settled into city life, then she'd stay away from them, just as she was certain they would wish.

City life. The idea was humorous, made her insides twist and palms sweat. The farm would be out of

148

reach, all those memories of the people she loved most in the world— forgotten. Her mother would be the only resident in her childhood home. Of course, it was a rite-of-passage for a mother to nurse her young and watch them leave the nest gradually, but she was supposed to have her husband there to make the loss bearable. Her mother hadn't got that luxury. Her husband and son were dead. Her daughter... as good as dead. Thea couldn't return once she'd left, couldn't just visit at the weekend for tea and biscuits. If she truly were to move to the city, it would be to free her mother of the disappointment she'd had to watch Thea become.

After she'd written the letters, Thea read over them until the words were imprinted in her mind.

A gentle touch to her right shoulder hadn't been anticipated, nor had the nervous gesture of Lizzie pressing her cheek against Thea's, peering over her shoulder. Thea must have been so invested in the letters that she hadn't heard Lizzie get out of bed and slip her dress back on. Thea folded the letters over and stared into the fire.

"Merry Christmas," Lizzie said into her ear, voice soft.

She'd forgotten.

A time for family and love. Angeline's favourite holiday, and Thea had just forgotten. Thea should be at home with her mother... it was all such a mess.

She cracked a weak smile despite her racing heart and the strange feeling of emptiness that had overcome her.

"I'm sorry I intruded."

"It's alright, my parents aren't due back from my grandmother's until later. It was nice to have... company."

Thea swallowed.

"You're writing?"

"I just arose early to write poetry of you, my dear," Thea teased in her best posh accent.

That was what would get them through this, Thea thought, denying the severity of the situation. But Lizzie didn't laugh, just stiffened.

"I'm sorry Lizzie," Thea whispered into the fire, too nervous to turn and face her.

"You mustn't apologise, Dorothea."

"This is all my fault."

"This?" Lizzie asked, leaning back. "Is that how you refer to what happened? Just... this?"

"I don't understand."

"You make it sound like I'm some vulnerable girl who can't make her own decisions. You make it sound as if we aren't friends, as if we can't simply work it out. You make it sound like you... regret it."

Thea bit her bottom lip, feeling Lizzie's eyes on her.

"Lizzie..."

"My God, you *do* regret it," Lizzie laughed, it sounded as if it was almost painful to do so.

Thea tightened her grip on the letters, still biting on her lip hard.

"I can't stay here," Thea whispered, defeated.

"What?"

"I'm going to ask some friends in the city of any places I can stay." Thea gestured to the letters in her hands, it wasn't far from the truth.

She'd just missed out the part about the fact they hadn't spoken in months and, in her mind, weren't likely to accept her request.

"You can't leave me," Lizzie blurted out.

"Lizzie—"

"You can't leave me," she repeated, pressing a hand on her heart as if it truly was breaking within her chest. "Please. We can forget it all if it means you will stay. Please. *Please*."

"My mother knows! I can't bear that look of disappointment in her eyes—"

"You're leaving me because of how your mother *looks* at you?!"

"What is it you do not understand? I cannot grieve my brother and father for eternity, people will start to ask questions. How long do you think it will be before everybody starts to wonder why the farmer's daughter hasn't ever been on a date? How long until they start to wonder why I won't settle and marry? How long until they all start talking about Dorothea Miller, who doesn't dress quite right, who doesn't walk quite right or act like she's meant to? The workers on the farm, Tom, and Bill, almost found out. I was just lucky that time. And really, Lizzie, it's only a matter of time."

"Tom and Bill? How would they know? You're overthinking this all, it's—" Lizzie began.

"That day you found me," Thea said, folding her arms and looking down. "Tom and Bill were trying to get those letters from me."

"You said they were from the evacuated boy, who stayed on your farm during the war."

"She wasn't a boy," Thea said. "If they had read her name if you hadn't come and stopped them..."

Lizzie rubbed her face, pacing.

"How do you know the city will be any different?"

"People come and go in the city, names are forgotten. I'll be safer."

"What about me?"

Thea tilted her head at Lizzie, who had stopped pacing to look Thea right in the eye.

"Have you ever thought of me at all?" Lizzie asked.

"Yes. I will be gone, and I will no longer be in your way of finding a husband."

Thea stepped forward, holding Lizzie's face like she'd done the night before.

"Once you're married, you'll have money and you'll be safe."

The conversation seemed all too familiar for Thea's liking. It was the same one she'd had with Angeline, now without the crushing jealousy. Thea didn't mind the idea of Lizzie moving on and being with a man. But Angeline...

"I don't know why I thought we'd be different... I thought you'd be... I thought you'd stay, and we'd meet at night and...." Lizzie stammered.

"It doesn't work like that; I learned a long time ago."

Lizzie pressed her lips together with a curt nod.

"Are you going to stay with her? The girl that you—"

"No," Thea interrupted. "No, I'm not lying. It doesn't work like that. I won't see Ang— her again."

Lizzie bit her lip, her hands coming to rest on where Thea cupped her cheeks. Thea leaned closer and pressed their foreheads together.

"I don't regret it," Lizzie whispered.

Thea let out a gentle laugh, stroking her cheeks with her thumbs. Thea knew that there was no place for her in Lizzie's life. Perhaps there once was if James had returned and married Lizzie rather than Judy... In another universe, where Thea wouldn't be this destructive presence. She'd be a sister-in-law rather than a scandalous, immoral woman that bedded her brother's ex-lover.

"I don't either, Lizzie."

CHAPTER SIXTEEN

Dorothea

They slept Christmas day away on Lizzie's makeshift bed. It was more like dozing than sleeping. This morning had been so special to Thea in her youth; she thought she'd always treasure it. Yet, that day she'd spent it mostly in silence, with no family around. She lay almost rigid, concerned about where she'd stay until Florence or Peggy responded to her letters, but Lizzie assured her it wouldn't be a problem if Thea stayed at hers.

"What about your parents?" Thea asked as she tilted her head to look at Lizzie, feeling the aching crick in her neck from sleeping on a hard wooden floor.

"They won't care, they're old and Pa's barely with it, Ma is too busy worrying about him. You can stay downstairs with me, we'll set up an extra bed."

It wasn't a good idea, Thea knew that. The more time she spent with Lizzie, the harder it would be to leave.

"Perhaps a separate bed wouldn't be a bad idea," Thea said, intending to sound confident but her voice wavered nervously.

They were staring at the ceiling with nothing but the backs of their hands brushing, but Thea could feel Lizzie tense up. Until she laughed, tilting her head to glance at Thea.

"Very funny."

Thea bit her lip and swallowed around the lump of guilt in her throat.

"Lizzie, I'm serious."

As Thea began to pull her hand away so she no longer touched Lizzie's, there was a shuffle of sheets as Lizzie took Thea's cold hand in hers without a word. Lizzie wasn't ready for it to end. She wasn't ready to let go. Angeline had been like this all those years ago. The morning she and her brothers were due to get a train back to London, refusing to let Thea get out of bed. Thinking back, Thea remembered feeling certain that was the last time she'd ever lay in bed with a girl, but it felt different laying with Lizzie, more like she was just comforting a friend.

Thea wasn't lying when she told Lizzie she didn't regret it, but if they were to live in the same house they'd have to get used to not touching. It could take weeks for Florence and Peggy to respond to the letters. She hadn't even posted them yet. The thought of having to sneak into the cottage when her mother wasn't around was daunting...

When Thea opened her eyes again Lizzie was staring up at the ceiling, her face blank.

"We need to get up, what if your parents come home?" Thea asked.

"Then we'll say it's goddamn cold and body heat works wonders. You overthink how people view your relationships with women. The truth is that people are often too ignorant to acknowledge that we even have desire."

Lizzie was still staring up at the ceiling, perhaps the aged wooden beams were easier to look at than Thea's eyes. But under the covers, their fingers were still laced together. Lizzie's expression remained neutral as Thea waited for what could have been minutes or hours of intertwined hands, thumbs brushing, and occasional reassuring squeezes, until she spoke again.

"My parents aren't coming home today," Lizzie admitted, lips barely moving as she uttered the words.

"It's Christmas."

"Is it really?" Lizzie asked sarcastically, her eyes still focused on the ceiling as her brow pulled together. "I told you my parents are old, so you can only imagine how old my Grandmother is. I can't bear seeing her and that's where they go every Christmas, so I just stay at home."

"So, you don't like seeing your Grandmother because she's old...?"

"She's dying," Lizzie said. "I hate to see her like that."

"You'd rather spend Christmas without your family?"

Lizzie shrugged, finally looking at Thea, green eyes narrowed, "Christmas is just another day."

"So, your Grandmother is dying, and you plan to never say goodbye?" Thea asked, a sad smile gracing her lips. "I wish I had the chance to say goodbye to James and my father."

Thea's tone wasn't harsh, just an honest comment that passed without a thought. Thea then realised they hadn't said James' name until then, and it hung in the air like a thick, humid fog that was impossible to respire in. Lizzie's hand slipped out of Thea's.

"I'm sorry, I just... I can't do goodbyes," Lizzie sighed, rolling onto her side to face Thea and resting on her hands like a pillow.

Mirroring Lizzie's position, Thea pressed her lips together in thought. This was a goodbye, a long-winded one that could last weeks or even months. Thea was effectively forcing Lizzie to go through an experience she'd just admitted to struggling with. Thea thought then that she should've just got on a train to the city and never looked back, it would prevent all this hurt she was causing. She wondered whether James had put Lizzie through a painful goodbye as well, or if he'd just left for war without a word.

Lizzie's eyes were downcast, and she was chewing anxiously on her chapped bottom lip.

"I think part of the reason I didn't tell you I was alone for Christmas is because I hate it when you look at me so sympathetically."

Stopping herself from instinctively apologising, because Lizzie would despise that, Thea let out a heavy sigh.

"I hate that you have to say goodbye to me when it pains you so much. Perhaps, if I was braver, I'd stay... I cannot help but think I am just as bad as my brother, leaving you behind."

Lizzie pressed a hand on her chest in uncontrollable laughter as if Thea had made some hilarious joke. But the sound was almost remorseful as she shook her head. She sat up as her chuckles faded gradually and tugged on Thea's hands, so she sat upright too. Lizzie turned serious.

"You are not like James. I did not kiss and... be with you, because you have similar genes. You are more than the farm your father left behind; you are more than just James Miller's sister. If I truly wanted, I could keep weeping and weeping at the thought of you moving to the city or even beg you to stay, but I won't. Because I know you are so much more than your past. You could be anything."

Looking into Lizzie's eyes Thea saw a rare glimpse of hope in her eyes. As if the one thing that gave her optimism was the thought that Thea would have a better life if she moved away. Thea knew better.

"Not in this world."

Pointless dreaming plagued her younger years, the false hope of a life where she could love freely and without judgment. It wasn't pessimistic to accept hopelessness, to acknowledge that a life like that could never be— Thea believed it was courageous to carry on living when nobody wanted her for who she really was. She didn't want Lizzie to trick herself into thinking everything always worked out, because it didn't for people like them. To deceive oneself was cowardly, to deceive others was simply cruel. Letters to Angeline stopped the day Thea came to terms with that.

Lizzie hadn't taken her eyes off her during the long stretch of silence, the faith she had for Thea still sparkled in her emerald eyes. Angeline always had that same look, up until the day she left. Thea considered how many weeks Angeline had managed without a letter before her hope melted away. One week? Two? Or was it easy to just forget for Angeline? It got easier for Thea to forget, with Lizzie to distract her. Guilt stabbed at Thea then as she wondered whether she'd just used Lizzie as a replacement, not intentionally but subconsciously... It would make sense. But then, to some extent, it could be argued that Lizzie had used Thea as a replacement for James. That didn't make Thea clench her fists and want to shout and cry. It made her smile.

She and Lizzie were just what each other needed at that moment in time, like a cast to stabilise a broken bone until it was strong again.

Lizzie raised a brow in question at her smile.

"You made me strong again, you know?" Thea said.

"I think I do."

*

The winter had never really bothered Thea, she prided herself on loving every season equally. Thea had registered the colder weather when working on the farm every time she went outside, and her fingers turned painfully red-raw. At least the cottage was well-insulated at the end of the day when she'd return, unlike Lizzie's small home and the drafts that were inescapable.

The build-up to meeting Lizzie's parents was nerve-wracking, but when Thea finally introduced herself to the short man and woman, with greying hair and deep smile lines, her tense shoulders dropped. They had the same body type as Lizzie; both like skin and bones as a result of their empty food cupboards and wallets. Thea felt pathetic for ever thinking they'd be opposed to her staying, they genuinely seemed joyous to have company. Well, Lizzie's mother did, her father just stared into space. If Thea was staring at him for too long, out of simple curiosity about what was wrong with him, Lizzie would glare defensively. Lizzie seemed guarded and quieter but other than that, the days that followed were easy. Lizzie's parents didn't talk all that much and didn't question why Thea needed a place to stay.

A few days before New Year, Thea went into the village to Henry's Greengrocers. The Millers had a weekly order that Thea's mother paid for monthly, so Thea took a few items from that. When Henry gave her a baffled look and questioned why she didn't take the entire order home, Thea ran out without a response.

Lizzie scowled when Thea dumped some cans, vegetables, and fruit on the wobbly table.

"We don't need that," Lizzie argued.

"View it as payment for letting me stay."

"I already told you it isn't a problem. We have enough rations to get by and Ma just went to pick up food from—"

"Oh, food!" Lizzie's father gasped, with a thick Welsh accent, from the rocking chair in the corner of the room.

It was the first time Thea had heard him talk. She didn't miss the way Lizzie's eyes sparkled. She went over to him, kneeling at his side and brushing his greying hair out of his eyes.

"Do you want something to eat, are you hungry now?" Lizzie asked.

He nodded vigorously and Lizzie stumbled back over to the table, opening some canned fruit, and retrieving a spoon from one of the drawers without meeting Thea's eyes once. She knelt back down to her father and fed him and sang to him as she did so. Her voice wasn't naturally soft in the slightest but, singing to her father, it had a gentleness to it that Thea had never heard before. It suddenly all felt too private, and Thea went for a stroll, around the parts of town that her mother never walked.

Some evenings were warm. Usually, once Lizzie's parents went upstairs to bed, Lizzie would avoid Thea's gaze and face away from her. On those nights Thea would make do with sleeping on the floor with a few sheets. On rare occasions, Lizzie's eyes would be on her; wide, pleading. And Thea would settle beside her friend with a whisper of sheets. Nothing happened. They'd just lay there stiff as logs, facing each other as they mapped out the shapes of one another's faces with their eyes, trying to figure out what the other was thinking. Thea never came to any conclusion, and she didn't think Lizzie did either.

But, the day that Lizzie's father had spoken, Lizzie didn't lie down once her parents went upstairs to bed.

"You haven't asked about him," Lizzie said, sitting cross-legged and staring into the fire.

Thea didn't have to ask who she was talking about.

"You didn't tell me, I'm not one to pry."

"James did," Lizzie laughed quietly to herself as she shook her head. "I invited him to meet my parents. I was never invited to yours, of course. But I let him see my house... after years of being so embarrassed because it's nothing like Judy's grand one. All he could say after he saw Pa in the rocking chair was, 'so that's why your father doesn't come to church. Is he quite mad? I thought I saw him drooling like a dog.'"

Thea scowled, sadly unsurprised.

"James always spoke before thinking."

"No, I think he thought about it. He just saw my father as nothing but a—"

"He's not," Thea interrupted her. "Your father is not mad, Lizzie."

"How would you know? You don't know why he's like that," Lizzie stated matter-of-factly.

"Madness is a response to an experience. If we were to blame a person for 'madness' surely we could blame a person for crying, too. Both are simply reactions to something that has happened."

Lizzie's teeth dug into her bottom lip.

"I was furious with James after that. We hadn't exchanged a word throughout the next few weeks, but suddenly everyone in the village was talking about him and Judy being perfect star-crossed lovers. I knew he saw the both of us, I knew I was his dirty secret, but people were saying they were to get married. I didn't know what it was that made him turn away from me. My run-down house? My deranged father? Or perhaps it was just because he'd never had a girl tell him that something he'd said wasn't right. James Miller would never admit to being wrong. And I just remember thinking..."

She shuffled around to face Thea, clicking her knuckles nervously.

"Thinking what?" Thea pressed, pointlessly trying to meet her eyes.

"I remember thinking I wanted it to happen to him," Lizzie looked past Thea, focusing on a spot in the wall with an emotionless gaze. "When he left for war, I just kept thinking how badly I wanted him to feel shellshock like my father's. I wanted him to spend his days in a rocking chair. I wanted someone to whisper that he was demented."

Thea sucked in a sharp breath. She'd learned more about her brother now he was dead than she had when he was alive. Still, he'd turned into nothing but a distant memory, a person that just looked a bit like her. Sometimes he felt like a memory Thea wanted to forget entirely, but he was still her brother.

Lizzie pressed her hands against her face and then raked them through her hair nervously when Thea's silence dragged on.

"Dorothea, I am so sorry. I did not mean— my father... he's always been this way as far back as I can remember. James laughed about it as if his trauma was just a joke. You said it yourself, my father is not mad. He just closes his eyes and he's back in the war, he's—"

"I know."

"—scared," Lizzie whispered. "I am too. I'm scared. I'm just some stick of woman who gets mouthy if anybody says a bad word about her father, who I still live with! And I always will... I'll never marry now, will I? You're in my head."

The apples of Lizzie's cheeks were red as her eyes that were flickered with the reflection of the flames from the fire. Thea felt her stomach lurch.

"In your head?" Thea dug her nails into her thighs. "Because that's what it was, was it? I... infected you?"

"I didn't say that."

"Oh, but you meant it."

"No, I wanted you the way I want men. You didn't start these feelings," Lizzie said boldly, though

164

quietly as her parents rested upstairs. She twisted a corner of her skirt. "It's not... a new thing for me... men *and* women. I... I meant you're in my head because you made me realise how it's meant to be."

"What are you saying?"

"I don't want to spend forever with you, quite frankly I think we'd kill each other, and you're not my 'person'. But you love so fiercely. I see it in your eyes, how much you loved that girl who wrote you letters. I'm just saying thank you, for showing me how it's meant to be."

The fire died down as they shuffled down to rest on their separate makeshift beds. Lizzie was humming the same tune she'd sang to her father earlier that day, it was familiar, possibly an old Welsh folk song. Thea could vividly picture her own father whistling a similar tune as he worked. In the midst of the mess Thea had created, she'd barely thought of him. She feared that her mind may one day forget his greying eyes and piano melodies.

In a way, seeing Lizzie's father made her grateful; her father died the man he always was, his life was not bound to a rocking chair, his daughter and wife carrying him upstairs to bed, feeding him, helping him go to the toilet. Not that it meant there was an absence of love. Lizzie's mother clearly still loved her husband, but it wasn't real life for him anymore. Her heart ached for the men and this war that took away their personality and stripped them of the life they had before.

165

Once Lizzie's tune ended, she let out a long sigh, glancing over to where Thea lay.

"It's New Year's Eve tomorrow," Lizzie said.

"Already?"

"Yes. You should visit your mother."

"Don't be absurd. I can't do that, Lizzie."

Thea clenched her fists under her thin covers, if she pictured her mother's face in her mind it was with glossy eyes and a disappointed expression, lips that ghosted the words: *I failed them.* As if James and her father could have prevented Thea's desires and her mother blamed herself, believed she was the one at fault.

"I'll sneak into the cottage one day when she goes into the village. I just need to find the addresses of the ex-Land Girls so I can send my letters."

She'd also have to see what a mess the farm had become since she'd left; she didn't doubt that either Tom or Bill would have jumped at the chance to be in charge of the jobs. They'd never run a farm before. Thea couldn't bring herself to care all that much, as long as the animals came to no harm, the harvest meant nothing to her now. She wouldn't be there to sell it when the time came.

"You'll sneak in and won't even say goodbye?" Lizzie asked.

"Just like how you won't say goodbye to your Grandmother. You said you understood the pain of goodbyes."

Lizzie's lips parted as if she had something to say to defend herself, but she refrained.

"What happens when you send those letters to your friends?"

"If they don't respond within a few weeks, then I'll set off on my own."

"And will you say goodbye to me, Dorothea?"

Thea hated how formally she'd phrased the question, as if she already knew the answer. If anybody deserved a goodbye it was Lizzie, to make up for the farewell James never gave her.

"My full name sounds so peculiar in your voice. After everything... I think you should call me Thea. And I thought you hated goodbyes."

"I do," Lizzie smiled sadly. "But I've never had a best friend before, and I should think if she is to leave me forever, it would only be right for me to say farewell."

The words 'it won't be forever' were tempting to say. But Thea had to prepare herself for the possibility that the village that she'd grown up in; the abandoned church with ivy crawling up the sides, the cobbled streets, the horses, Henry's and golden cornfields, were soon to be nothing but a faded image of a life she had to flee.

CHAPTER SEVENTEEN

Angeline

There was a little black sign, outlined with white and the university's red badge in the right-hand corner: *Keep off the grass*. Angie couldn't help but glare at the sign. It had been too long since she'd seen so much greenery, all spread before her like nature's welcoming blanket. And yet, it didn't seem like it belonged to Mother Nature anymore, because some privileged person thought the grass wasn't for walking on, apparently. At least there was a lot of grass. At least the air felt less like it was clinging to the walls of her lungs. But her chest still felt tight, not with smog but with anticipation and anxiety.

Angie didn't know a soul that walked these grounds. She was sure making friends wasn't going to happen anytime soon because of the judging eyes that felt like they were piercing her skin as she approached the arch design of the large doors to Edinburgh University.

Everywhere seemed overdramatic. The towering pillars around some of the buildings had strange little faces, like the gargoyles perched on the roof outside the church back in London, the ones that ward off evil spirits. Angie wondered why they had them on a university campus because it wasn't like the devil would want to sneak inside and watch students write equations as long as a short story, speak fluently in different languages or recite Shakespeare.

Angie kept looking down at herself as she stumbled her way up the steps and through the entrance. Well, one of the entrances.

She'd worn something slightly ambitious, unlike the clothes she usually wore; high-waisted beige slacks and a white open-neck blouse with pretty floral lacing on the collar.

Her roommate wouldn't be arriving until later in the week, taking a few extra days for the Christmas holiday, apparently. Angie was thankful for the time to settle by herself, to get used to all the strangers staring at her.

There was no reason for them to be staring so much. Perhaps it was down to her gender, most of the students that passed her were men with expensive clothes and hair that was thick with pomade. It wasn't that unusual for her to be on campus, women had been allowed to study at Edinburgh, and most other universities in the UK (aside from the ones with superiority complexes) since the late 1800s. But, then again, the percentage of men against women was strikingly higher. She hoped she wouldn't be facing any problems surrounding her gender in the coming years.

Though some more first-hand experience would undoubtedly aid her in her plan to make every essay she wrote about gender roles in society. Perhaps she'd post a few back to her family, in hope that her father would read them and feel great disappointment and embarrassment for his daughter's radical opinions, which she very willingly announced to the world.

The thought of him still made her skin crawl.

Her mother had been insistent that she'd be fine without Angie, that they all would, though they'd miss her. Charles the most, but perhaps this was what he needed, a reality-check to understand that Angie wasn't going to be around forever. Leaving the boys wasn't at the forefront of her mind, mainly, all she worried about was the fact she'd left her mother behind.

She'd hugged her family goodbye at the train station, boarding the carriage to lean out of the window. She watched the wobbling silhouette of her brothers and father through teary eyes. Once they were out of sight, Angie pressed her clammy hands together and squeezed her eyes tightly closed, silently praying.

But after all, this was what she'd wanted. This selfish decision would define her now. If she had got married, she'd still be in London, looking out for her family. This ambitious choice to pursue a higher education and rebel against her father had overridden her duty as a daughter and a sister. Angie didn't think she'd spent more than a night away from her brothers since they'd been born, and the memory of Charles sobbing until his face was so blotchy, he looked like he had a rash, his throat so raw he winced when he spoke, was an inescapable thought.

Approaching the front desk at the university's reception, Angie feared her throat was too dry to speak. She was certain the receptionist was used to nervous students, but Angie was overcome with more emotions than just a little anxiety. And there wouldn't be many students joining in January, which only added to her worries. They'd already been there for a term, then gone home for their Christmas holidays.

"Angeline Carter," she croaked, almost inaudibly.

"I beg your pardon?"

"My name is Angeline Carter; I've applied for the English Literature and Language course. I wasn't able to start in September because—"

"Here are the final forms," the receptionist interrupted, shoving a pile of papers into her hands.

Angeline retreated from the building, clutching the papers to her chest so they didn't fly away in the wind. She walked across campus to an area with more people, where she could disappear and become nothing but a face in the crowd.

There was a grand fountain, flowing with clear water that twinkled in the sunlight. Perching herself on the side of it, Angie half-sat on the papers and picked up the first one as she read through the small text with squinted eyes. It outlined what the course entitled, campus rules, confirmation of identity, all things she'd already gone through back at home.

The background sound of chatter as students passed was calming, less people stared, and she blended into the abundance of people sitting studying on benches.

A man sat on the wall around the fountain, a few metres apart from Angie but he didn't appear to be studying. Glancing up, she took in the sight of the awkward-looking dark-haired bloke who fiddled with his hands. Angie shuffled away from him slightly. The man moved closer, his hands now resting at his sides.

Reading the information on the papers was difficult with this stranger's gaze on her.

The man cleared his throat, rubbing his hands on his thighs nervously. Angie pressed her lips together, gloved finger trailing along the words as she read them, but it didn't seem to help, she wasn't taking a word in. And he kept watching.

"Can I help you?" she finally blurted out.

His face lit up red, looking like one of her brothers when they'd been caught with their hand in the biscuit tin.

"N-no. No! Y-yes, yes. That doesn't mean that you *must* help me. Well, help isn't quite a suitable word. I suppose it could be... in a different context. I would like to ask you something."

Angie stared with wide eyes as the bespectacled man stuttered.

"I have not seen you before. I suppose I haven't seen every person that attends every course at this entire university. But I am quite a curious man, I tend to be rather aware of people. Not in a way that's intrusive or prying. I'm not like that. But I haven't seen you here before and… well I think I would remember if I had."

Angie didn't know whether that was a compliment or not. But she was busy, and this rambling man was interrupting her, at this rate she wouldn't have the papers signed for a while. Angie wanted to get the first day over and done with, so she kept her eyes down.

"I'm new. You haven't seen me before because I just arrived yesterday," Angie said, tone nonchalant despite her frustration.

The man looked amazed as if he hadn't expected Angie to respond.

"Is there a reason you didn't start in September?"

"I don't know who you are, I don't think it's appropriate to be asking me personal questions," Angie snapped, looking up from her papers.

The dark-haired man jumped, eyes widening as he stumbled over apologies,

"I-I- I'm sorry, Miss. I wanted to get to know you, that's all. Oh goodness! That was forward of me… I… people here don't like me, and I thought perhaps you'd be my chance of a friend… you have a kind face. But I shouldn't have asked something personal right away."

Angie pressed her lips together. His uncertainty was almost comforting in a strange way, knowing there were others around her that were just as nervous as she was, was somewhat calming.

"Don't worry," Angie forced a smile that made her cheeks ache with unfamiliarity at the gesture. "I shouldn't have been so harsh. My name is Angeline."

His face lit up again like somebody had just told him he'd won a bet.

"How wonderfully unique, as if you were to be called Angelina but then without an 'a' at the end. I do believe it is of French origin, coming from 'angel,' are your family of that heritage?"

Normally when telling a person your name, they would simply give theirs in return. But this dark-haired man with imperfect skin and wide-rimmed glasses was clearly an exception. Angie gathered her papers together and folded them over as she thought of how to respond.

"Distant relation, possibly. But my name is for my mother, wanted a unique name for her firstborn," Angie explained, trying to meet the man's eyes but they were darting around everywhere. "What's yours?"

The man hummed in thought, looking at the ground.

"You know, I don't think I've ever asked about my family heritage. It seems all they care about is being perfectly pure and British."

Angie understood what he meant, it sounded like a belief her own father had.

"Sorry, I meant what is your name?"

"Oh!" he squeaked, closing his eyes, and shaking his head frantically. "Of course, you did! Of course. My name is Alan. Short, simple, boring. A little like myself."

He laughed to himself then furrowed his brow.

"I shouldn't have said that, now you shall never wish to be my friend."

Despite all of his confusing words and his appalling social cues, Angie decided that she very much liked Alan. Even with his peculiar glasses and hair that stuck up on one side. She imagined Charity Smith or any of her friends back in London wouldn't be caught dead talking to a man like this. And that only made her want to talk to him more. His dark hair and awkwardness felt familiar.

"I should hope you would allow me to make that decision for myself," Angie said, a small smile gracing her lips that, for the first time in months, did not feel fake.

He smiled wide, showing his teeth.

They continued a light conversation, well, if it could be considered light. Alan was quite philosophical, almost poetic, which meant his sentences tended to be very lengthy and he sometimes spoke so much that he became out of breath. Which was perfect, as Angie herself didn't have to talk much. He took her around the campus, to the English block where she would study. He discussed his own course and the college he was attending, which was only a short walk away from Angeline's. As the pair walked back to the fountain where they'd sat before so Angie could fill out her forms, he told her he wanted to be a writer but told her his father didn't think poetry was 'proper' enough.

"I don't think we should listen to our fathers," Angie said.

"I wish it was that simple," Alan sighed. "I do sometimes wish that we could choose our own families. Those people that we meet in life when the label of a friend or a partner doesn't quite express what they are to you. I wish those people could be family."

Angie absorbed the words, letting them sink in as she sat against the fountain. She unfolded her papers and retrieved a pen from her satchel to tick the right boxes and sign her name. What Alan had said kept echoing in her mind, making her heart ache. Alan kept quiet and didn't pressure her to say anything, his eyes kept flickering up to look at her then snapping back down again, he'd clearly sensed her sudden sadness.

"I had a family," Angie said when she'd finished with the papers. "A family I chose."

"Who?" Alan asked, voice not demanding but gentle, giving her room to ignore the question. But she didn't want to. Angie hadn't spoken of her life on the farm in so long.

"When I got evacuated, they lived on a farm. I fell in love... with the place. It was home." Angie bit her bottom lip, "I fear they have forgotten me. I can feel it in my heart, this strange... emptiness."

"If they were your family, they couldn't forget you."

If that were true, then why had there been no letters? Why hadn't Peggy written, or Florence, or Mrs. Miller? She wondered then whether had been family at

176

all. She wondered whether it had all been a fantasy, a way to cope.

"Do you think one day I could find another?" Angie croaked, throat feeling tight.

The question was ambiguous. She could mean another family of her choice, she could mean another friend, she could mean another Thea.

"I think this is a whole new chapter," Alan said. "I think you can do whatever you want. It's a perfect chance to simply start again."

Angie looked down at the papers she held tightly in her hands, looking over at the university reception. She had to hand them in, she told herself, then the new chapter would begin.

CHAPTER EIGHTEEN

Angeline

Angie's new accommodation wasn't anything to write home about. The brown-red carpet was so worn that the cotton of it had become almost rock-hard, Angie could tell when she still had shoes on so she wouldn't dare walk across it barefoot, or even socked. It had off-white walls, wooden skirting boards, and a thick oak frame around the window that was too large for her liking. Big windows used to be favoured but after blackout regulations during the war, Angie had become accustomed to the limited light of day. The winter light from the window provided no warmth, cold nipped at her skin as she removed her coat, hooking it on the back of the door.

Alan, being the gentleman he clearly was, walked her home. Home was a term to be used lightly as it certainly did not feel like it yet, perhaps it never would. Angie had handed in her papers and exchanged them for her timetable that she placed on the chest of drawers that she'd filled with her belongings the previous day. As she read over the timetable, she realised that it had an abundance of empty slots. She'd been out of education for years but thinking back to her childhood days Angie recalled short breaks and plenty of lessons: typewriting, sewing, cooking, bible studies, domestic subjects... This timetable entitled the subject she loved most and nothing else. That was equally exciting as it was terrifying.

It left a lingering concern, a fear that it would not live up to its expectation. And, Angie wondered, what was she to do during the long breaks? Socialise? With one friend? Their timetables and breaks wouldn't match up perfectly, there'd always be times when she was available, and Alan would be attending a lecture or something of the sort. Plus, the prospect wasn't all that pleasant despite the liking she'd taken to Alan, he was sweet, but he talked a lot. He asked questions. Angie wanted the type of friend that you could sit in comfortable silence with... but she hadn't experienced that in months.

Glancing to the empty bed on the other side of the room, Angie pondered the thought that perhaps she'd find companionship in her roommate. It wasn't certain they'd get along, but Angie didn't think it would be possible to live in such close quarters with another person and not find at least one thing in common. Angie still had a week before her roommate was due to arrive, so she'd settle for having Alan as her only friend because she had no plan to intentionally meet new people, even though that was intended to be an essential part of university life.

Leaving her timetable on the side, Angie padded over to an ugly chair with dramatically royal-red cushions. She slouched against it and closed her eyes to think of her family. It was evening, her brothers would be playing in the garden until a maid would drag them inside for an unwanted bath before supper, her father would be in his office as he always was, and, if she hadn't altered her ways, her mother would be sat in her room, fully-dressed and staring out the window like a woman frozen in time. Angie refused to end up like her mother, staring out windows with no purpose and in an unhappy marriage. Perhaps if it became a last resort to save herself, then she'd marry as her father wished, for money and not for love.

But until then it would be a fight, and Angie owed it to herself to try.

*

The days are longer here, they stretch and stretch. Angie wrote as the English lecturer spoke, his deep voice becoming nothing but vibrations as she lost concentration. Her notebook was covered in words, which should have been noted from what she was being taught but were not.

It had been mere days and she was already losing interest in her course. She'd teach it to herself, she thought, it wasn't difficult to analyse meaning.

I cannot learn faces anymore. Perhaps I do not care enough to remember them. Her writing was messy, only readable to herself. She hoped. *Alan meets me at lunchtime, and we walk. I keep hoping the rivers and canals will turn into a lake, the old gas lamps will turn into trees, the buildings will turn into the farm, the people will turn into sheep and Alan turn into Dorothea.* The name felt unfamiliar, she hadn't seen those letters beside each other, forming that beautiful word in so long. *Dorothea. Dorothea. Dorothea. Dorothea. Dorothea. Doroth–* No. She crossed it all out. Re-writing, *Alan meets me at lunchtime, and we walk. I keep hoping the canals will turn into streets, the gas lamps will turn into lampposts, the buildings will turn into my house, the people will turn into my brothers and Alan turn into my mother.*

That was what Angie should be missing, months of missing the farm had already been wasted away and she wasn't here to start that all over again. If she were to miss anything it should be her family. Not some farm girl that didn't care about her enough to write her a letter.

"It is thrilling to know you are so actively engaged with this topic."

The deep voice that had become meaningless vibrations, suddenly became words.

Angie snapped her head up, slamming her notebook so hard her fingers got caught between the pages. The professor was looking at her with piercing opal eyes, his bushy, greying eyebrows raised.

"Sir—"

"What is your name?"

"Angeline Carter."

181

"I have never had a female so engaged in her studies," the man said, his thin smile told Angie he was not being sarcastic; he truly thought she'd been making notes.

Well, who was she to tell him he was wrong?

"I am honoured to be here learning of a subject I adore."

"I should think so, girl," the man said the word 'girl' as if it didn't taste quite right in his mouth. There were sniggers coming from students.

Angie dug her teeth into her bottom lip to refrain from saying anything to the people around her. It was no surprise they were scoffing, they were mostly men, private school Oxford-rejects.

She opened up her notebook to a clean page. And she made notes as she listened to the man ramble on. The distractions would fade away eventually, she thought, and she'd become focused. But it always felt impossible to stop thinking of the lives she'd left behind, now with more free time and less company it became more difficult.

Alan met her for lunch. He brought a paper bag with meat sandwiches on fresh seeded bread with tough crusts, the rest soft and flavourful. Bread in London did not taste this good but bread in Wales tasted better. The meat tasted like a paste of some sort, rationing still being prevalent meant a ham sandwich wouldn't be the norm for some time, Angie presumed. They had an apple each, the sourness of the green fruit made Angie squint. Alan was still eating his sandwich as he struggled to balance talking and eating as they sat on a bench, on a bridge overlooking the Union Canal. Angie stared out into the distance.

"Angeline," Alan said, the first word he'd said that Angie had acknowledged.

She faced him, half-eaten apple still in her hand making her fingers sticky. Angie did not have the heart to tell him it was far too sour for her taste; she was used to sweet red apples.

"Alan?"

"I fear something is the matter," he said.

"You would be wrong."

"Is your subject enjoyable?"

"Yes."

"Are you missing home?"

"Yes."

"Which home are you missing?" Alan gave her a knowing look.

He was the first-person Angie had opened up to about her life on the farm in a long time, she'd told him more than her childhood best friend Charity Smith. But Alan seemed to speak so openly of his emotions, seemed so in touch with his sensitive side that Angie felt like she owed him some truth about what mattered the most to her. She'd only told him a very brief overview, but the man seemed to have grasped the idea that she missed them like a family.

"Not the home I should be missing," Angie whispered, looking down.

"Who's to say you should not miss the farm more than London?" Alan smiled. "I say you should miss what your heart tells you to miss."

It's more than just missing, Angie wanted to sob. *It's longing, needing.*

"I need to end this..." Angie closed her eyes, waving her hand as she tried to explain. "This isn't how a young woman should spend her days, grieving a life I won't get back. I should be thinking of my poor mother."

Alan put his hand on her arm; Angie met his grey eyes and saw nothing but friendship and care. She hadn't looked into a man's eyes and seen that before.

"This is *your* chapter," he said. "If it is your quietness and detachment, you are worried about, please do not. I haven't had the company of a friend in a long time. I wouldn't even mind if you went entirely mute."

The corners of Angie's mouth turned up; Alan patted her arm before removing his hand. Angie couldn't stop thinking that she didn't deserve a sudden friend like this.

"You are a kind man."

"Surely if I was so kind, you would not be frightened to tell me you aren't enjoying the apple, I bought you."

Angie blushed. "I'm not used to the sourness."

"That's alright," Alan laughed, taking the apple from her hand, and putting it in the bin beside their bench then faced Angie again with his dimpled smile and twinkling grey eyes that made her feel safe.

184

"I acknowledge that this is my chapter and a chance to start over," Angie admitted after a while, "but my mother was in a bad way when I left London, I suppose it's been a cause of anxiety."

Alan took a bite of his sandwich as he listened.

"And my brothers... especially my youngest brother, Charles, I believe he needed me for the times that my mother was... when she wasn't feeling like herself."

Which was most of the time, Angie thought to herself as Alan finished his mouthful and swallowed.

"So, you feel that you should be worried about them, and yet in truth what you think of most is the farm," Alan guessed.

"It's ever so silly."

"No," Alan sat up straight and shook his head. "No, Angeline, it isn't. Your guilt about it is just proof of the person you are."

"And what type of person is that?"

"One that needs to try putting herself before others for once," Alan chuckled.

That wasn't right, Angie thought to herself. Alan didn't know the full story. He didn't understand that her thoughts and hopes about the farm were pointless, that the whole thing was just as good as a fantasy. She may as well pretend it had never happened.

"They don't even write to me, Alan," Angie bit her lip. "It's all better forgotten."

Alan shrugged, putting the crusts of his sandwiches in the bin.

"Alright then, so forget it."

"I can't just..." Angie laughed. If only it was that easy.

"Nobody said you had to forget it right now, Angeline," Alan explained. "You should take all the time in the world you need to make new memories that are just as good."

"Will that work?"

"If you believe it will."

Angie pressed her lips together, mulling over the idea. New memories to replace the old. That had been impossible in London where the people were so square, but here, Angie could take the reins and make it feel as if the whole world was in the palm of her hand... even if it was just an illusion.

CHAPTER NINETEEN

Angeline

Over long days and nights, she'd become accustomed to the hardness of the mattress beneath her as she slept, the bland four walls of her dorm, the muddy colour of the canal that looked nothing like the sparkling water of a Welsh lake in summer. In Edinburgh, there were no steppingstones in nearby streams that she could stumble over and there weren't as many trees, casting patterned sunlight on the twinkling water.

Angie's walks in Wales had never been short, not when she was always finding unfamiliar plants, eyes filled with wonder as she looked behind her at Dorothea and said, "What's this one called?" Angie couldn't remember the name of a single one now. Perhaps she had never retained them at all, just liked seeing Dorothea's eyes narrow as she sat by the side of the stream, Angie beside her and their toes in the clear water that lapped at their bare ankles. Dorothea would hold the plant up to the sunlight to study it and Angie would rest against her until Dorothea remembered the name. It felt like a final puzzle piece falling into place as if beside Dorothea was where Angie was destined to be. Dorothea would stand. She'd look around to check they were alone, then bring Angie's hand up to her lips, eyes fixed on hers as she'd kiss across her knuckle, her wrist, then squeeze her hand before they'd carry on walking.

On a bad day, Angie didn't push her to talk, didn't say anything when she sat alone in her father's office for hours on end, or when she kept her bedroom locked at night. The grief Dorothea faced came in stops and starts, like the Miller's unreliable tractor.

Some days she'd play football with the boys, take Angie to her favourite spots, kiss her softly right up until the morning light broke them apart. But when her mood dropped, her eyes were fixed on walls, and she'd flinch whenever Angie touched her. She'd fold into herself, into this unrecognisable self-loathing character, mourning her father and brother as if they'd died the day before. Then the good days came, and it was all forgotten.

It only really dawned on Angie then that her own disordered good and bad days were like Dorothea's. Now she was without her, Angie grieved too.

She allowed herself these moments in the early morning, with a tea warming her hands as she watched the condensation drip down the dorm room window. It was healthier to reflect rather than push out the memories altogether, Dorothea had her time to grieve her father and brother and gradually her bad days became fewer and far between, perhaps the same would apply to Angie.

Despite knowing Dorothea didn't love her anymore, she was thankful for the closure. The lack of letters meant it was over; there wasn't any doubt about that. And just as Alan said: new memories had to be made to replace the old, because no new memories were to be made with Dorothea. In a strange way, Angie was grateful Dorothea wasn't grieving over the Carter's absence because she'd had enough loss for a lifetime. If Dorothea didn't need Angie anymore, that meant she'd moved on, that meant she was happy. She prayed that Dorothea had learned to love herself.

She finished her tea, leaving it on the side as she retrieved a towel from the cupboard to wipe the condensation from the windows. She started making her bed with practiced ease that she was proud of considering she'd only been doing it for the past week - it was muscle memory from when she'd had to do it on the farm. Angie spent the rest of the morning cleaning because she wanted to make a good impression when her roommate arrived later in the day.

Alan knocked just before midday to walk to their lectures. Angie hadn't had a chance to fit in any studying that day but was feeling confident with her degree so far. Hopefully one morning wouldn't result in a drastic falling behind. Alan was early, so they walked the long way to the English department, past all the grand buildings that Angie wasn't yet used to seeing. It was frustrating that men weren't allowed in the women's dorm rooms because Alan was just a friend, and it was cold in February and there wasn't really anywhere else to sit inside to eat and talk. So, they had to spend most of their time together walking. There were libraries and places like that, but Angie didn't fancy sitting in silence. Thankfully, Angie had wrapped a woollen scarf around her neck and had a warm coat on, so the walk was pleasant. That, along with the excited anticipation of meeting her new roommate, meant she was walking with a skip in her step.

"You seem jolly today," Alan smiled.

"Just your company making me happy, dearest."

Alan never seemed to blush when Angie made jokes like that, he'd just roll his eyes or chuckle. Angie couldn't quite believe how lucky she was to have met a man with the same gentle look in his eye that her brothers had, the same care that wasn't too over-protective or overbearing. Alan had also stopped rambling so much now and didn't seem to ask as many questions. It was as if he'd accepted Angie wasn't going anywhere and that he didn't have to talk at the speed of light anymore just in case she got bored of him.

"Have you asked her name?" Alan asked.

"Who?" Angie thought playing the oblivious card would make it less obvious that she was desperate to meet her new roommate.

Alan raised a brow.

"No. The lady at the desk said, 'You are sharing quarters with another girl, but I don't suspect she will arrive until next Monday.'"

"So, she may not come?" Alan looked optimistic about the concept.

Angie pouted, linking her arm into Alan's as they came up to the English building. "I won't replace you."

"I wasn't thinking you would."

"Well good, because I'm sticking with you."

Smiling, Alan walked her right up to her lecture hall. There were a few people there already, Angie assumed they too were studying English. She didn't recognise their faces, but the furrow of their mocking grins made her insides twist. Alan's face always seemed to light up when there were people around to see them together, like he was proud that he finally had a friend and people could see it. Alan gave her back her satchel, which he always insisted on carrying, as Angie slipped her arm out of his and waved as he went off to his Classics lecture.

"Miss Daydream and Specky: an unlikely pair," a student said, his voice was rough and mocking.

There were a few quiet laughs as Angie narrowed her eyes and cast a scowl at the man who'd spoken. He had a grey waistcoat that looked too tight on his form; his red hair looked wet with pomade. Angie didn't mind that he'd called her a daydreamer, she did often zone out during lectures, but she wasn't letting this man be cruel to her friend. With long limbs and the awkward way he held himself, his imperfect skin, and crooked smile, Alan wasn't much to look at. But that didn't determine a person's worth. Alan had mentioned how he'd made a reputation for himself amongst the students by barely saying anything, people simply looked at him and decided he wasn't worth talking to.

"Teasing people for having glasses? Forgive me if I'm wrong, but that isn't the intellectual insult I would expect from someone receiving education at a university like this."

The red head looked shocked that Angie had dared to speak back, mouth gaping like a goldfish for a moment. Angie plastered on a heavily sarcastic smile, folding her arms as they waited for their lecturer. The rude redhead barged passed Angie when they were welcomed into the lecture hall, but she didn't let it get to her.

*

There was a man standing outside Angie's room when she returned after having lunch. He was arguing with a petite woman who had a flushed face and an angry expression. The man was attempting to pry boxes out of her hands. Concerned for the distressed woman, she approached them. Angie wasn't one to walk away, not anymore.

"Excuse me," Angie said, "men aren't allowed in a girl's accommodation."

He loosened his grip on the box and the short woman snatched it back.

"I don't need your help," she murmured to the man as she fumbled in the pocket of her coat for keys to try and get into Angie's lodgings, which meant that...

"We're sharing a room," Angie smiled at the woman whose eyes softened. "Oh! It's lovely to meet you!"

Angie turned her attention back to the man, "Is he bothering you?"

"Yes, he's been following me all day and it's concerning me. I might call the authorities," the woman said, though she looked as if she was suppressing a laugh.

"All day?" the man scoffed. "I've been looking out for you since the day you were born."

Confused and slightly uncomfortable by the man's statement, Angie's lips parted but the woman cut her off before she could say anything.

"Stan is not causing any major issues besides annoying me," the short woman explained. "That is a brother's job, I suppose."

Angie pressed her lips together, her cheeks reddening when she realised that the man was not trying to steal boxes, he was helping his sister move into her new dormitory. Upon inspection, she felt quite embarrassed she hadn't noticed the resemblance between the man and woman sooner, the same bronze skin and dark eyes.

"I'm Lottie," the short woman introduced, Angie thought she was trying not to laugh. "I have to say you've made quite the impression."

"Angeline. And sorry, I thought he was trying to steal from you."

Angie ducked her head, avoiding eye contact with Lottie's brother.

"It wasn't necessarily a bad impression, just unexpected: A brave and fearless girl who is ready to fight off powerful, muscly men that steal boxes," Lottie's brother smirked.

"Yes, well, girls can be fearless too," Angie said.

"And don't hold yourself to such a high standard, Stan," Lottie scoffed. "You look like those thin spring beans father grows on the allotment, not a muscle in sight."

Her brother nudged passed his sister and into the dorm. Angie acknowledged that Lottie wasn't incorrect; his arms and legs were thin much like Alan's, but unlike Alan, he held himself confidently, with self-assurance. It should have been expected, Angie thought, given his handsome appearance. He leaned against a cabinet and watched Lottie struggle with her armful of boxes that she dumped on the floor. She pulled out folded piles of clothes, books, a hairbrush, and an alarm clock. Angie couldn't help but think it strange that she'd packed her items into cardboard boxes rather than a suitcase. Not that she was one to judge, but they struck Angie as a strange pair. Lottie looked up at her brother, pieces of curly dark hair out of place due to her exertion.

"I can handle this alone, Stanley."

"I know," her brother— Stanley— smirked, "I'm just here to watch you struggle."

194

For a moment, the sibling's bickering made her heartache for her home in London for the first time since she'd arrived.

"So, where are you from?" Angie asked.

"Near Liverpool," Lottie said.

Angie didn't know much about the place, she only knew there were docks. She nodded.

"It isn't near Liverpool, there's a river between home and Liverpool," Stanley argued.

"It's easier to say Liverpool!" Lottie whacked his arm on her way to the wardrobe. She looked back at Angie. "Can I put a couple of dresses in here?"

"Of course, we share the room," Angie said. "There are spare hangers just to your left."

Angie perched herself on the side of her bed, feeling her heart beating against her rib cage. Meeting people never used to make her so nervous.

"Where are you from?" Stanley asked.

"London."

"Did you like it?"

Angie chewed her lip, shaking her head.

"They had high expectations, I couldn't live up to them and that's why I'm here."

"University doesn't count as a high expectation?" Lottie laughed from the corner of the room where she sorted her clothes.

"Not for my father," Angie said. "He wanted me to marry."

"Well," Lottie span around with her hands on her hips. "Here is what I say to that: It is 1945 and we

195

won the bloody war! There's a future for us with endless possibilities, Angeline, I am sure of it."

Angie couldn't help thinking of her mother and how she would have thrived in a place like this, rather than remaining frozen in her unhappy marriage.

"I hope you're right."

"What I've unfortunately come to learn, is that Lottie is rarely wrong," Stanley admitted reluctantly.

"That is where you are wrong, dearest brother," Lottie pointed a figure at him before flashing a grin at Angie, "*women* are rarely wrong."

Unable to keep herself from smiling, Angie watched as Stanley rolled his eyes, though not maliciously.

Whilst Lottie unpacked and Stanley argued with her, Angie tried to calm herself down. She reflected on her first encounter with her roommate, concluding that it could have gone a lot worse. Lottie was witty, bubbly, and clearly quite a stubborn character, but the thing that comforted Angie the most was that she felt like someone almost... homely.

She felt like she could be a friend.

CHAPTER TWENTY

Angeline

Stanley Turner did not attend any of the colleges in Edinburgh, he explained as Lottie stuck up posters of an American jazz band on the wall. It seemed he had moved there with the sole purpose of looking after his younger sister, which seemed absurd. Angie didn't think she'd ever met a woman like Lottie before, one who was so clearly prepared for what university would have in store for her. The fact Lottie was taking a science, specialising in something that Angie couldn't pronounce or spell, was evidence that Lottie was smart enough to fend for herself. That combined with her conspicuous maturity and political awareness, left Angie thinking Lottie should really be the one looking out for Stanley, who had perched himself on the windowsill, asking Angie dull questions and occasionally chipping in to tease his sister.

"So, I presume you have a job in mind, something to pay for rent whilst you stay in Edinburgh?" Angie questioned Stanley, partly because she was curious and partly because she was wondering why he was so entitled to be teasing his sister about her life.

Stanley cleared his throat, and with a ducked head, muttered something.

"Sorry?"

"I said I'm not exactly employable," Stanley snapped.

Lottie rolled her eyes, strolling over to Stanley and sitting beside him. The dormitory was mostly tidy now. All of Lottie's clothes were stored away and the only new additions to the room were her posters that provided some well-needed brighter colours to the off-white walls, a slightly rusted alarm clock on her bedside table, a picture frame, some books, and a mirror. Lottie nudged her brother in the side, a soft smile gracing her lips.

"He's not unemployable," Lottie told Angie.

Angie held her hands up in surrender, "I didn't think you were I was just wondering what brought you to Edinburgh."

Stanley lifted his head up slowly, shooting Angie a curious look.

"Do you have any siblings?" he asked.

"Yes."

"Younger?"

"Four little brothers," Angie replied.

Stanley hummed in acknowledgment, "I think then, that you should understand."

Did she? Would Angie follow her brothers anywhere to protect them? She'd never come across the necessity to do so before, they'd never been taken away from her, she'd moved away from them. Even during the war, they had been together... It then occurred to Angie that not all siblings were as lucky as she had been, being evacuated to the same place, knowing her brothers were safe for those long years.

Angie had estimated Stanley was a few years older than her, and he was a man. Being over eighteen in 1939 meant Stanley would have been eligible to be a soldier, but Lottie would have either been evacuated or forced to stay at home. Angie watched him ruffle Lottie's hair, Lottie retorting by poking him in the side and Angie saw the two of them laughing and the way Stanley's eyes lit up. Stanley wasn't lingering in their dormitory or moving to Edinburgh because he felt he should be protecting his sister. Angie decided that he must be here because he had missed her.

"Anyway, where's a good place to get a drink around here, London Girl?" Lottie flashed her an excited grin.

Angie hadn't been out drinking yet, there were plenty of pubs lining the streets, but she didn't know if she'd planned to even drink at all. Angie presumed it was early evening... she'd planned to get some work done but...

"There are plenty of pubs. Could my friend Alan come along?" Angie asked.

"Yes!" Stanley clapped. "I will no longer be outnumbered!"

Lottie rolled her eyes, manhandling Stanley towards to door.

"Angeline and I will get ready and meet you at the reception in an hour," Lottie told him.

Angie watched Stanley pouting as Lottie pushed him out the door. His scruffy shirt and slacks were creased, his dark hair a mess across his forehead. Strangely, the messiness seemed fitting if anything it made him appear more at ease, handsome, even. Angie had never really thought of a man as handsome before.

The door closed on Stanley's sulky face and Lottie clasped her hands together excitedly before running over to Angie, who was standing beside her bed, nearly fell over when Lottie pulled her into an unexpected, crushing hug. She squeezed Angie's waist tightly and she could feel Lottie laughing joyously into her shoulder, "Oh, this is so lovely. I haven't had a girl friend in so long."

Angie hugged Lottie back, breath caught in her throat because she hadn't had a *hug* in so long.

"Me neither," Angie managed to reply as Lottie leaned back, clutching Angie's hands with an excited squeal.

"We are going to be such good friends," Lottie told her. "Oh! We should let your friend Alan know what time we are meeting."

Angie hadn't thought that far ahead, she wasn't even certain he would be willing to come along. But the prospect of Alan proving to all the people who called him 'Specky' that he did in fact have friends, was always thrilling.

Angie knocked on Alan's door whilst Lottie was in their dorm doing her makeup. Alan responded within three seconds of Angie knocking, as he always did, with a smile and a wave. She told him where to meet and he cut the conversation short, scuttling back inside to get ready. He'd be nervous, he'd talk a lot, but that was just Alan, and Lottie seemed nice enough to be courteous to him. Stanley had been expecting a male friend for company, perhaps he had the idea of one that was willing to talk of sports and women in his head. Alan would be a surprise for Stanley, but if he said a bad word about him, he'd have Angie to deal with.

It had been a while since Angie had had a genuine reason to wear something pretty, darken her eyes, and colour her lips. Looking at her reflection and the way the material of her red dress hugged her curves in the right places, she felt... beautiful. In a way that made her feel powerful. She'd grown up a little later than everybody else. She was still curvy but had grown a little taller and the chubbiness of her face hadn't really gone but she looked older now. Angie wondered, for a brief moment, what Dorothea would think if she saw her now. She banished the thought as quickly as it came.

Behind her, Lottie applied her lipstick and smiled at Angie in the mirror.

"You alright?" Lottie asked.

"Yes, it's just... been a while since I've socialised properly."

Lottie faced her with a sympathetic smile and started twisting Angie's golden hair back, pinning it out of her face so she could see.

Lottie's curly hair needed no pinning back; the naturally tight ringlets fell perfectly into place and bounced with her every move. But the gesture felt so familiar, similar to something Angie and Charity Smith would have done back when they were still friends.

"Is it Stanley? You don't mind him coming with us, do you? He'll make friends with people his age soon, I'm sure, but in the meantime—"

"I like Stanley just fine," Angie interrupted.

She hadn't actually known him long enough to decide if she did or did not like him yet. But he had a kind smile and clearly loved his sister dearly, so Angie thought he couldn't be all that bad.

"There," Lottie said when she was done with Angie's hair.

The pair looked at their reflections in the mirror and smiled.

Angie slipped on her cardigan, knowing she'd be cold, but it was a sacrifice women had to make. A thick, warm coat and delicate dress would look laughable.

Lottie and Angie waited at the bottom of the stairs by the reception after an hour had passed, the sun was going down and Angie couldn't help but feel nervous anticipation for her first night out at university.

Stanley showed up first, wearing the same creased green shirt and dark trousers as before but his curls had been combed back with pomade. Angie wasn't sure why, but she thought he looked much better with it messy. Stanley's eyes lingered on Angie's dress, his gaze only interrupted when Alan appeared, red-cheeked and smelling strongly of aftershave. Angie watched Stanley for his reaction.

"You must be Alan!" Stanley smiled widely but it didn't seem to hold any maliciousness.

There wasn't a hint of mocking as Alan held his hand out and Stanley shook it. Unjudgmental, even despite Alan's awkward stance and huge glasses. Angie was beginning to suspect she had severely underestimated Stanley.

They found a pub with a name involving a 'lion.' Angie realised it must have been a common name because she'd seen countless pubs in London with a similar one, even in Wales too.

The air inside was humid. It was bustling with students and people of various ages, all dressed in somewhat expensive clothes, nothing like the types of people you would find in bars back in London. Angie had to bite back a smile thinking of how shocked her father would be to see her now, a pint of ale in her hand, in a sweaty pub.

Alan was sitting on Angie's right and his shoulders weren't tense as they so often were. He appeared at ease, especially with Stanley whom he'd been chatting to since they'd arrived. Stanley was on Angie's left, his brown skin looked as if it had a golden glow in the low light. He looked relaxed and Angie's slightly drunken mind started wondering how many years he'd gone without happiness and if her suspicions were correct and he had in fact been a soldier. A soldier making up for lost time.

*

"I think that we should go dancing," Stanley suggested, later into the night when Lottie and Alan were talking enthusiastically about a singer Angie had never heard of.

His voice was gentle, inviting in a way that left Angie feeling as if she had the right to say yes or no without any consequences. Angie was certain it was the beer, the alcohol in her system, lighting up her veins and making her drowsy enough to mistake Stanley for a type of man that only existed in novels.

Angie scoffed, leaning into Stanley without thinking about it. The smelt of sweat and lemonade. He wasn't even *drinking*. This had to be an act.

"I'm not dense."

"No, London, I didn't think you were," Stanley replied, leaning back to look at her, a brow raised curiously.

"Why is it you want to go dancing then?" Angie took a sip of beer, eyes on Stanley as she drank.

Her eyes lingered on him without her consent.

"Because it's too loud in here to think," Stanley said.

"And why would you need to think?"

"Because…" He ducked his head and mumbled something to his hands that he'd placed in his lap.

"I can't hear you."

"I need to think so I can talk to you."

204

"Why do you want to do that?"

"You ask a lot of questions."

Someone had said that to Angeline before, but she couldn't remember who or what the context had been. It sent a spark of exciting electricity buzzing through her.

"That's how a conversation works, you wanted me to talk," Angie pointed out.

He threw his head back in a laugh and Angie noticed how long his exposed neck was. The skin there was smooth, apart from a freckle just below his Adam's apple. Her mind ran away with thoughts of him, so fast she couldn't catch up. Her mouth formed the words before she could even process them:

"I think that we should go dancing, too."

*

The February air that filled her lungs tasted faintly of tobacco, a flavour that lingered from the densely packed pub that seemed to have been void of any oxygen. With her legs feeling like jelly and her mind a fog, she held tightly onto Stanley's upper arm as they stumbled along the cobbled streets of Edinburgh in search of the dance hall.

Stanley had loosened up since leaving the bar and it made Angie wonder whether it had been his sister that was making him anxious. There was plenty of reason for her to; Lottie was clearly the smarter sibling and got on better with people. Stanley hadn't spoken much to Alan, but she didn't think that was due to him being judgemental but rather that Stanley himself had been nervous. Whatever worries Stanley had faded away, evident in the way he rambled on with his thick and unfamiliar accent.

"You speak strangely," Angie interrupted him; she hadn't been listening, too busy trying not to trip up.

"Oh." Stanley stiffened.

"Sorry," she giggled.

Stanley forced a smile before pressing his lips together to form an uncertain expression. It seemed he was either ignoring or just allowing Angie's insult.

"It isn't a bad thing," Angie protested, patting Stanley's arm, the one she was holding tightly onto. "It just so happens that I like people with funny accents, I've met people who speak even stranger."

With rosy cheeks, Stanley walked a little faster, almost as if he believed if he picked up his speed, he could run away from the compliment Angie had given him. It was a peculiar notion, one that Angie rarely saw in men, most responded to compliments with a smirk or flirtation.

They approached a building that looked slightly like the town hall back in London, but with flowers in plant pots that Angie could only just make out in the dark. They lined the path up to the arched double doors of the entrance.

"I'm not sure how people will react in there," Stanley cleared his throat, slipping his hand away from Angie's. "I mean with our different... heritage."

For a long moment, Angie failed to understand what the man was referring to. Until a couple stumbled out of the double doors, the man with his arms tightly wrapped around the waist of his lover, who wore a darkly coloured, puffy, poker-dot dress. It contrasted drastically with the pale white of her skin and the skin of her partner. The penny dropped as Angie looked up at Stanley in the ghostly moonlight that cast a glow on his youthful facial features.

Angie felt a tug on her heartstrings as she took his calloused hand in hers, wondering whether their rough surface was due to dock-work.

Angie smiled at him confidently and led the way, lifting her chin up and widening her eyes to convince herself that she was sober, needing to be aware to shoot glares at anybody that had something negative to say to them. They passed through the crowd freely, people seemingly too immersed in their dancing. With a talented band playing songs Angie recognised from before the war, it was difficult not to be.

Hesitantly, Stanley placed his hands on her waist and Angie couldn't deny the warmth she felt in his embrace. Buzzing from alcohol, adrenaline, and anxiety, Angie closed her eyes and let the music guide her, lips mouthing the words of a song she knew from years ago.

They moved together and Angie acknowledged the shape of their bodies, the way his bigger hands felt around her small waist. Something uncomfortable stirred at the thought, guilt for all the years Angie had believed she preferred being this close to a woman. And here she was, realising that she enjoyed dancing with a man too.

"Spin me," Stanley interrupted her thoughts, prolonging Angie's spiral of guilt.

"What?"

"Spin me around."

"I'm… not the man," Angie raised a brow.

"You're definitely the man."

"What does that even mean?!" Angie squealed with laughter when Stanley let go of her waist to spin around.

"You've got something about you," Stanley continued, when he moved back into her embrace again.

There was a moment of silence between them whilst Angie thought of how to respond, debating whether Stanley's compliments were genuine.

"You've got something about trying to make people dislike you," Angie giggled.

Stanley leaned in close, his warm breath brushing the shell of Angie's ear; it was then that she saw a snobbish side glance from an older-looking woman to her left. It was selfish, but Angie was too caught up in the moment to say anything about it.

"I just wanted to hear you laugh," Stanley said before leaning away.

Stanley was definitely a fictional book character.

The world faded away for a short while. Moving and humming, singing, and swaying, an invisible bubble encased Angie and Stanley inside and Angie let her inhibitions fade away. Happiness had avoided her for so long that Angie was too afraid to let it be chased away.

It didn't last for long. It never did. The bubble always popped. Two notes into Vera Lynn's *We'll meet again,* and a woman's grieving cry rattled the room. Angie met Stanley's apprehensive eyes. Their gaze never faltered as they listened to the words that had somehow managed to capture all the feelings of 1943.

"*...keep smiling through, just like you always do,*" Angie whispered, not quite singing, not quite speaking.

Stanley's eyes glistened in the dim light.

"I took you dancing to make you smile," Stanley said with a frustrated sigh, loosening his grip on Angie's waist.

With a spinning mind that could not quite distinguish her feelings, Angie put her hand on top of Stanley's, afraid he'd let her go. Because people, well, they always seemed to let her go.

"I haven't smiled," Angie croaked, "not really, not since... not..."

Alan made her smile, having Lottie as her new roommate had made her smile, and even Stanley had. But nothing felt quite as real as the whisper of the wind in the trees, the melodic sound of the Welsh accent, and that sense of hope she'd had for a few fleeting months when she'd thought perhaps, she would meet Dorothea again. It all came rushing to the surface, like crashing waves at the beach on a windy day— violent waves, frothy and grey under an unforgiving sky and heavy rain.

"God," Angie pressed her forehead against Stanley's sturdy chest as an ocean wave of nausea took her under the surface.

"I'll walk you home," Stanley responded, Angie couldn't establish what tone laced his gravelly voice.

*

They were almost back to Angie's room when she acknowledged where they were going. Had she been returning to an empty room, a place to be alone and cry, Angie would have allowed herself to be led. But not if Lottie was there, a new person she didn't quite have the courage to trust. She didn't know why she'd chosen to trust Stanley and yet here she was, clutching onto his arm.

"Don' walk me back," Angie slurred.

"Angeline, you trust too easily," Stanley said, of all things.

"That is not true."

"You don't know me yet," Stanley said.

"But I want to."

It had been the first thing Angie had said without slurring her words since they'd left the hall, and it must have been why the corner of Stanley's thin lips rose and he stopped walking. Angie let go of his arm.

"I want to," she repeated.

He nodded, his hand coming up to her cheek. He held it, looking into her eyes in search of something. Angie let out a shallow breath.

"Time isn't going anywhere, you know?" Stanley said. "We have time. I'll give you time."

210

Growing up wealthy, Angie had received many gifts throughout the years. Time seemed to be the greatest one yet.

CHAPTER TWENTY-ONE

Dorothea

Wheels screeched as carriages came to a halt before her. She stood behind the faded white line on the train platform. She grasped a small suitcase filled with some spare clothes Lizzie's mother had given her, and the money she'd got out of the bank before leaving. Thea hadn't known what else to pack.

She had travelled very few times in her life, only ever for a summer's day to the sea with her family, or a daytrip to a neighbouring town. Short journeys when her father would rub her back as she vomited into a paper bag.

Thea hated trains.

Cars were bearable, though the Miller's only owned a tiny old one with rusted red paintwork that they rarely used, one that her father had only ever driven about as slow as riding a bicycle. But trains... trains were fast. Trains made Thea throw up. But she had no other choice.

A whistle was blown, and people walked passed her to board the carriages. One red-headed little boy who was holding his mother's hand stared at Thea with a confused expression, clearly wondering why Thea was motionless, staring at the train as if it had killed her entire family, whilst everybody else boarded it. Thea was trying to tell her feet to move but it was proving difficult as her stomach continued to twist itself into anxious knots.

Thea had received Peggy's letter two days ago, one week after she'd posted it. She had left before receiving a response from Florence, but imagined she'd welcome Thea just as Peggy had; enthusiastically, with a quickly written hand that was so messy in some places that Thea had to ask Lizzie to help decipher the words letter by letter. Peggy sent Thea her exact address, the train station to get off at and said Thea could show up whenever she pleased.

The welcome was slightly unexpected, coming from somebody whom she hadn't spoken to in at least a year. But Peggy had practically become family during the years of the war, so when Thea needed help, she hadn't even questioned the reasoning behind it. Although Thea didn't think that meant the subject would be dropped, she was prepared for Peggy to psychoanalyse her when they reunited.

Sneaking into her own house to find Peggy and Florence's addresses had been a nerve-wracking experience. It hadn't been difficult at first. Thea had experience of sneaking around with Angeline.

She'd snuck in once her mother had left to go into the village, using the spare key they kept hidden in an empty plant pot. The addresses were written on a small piece of card, exactly where Thea had anticipated they would be, in the drawer in the kitchen that was filled with bills, receipts, notes, old letters and something Thea had not anticipated. Telegrams. Her breath hitched in her throat when she saw them and she was tempted to take them with her to the city, so she could have just a small part of her brother and father with her. But she couldn't do it.

Before sneaking back out, Thea had traced the ugly floral paper in the hallway with faded colours, marks, and scratches. There was a lump in her throat that she couldn't swallow around, one that got worse when she'd walked a few yards away from the cottage, turning back around when she shouldn't have.

Green plants had grown up the sides of the cottage. Thea had once found them beautiful, but they now appeared less like welcome guests and more like intruders. She could picture the plant taking over the whole cottage until it was entirely unrecognisable, engulfing her mother inside. She could picture the cottage collapsing, the roof caving in on the small rooms she grew up in, picture frames smashing, piano keys breaking, the memories fading.

Tears trickled down her cheeks on her way back to Lizzie's, and the lump of guilt in her throat remained.

"Thea, you should at least leave her a letter," Lizzie had said.

"No."

"She'll never forgive herself."

"My mother did nothing wrong," Thea had replied, defensive.

"She doesn't know that, what if she thinks she pushed you away?"

"I pushed myself away, like I should have done years ago."

"You don't need to push people away."

Thea ignored the statement.

"I have to leave, and I may never come back. She was all I had left, and I can't even say goodbye. I'm not even strong enough for that."

"This is the strongest, bravest thing you could possibly do."

"If I was brave, I would stay."

And yet there she was, ticket in hand, finally putting one foot in front of the other to board the train. Leaving her old life behind and running away like the coward she believed herself to be.

She stored her case in the compartment above where she was to sit. Her stomach lurched when she slid into a carriage booth, feeling the floor move beneath her as she sat down with elbows on her knees and her head in her hands, swallowing the acidic bile that rose her throat.

Thea couldn't have been in that position for more than five minutes before she felt the hairs on the back on her neck stand, her mouth filling with saliva as she gripped the material of the seat, digging her nails into the worn fabric and supressing the inescapable urge to gag. Had she not been forced to eat breakfast by Lizzie's mother, perhaps she wouldn't have struggled so much. Then again, Thea hadn't been able to cope with her travel sickness even with her father's gentle reassurances, getting through it alone was bound to be impossible.

Lizzie had offered to travel with her to keep her company. But she'd said it with a worried look on her face that told Thea Lizzie didn't want to leave her parents. And could Thea blame her? If the Miller's farm on the hill had returned to what it used to be; Mr and Mrs Miller with their two innocent children who were untainted by the horrors of life, then Thea wouldn't consider moving away from her parents either. She'd have no reason to leave such a perfect life behind. James would marry Judy Tucker and Thea would have her family. She didn't need anything else to be happy.

At least she wished she didn't.

Living with the absence of lovers was something Thea wouldn't be capable of doing. Even if her brother and father had returned, even if the war hadn't happened, Thea would still have unnatural desires. It wasn't a subject she thought about often and perhaps contemplating it whilst travel sick wasn't a smart idea. But her thoughts spiralled as she considered where it came from, and what caused her to feel this way. There was nothing wrong with any of her other family members so it couldn't have been in her genes.

The train came to its first station and a blonde woman with an elegant skirt that framed her body in a way that normal girls would be jealous of, rather than admire in a way that made their head spin and heart race. It was then that she remembered the reason. The answer to why Thea felt this way for women could be answered with one word, the sweet-sounding name she had struggled to forget. The 'angel' at the start of her name was deceiving when she'd sown the seeds of Thea's unholy desires.

The woman didn't look much like Angeline, though Thea couldn't be certain of that as she hadn't seen her in months, but she looked similar enough that Thea had to hold back the urge to walk over to her. She looked familiar enough that Thea's shoulders were no longer tense, and her nausea had almost entirely subsided.

Thea closed her eyes and rested against the window when the train started moving again. Her father wasn't there to help her through her travel sickness and yet the blur of the world outside didn't scare her now. Because the wood of the trees that passed by were the same shade of brown as Angeline's eyes, and the winter sun lit up the world in gold. Thea closed her eyes and saw *her* again.

*

Sleep wasn't something that had come easy to Thea in the past weeks, but, in between trains transfers, the movement of the final train had lulled her into a dreamless sleep. The travel sickness was gone, and Thea convinced herself it was because, after sleepless nights, her body had finally crashed. She tried to assure herself that it had nothing to do with the thought of Angeline. And how, even after years, she still felt like the equivalent of a warming hug, like tea on a warm day, capable of ridding Thea's body of any anxieties. It was nothing more than the curse of a first love; Angeline was an inevitable handprint on her soul, burnt into her memory for all eternity.

Unforgettable, like all first loves were.

Blinking hard so her eyes focused on the world outside the train window, Thea felt her palms begin to sweat. The train was gradually slowing as she took in the unsettlingly unfamiliar environment around her. They passed a multitude of old empty carriages, rusting and rotting on the unused tracks that led into what Thea presumed would be the station.

There were thick, strange wires overhead, tall lampposts that looked nothing like the ones at home and variously sized silhouettes of buildings obscuring the horizon from view.

They passed through a tunnel that turned the world dark; heading towards the light ahead which, as they came to a stop, Thea realised was a station bustling with people. It was underground.

Her travel sickness was then replaced with claustrophobia. It felt as though her ribcage was caving in, squeezing air out of her lungs. She grasped the rickety table in front of her and stumbled to her feet. People rushed passed to exit the train and Thea tried to spot somewhere where daylight was visible, petrified of the concept that they were metres below the ground. As if she was in a grave.

Disorientated, she grabbed a stranger's upper arm.

"Where are we?"

The man she grasped looked as if he was in his mid-thirties, with dark eyes and a flat cap that sat lopsided upon his head. He studied her expression.

"Are you quite alright, Miss?"

"It's hard to..." Thea grasped her shirt at her chest, feeling how quickly it rose and fell as she tried to let out steady breaths that kept coming out as weak rasps. "Why are we underground?"

The stranger's lips turned up into a faint, understanding smile as he pointed outside the window to the train platform.

"The stairs are just through those doors," the man said. His accent was unfamiliar, not posh, and certainly not Welsh. He sounded as though he wasn't from Britain at all. "I'm going to assume you haven't been on a train station that's underground before."

Thea shook her head, fiddling with the hem of her shirt before blurting out, "I've never been to a city before."

"Well, isn't that something," he laughed, not unkindly. "I've been to cities all around the world."

Thea didn't want to ask why; something told her he was running from something.

"Is London a pleasant one?" she asked, the conversation distracting her from her panic.

The man pressed his lips together in thought, pulling down Thea's case from where it had been stored above her head. He handed it to her, meeting her eyes.

"If you know what you are looking for."

"And if I don't?" Thea clutched onto her case.

After a brief pause, the man replied, "I wish you the best of luck. Because you're going to need it."

CHAPTER TWENTY-TWO

Dorothea

February air had never felt this close and muggy. It stuck to her lungs like *Wrigley's Spearmint Gum* to the bottom of a shoe. Thea was surprised she'd even managed to find her way out of the labyrinth of corridors and stairs that made up the train station.

She thought she'd finally got out when she saw daylight peeking through overhead windows, but she still had to weave her way past bookstalls, tea rooms and countless clocks ticking to the beat of the chatter, to finally find an exit.

If it could even be called that— Thea did not feel like she had exited anything.

The reds, golds and oranges of advertisements were plastered inescapably against every lamppost, every bus, every wall; shouting at you to buy *Gordon's Gin*, to smoke these cigarettes and buy that perfume, telling everyone that '*Oxo cubes are the Best of The Best!*'

The cars and buses flew past so quickly they became a mere blur of colour, a man with a neat moustache started yelling at her in a language Thea didn't understand. Or maybe her overwhelmed senses made people impossible to understand. Her mind was screaming. London was screaming. Thea was fighting back tears, holding her breath as she marched with her head down so London would stop telling her that *'Guinness is Good for You!'* and that *'Weetabix is more than a breakfast food!'*

There was an alley way.

Long and narrow, posters still preaching at her as she slouched against the wall and squeezed her eyes shut to finally let out a shallow breath. Thea lowered her case to the ground, fumbling in the side compartment to try and find the slip of paper with Peggy's address. She silently prayed that there was somebody in this mad, mad city, with a heart to give her directions.

Like a lion from *Oz*, Thea found the courage to pick up her case and leave the alley, finding a man with patchy hair, pointy ears, and a scratchy sack he clutched closely to his body to keep him warm. Thea didn't know why he was sitting in an abandoned shop window, and his face was practically black with filth, she wondered why he didn't go home for a bath.

"Sir?" she asked in a voice so high-pitched she hardly recognised it as her own. "I was wondering if you could help me with directions."

His tired eyes met hers; a tally-chart would have to be made to count the wrinkles on his face. After looking her up and down in a way that made Thea want to hide away, his eyes softened.

"Young little Land Girl how was your time in the countryside?" he smiled and Thea didn't know if it was her creased blouse or muddy shoes that indicated her occupation.

Putting her bag down, she kneeled beside the man as she began to explain, "I'm not from the city, I live in the countryside, Wales. Well, I... I did."

The man shook his head, putting a shaky hand with a fingerless glove on her arm.

"Poor, poor country girl."

"I... I really am quite alright." Thea stiffened under the man's touch.

As if knowing what she was thinking, he removed it.

"London isn't for gentle souls," the man said, head lolling against the empty shop's window. "You are gentle. Gentle, gentle. Like sweet Sylvia. My sweet Sylvia..."

Thea realised, upon noticing an empty bottle of whiskey beside him, that this man was either crazy, drunk or both. And yet, Thea found herself seeing more life in him that any other person she'd walked past in the bustling streets. He had a kind look, resembling that of Lizzie's father and a slight hint of her own.

So, Thea found herself sitting beside him.

"Who's Sylvia?"

"My beautiful wife," he whispered. "I left her behind. I had to... I was recruited but that German scum... took m-my..."

Perhaps it was selfish she didn't want the full story, but enough grief had followed her around.

"I understand."

The man forced a smile, opening his eyes with great difficulty.

"Do you know a lot of love?" he croaked.

"Yes."

He sighed contently.

"Oh, that's good. The directions I help you with, will they lead you to love?"

Thea unfolded the slip of paper from where she'd tucked it up her sleeve, she read the street name over and over, counting the letters and tracing the edges as she thought of a reply.

"I lost my love."

The man let out a pitiful sob, pressing the heels of his hands to his eyes. For a moment, Thea wanted to scrap the idea of finding Peggy. Perhaps she'd be better off, here with this man, hiding her face behind her hands as she cried her throat bloody. Yearning like a dog with a dead owner.

"But these directions," Thea said. "If I find this house I have a chance again, sir. You see, I will find my friend, my family."

He looked up with desperate eyes.

"And what is it we do, when they are all dead?"

The question pounded her head, like two rocks whacking hard against each other until eventually one of them cracked.

"I will tell you the way," the man said hopelessly, taking the paper from Thea's frozen hands.

*

The city filtered out into fewer roads and more houses, a rare scattering of trees and a few rivers. Thea nearly fell to her knees when she arrived at the little house, the number painted on a slab of slate made her let out an audible laugh of relief. But the face in the window was ultimately what made her knees give way.

In a flash, Peggy was there. Peggy was hugging her tight, stopping her from falling. Thea cried into her shoulder. She smelt like tea and cake. The image of her in the kitchen, doing something as mundane as baking whilst she smiled and smiled, made Thea hold her tighter. It was almost as if the time apart had led Thea to convince herself that the war had been a dream.

"Oh, darling," Peggy hushed, stroking the back of her head. "You're safe."

The tears stained Peggy's dress but Thea refused to let go. No more words were uttered in that moment, because no more needed to be said. A reassuring arm laced around her, and Peggy led her up the path and into the house.

An aroma of baking filled her senses, the flickering fire in the living room catching her attention the moment she entered the room. With her overwhelmed senses, Thea had hardly noticed how cold she had been, wndering through the streets of London with nothing but a blouse, trousers, and a suitcase in her hand. Her fingertips stung as they warmed up.

She perched by the fire instinctively, dropping her case haphazardly beside herself. The fire became nothing but a blur of yellow through her teary eyes. Perhaps she was crying from relief, perhaps it was from the heat of the fire. Thea wasn't quite sure. But she liked it by the fire. It was familiar. Most of her days at Lizzie's were spent there. For a moment, Thea thought she'd turn around and see her dear friend smiling. When she did look behind her, she was met with another dear friend, but her smile said a thousand words. Where Thea couldn't read Lizzie, Peggy's sympathy and concern radiated from her.

Thea sat on her hands, waiting for Peggy to say something from where she hovered in the doorway.

"Peg?"

A voice called from the other side of the house, distinctively male but soft.

Peggy called back, "Thomas, Dorothea is here."

There was a moment of awkward shuffling and a red-cheeked man appeared beside Peggy in the living room doorway. He was wiping his hands on his... apron?

"I failed to mention in my letter," Peggy spoke timidly. It was strange, hearing her usually confident voice like that. "Thomas is my fiancé."

Thea's mouth fell open and she stumbled to her feet. Peggy *had* failed to mention her engagement. It made Thea's stomach churn with guilt; her own problematic life had overtaken the joy Peggy could have shared in her letter. Thea's head pounded from the roller-coaster of emotions she'd been on, she was certain it would be the last surprise, at least for that day. And how pleasant to end on a positive note, Thea thought. It was much needed.

"Peggy, I- Wow! I'm so happy for you and, Thomas, it's nice to meet you!" Thea said it with a laugh, grinning between the pair. "I feel terrible, Peg. You must have so much planning to do and here's me taking up your personal space."

Peggy looked up fondly at Thomas as he wrapped his arm around her waist, pressing a chaste kiss to her forehead. Thomas had bright baby-blue eyes, which sparkled with love for his fiancée.

The words the homeless man had said to Thea earlier that say, echoed in her mind, *'Do you know a lot of love?'* The fact was, Thea had known a lot of love before, and she very much still did.

When one surrounds oneself with beautiful people with beautiful souls, love becomes inescapable.

Her father's love for her mother, Lizzie's love for her parents and now Peggy and Thomas. Thea knew a lot of love, she just hadn't felt a lot, or, more accurately, had not allowed herself to feel a lot. Romantic love was off the cards for her, but Peggy was her family and, judging by Thomas and his sweet smile, he, one day, would be too.

"Actually, all the planning for the wedding is done," Peggy chuckled.

"Oh?"

"It's happening next month." Thomas nodded, looking shyer than Peggy. "I must say, your arrival has been timely."

"We've baked a cake to celebrate the end of all our planning!" Peggy brushed the flour off Thomas' apron.

"Not to mention, you have just enough time to get fitted for a dress," Thomas said, Peggy's eyes flew wide, and she swatted his chest. He didn't stop talking. "Peggy's enjoyed looking for bridesmaids' dresses, haven't you, love?"

Colour drained from Thea's face. Peggy glanced at her cautiously, anticipating a negative response.

"You want me to be a bridesmaid?"

"Yes," Peggy sighed, tutting at Thomas who uttered a quiet 'oh.' "You, Florence and..."

The world span on its axis and the crackling of the fire sounded like the beating of a drum. Thea swallowed despite her impossibly dry mouth.

"...and Angeline."

CHAPTER TWENTY-THREE

<u>Angeline</u>
Angeline found herself almost in love with Stanley Turner within a month. Alan took pleasure in teasing her, almost as much as Lottie, who took their coupling surprisingly well. Angie told Lottie after a busy day of classes, when she'd been daydreaming about Stanley's fingers intertwined with her own, his soft laugh, the way his slightly crooked nose would crinkle when he smiled.

"I should have guessed my brother would woo a girl here, but it wasn't meant to be my bloody roommate!" Lottie had said, the pair laying on the floor with a record humming in the background.

"He isn't... wooing me," Angie had chuckled, cheeks reddening at the sound of her own laughter.

It felt like she was split down the middle. One side of her loved curves, long lashes and soft lips, the other liked calloused hands, flat chests, and a body entirely different to her own.

"There's something on your mind," Stanley said one Sunday afternoon.

Lottie was off running some campaign. She'd taken Alan along. For company, or possibly because she saw that passionate voice and those thoughts he kept hidden behind his shy demeanour and poetry. Lottie could be his temporary voice.

"Hm?"

Angie didn't mind the apartment to herself. It gave her and Stanley some time. He'd found himself a one-room place and a job unloading packages at a local shop. His accommodation was appropriate for him to have a mere night's sleep, but there wasn't exactly living space.

When Stanley and Angie spent time together it was walks, picnics or cafes. A perfect post-war romance with a perfect gentleman and beautiful blonde girl.

Perfect was what it should have been.

"Your mind is always racing," Stanley said.

Angie lay on his chest. They hadn't even kissed yet, but somehow always ended up touching like this; in comfortable silence with his hands threading through her hair. As if they'd been lovers for years.

"I just don't want you to be this emotional crutch for me," Angie whispered. "We spend time together and I always fall silent."

Stanley let out a sigh. She felt him shift, tilting his head down to look at her.

"I promised you time, Ang."

A nickname for her nickname.

"I know."

She did. But wasn't quite sure whether she was taking her time, so he'd give up and leave her, or as a test of loyalty.

Silence flowed between them, Stanley twirling and looping golden strands between his fingers.

"Tell me about your hometown," Angie muttered timidly, feeling a little guilty that she hardly asked Stanley anything.

A part of her thought that if she kept him mysterious, almost anonymous, she wouldn't get too attached. Almost as if she was saving herself for a person that must have forgotten her, as Angie should have too.

"It was grey, obviously. That's Britain for you," Stanley laughed lowly, vibration against Angie's ear on his chest. "Not far from North Wales. Quite a few hills, forests."

"Nothing like London, then?" Angie grinned up at him, ignoring the word 'Wales' and the thrill it sent through her.

"No. Nothing like Edinburgh, either. I miss it, a bit. My friends, the docks. Lottie actually got a letter from home." The tone in his voice was indetectable. "There's not a lot going on at the moment."

Humming in acknowledgment, Angie pondered on her own family: whether William was enjoying his role as the oldest sibling, whether Peter was still following his father around like a lost puppy, brown eyes gleaming with admiration. And she wondered if her mother was focused on nothing but the ticking of the clock in her bedroom, whilst life moved on and nobody stopped to question it.

"I haven't received a letter yet," Angie muttered.

She hadn't bothered to call either, or write a letter herself. Her intention to rewrite her life was perhaps selfish, but it got her further away from the memory of Dorothea.

"Neither," Stanley chuckled. "The letter was addressed to my sister."

Angie leant up on her elbow, resting her chin on the palm of her hand.

"Your family don't write to you directly?"

Stanley's mouth twisted into a frown, looking down at the crumpled sheets they lay upon, rather than meeting her eyes. She put her free hand on Stanley's chest, tracing along the creased material of his white shirt. He didn't speak for a short while.

"Your family must have high expectations for you," Angie guessed.

"And I let them down," Stanley shrugged, pretending he didn't care.

"They let *you* down. Families are meant to care no matter how you turn out."

Stanley flashed a white-toothed grin, one Angie was sure had all the girls swooning. It had her a little breathless herself. He raised his hand from where it lay limp by his side to cup Angie's cheek, brushing a thumb against the soft surface.

The tenderness, the familiarity of that touch from another lifetime, another person, brought tears to her eyes. It must have been something about the way his dark hair framed his face, the way his eyebrows were carelessly bushy, and the way a cocky smirk graced his lips, that had Angie leaning in to kiss him.

*

The letter arrived a few days later. Scruffy handwriting that clearly did not belong to her father or mother. Angie took it to the window, letting the afternoon glow light up the crinkled paper. Stanley's arms wrapped around her from behind, peering down at the envelope.

"Family?" he asked.

"No... it's—"

"Is the whole touchy-feely thing really necessary?" Lottie teased from the other side of the room, where she lay on her front with her nose in a comic book.

"Shut up, Lott," Stanley said, loosening his grip all the same. "Angie's got a letter."

"It's from..."

A past life, Angie almost said, biting her tongue to stop herself. Peggy's scratchy writing covered the letter that had been delicately designed with a floral boarder, one that would only decorate letters on special occasions.

Angie could have stayed in her head for hours, the only thing drawing her away was Stanley's warm breath on her neck and a soft, "You alright?"

"Yes," Angie rushed to say, tearing up at the overwhelming feeling of joy that she hadn't felt in too long. "One of the land girls I lived with during the war is getting married. She wants me to be a bridesmaid."

Lottie clapped excitedly, rushing over to Angie, and taking the letter from her hands as she bounced around like an overexcited child on Christmas day.

"*Please* say you can bring a plus one!" Lottie beamed. "There hasn't been anything remotely exciting going on around here for weeks!"

"You're in full-time education, of course it's boring," Stanley chuckled.

"Yeah, how's unloading cans and jars from lorries, Stan?" Lottie teased. "So much more thrilling? Or maybe it's just the old ladies flirting with you—"

"You won't be teasing when I've got more money than you!" Stanley replied, red-cheeked.

Amongst the petty squabbling, Angie had found herself entirely zoned out, distanced from any sense of reality.

She wondered whether Peggy had aged, whether she had wrinkles around her almond-shaped eyes. Did people age that quickly? Even if Angie tried, she wouldn't be able to work out how much time had passed, after spending so long trying to forget.

She wondered whether Florence and Heather would be there. Or even Scary Mary. Saliva thickened in her mouth, and she swallowed hard, Dorothea wouldn't even consider going, not to the city. The thought terrified her, would that merely be an excuse so she wouldn't encounter Angie?

"I'll go alone," Angie said, cutting Lottie and Stanley's arguing off.

Angie folded the letter back up, slipped it into the envelope and went to leave the room.

"I'm going for a walk," she said before she closed the door behind her, heading straight for Alan's.

He opened the door almost instantly, shaving foam around his mouth, joyous jazz music playing in the background, a record Lottie must have lent him. His mouth fell open and he wiped the foam off his mouth with the off-white towel he had hanging from his shoulders.

"Angeline are you quite alright?" he asked desperately, already knowing the answer judging by his expression of sympathy.

"I told you, about the family I chose," Angie stammered. "The ones from the farm, how I thought they'd forgotten me."

She raised her trembling hand with the crumpled letter encased inside it, struggling to form words. Years and years came back, as if she'd been pinched and woken up. Starting a new life was a feeble attempt at moving on, one person associated with her past life, and she was taken back to 1943 in an instant.

It wasn't that Angie wasn't over the moon for Peggy, her tight throat and feeling of nausea was perhaps a result of jealousy that Peggy's life post-war had been so simple; a closed-minded approach, but one that was inescapable given the hardship she'd gone through with Dorothea.

Dorothea.

Alan brought her out of the hall and into his doorway, hugging her with strong, reassuring arms. Like a brother.

"Nothing terrible has happened," Angie sobbed into his shoulder, his shaving towel having fallen to the ground. "It's a wedding. I just can't... it... brings everything back."

"Everything?"

Her gut twisted, leaning back to look Alan in the eye.

"God, I want to tell you, I do."

"So, tell me."

He took her hand, pulling her into the apartment and closing the door behind her. She went to the window, it seemed she always found herself there.

She was safe and loved by her friends. No man had done her wrong, no person. She'd had it so easy in comparison to so many people, and yet she discarded her luck unthankfully, still caught up on a person, a life, which had gone.

"Peggy is getting married," Angie spoke softly, watching an icy morning in Edinburgh outside the window, faces and people blurring together into a picturesque painting. "A Land Girl, I once knew when I lived on the farm. The beginning of '43 to '45. I became a woman on that farm, watched my brothers grow up. I don't think my mother ever really forgave me; Charles was only four at the time, when he used to cry it was always me, he ran to, even when we went home. I'd stolen her role."

Angie closed her eyes. She knew she was rambling, avoiding the point. Alan didn't pressure her.

"Two years is a long time, when you fall so desperately in-love with a place." She sighed, watching the memories replay beneath her closed eyelids. "And you grow close to people, too."

"Were you good friends with the land girls? Are you nervous to see them again?"

"We were close, yes. But... it was... Mrs Miller, the farmer's wife, she had a daughter."

Angie took a shaky breath.

She could picture Thea's hands as she held her face, and whispered softly against her freckled cheek, *"I'll always love you."*

"She was..."

Angie could still recall those blue eyes; blue eyes filled with tears, blue eyes sparkling with happiness.

"Alan, I like Stanley," Angie blurted out, facing him with pleading eyes. "I really do."

"I know," Alan smiled reassuringly, holding his hands up. "I believe you."

Angie sucked in a sharp breath. It didn't matter who she told. Dorothea wouldn't be at the wedding, wouldn't write to her. Scary Mary wasn't lurking around corners, waiting to catch her out. And Alan was good, Alan had nobody to tell. And so the words passed her lips with ease,

"I loved *her* first."

CHAPTER TWENTY-FOUR

<u>Dorothea</u>

They didn't talk about it.

Peggy let her sleep in until after midday and didn't make her come downstairs. Thomas must have suspected Thea was quite mad, or just rude. Neither were that far from the truth.

She'd arrived at an old friend's house with nothing but an old case, mucky clothes and a total lack of gratefulness for the fact she'd just been asked to be Peggy's bridesmaid. Even contemplating how ill-mannered she was being didn't give Thea the energy to move, to go and make it right.

All Thea could bring herself to do, was watch how the light changed in the bedroom throughout the day, read the titles of books Peggy had on the shelf until she could recall every one, count the cracks in the ceiling and sleep on and off, trying to ignore the fact there was a possibility she'd be reunited with Angeline Carter in less than a month. The fact she'd be forced to see the very person that had plummeted her into years of feeling she would never feel happiness again.

Without the farm, Thea suspected there would have been many days throughout her life when she would have found herself bed-bound by her emotions. It was difficult to wake when one had no purpose, and when her mother wasn't shouting her for breakfast.

Missing her mother wasn't something that came all at once, not like missing her father. The feeling came from little things; seeing how Lizzie had been with her mother, having a piece of shortbread as a snack on the train, something that had tasted nothing like her mother's. Even hugging Peggy reminded her of home.

Thea didn't have any concept of time. Sleeping on and off, she sometimes woke up to see cold toast and water by her bed. She'd eat and go back to sleep. For two weeks, Thea was merely surviving.

Until Peggy had had enough.

On a chilly morning in early March, her blinds were opened before midday and Thea hissed like a vampire from a gothic novel upon seeing daylight. She pulled the covers over her head.

"That's it," Peggy said, her voice laced with authority.

Thea groaned, rolling onto her front, and burying her face into the pillows.

"Get up, or I'm calling a doctor," Peggy ordered.

"I'm quite well," Thea grumbled with a hoarse voice, it must have been the first thing she'd said for weeks.

Peggy ignored her, going to the door to call down the stairs, "Thomas, are those eggs almost ready?"

"Yes, love."

Thea thought she'd vomit at the thought of food.

"Food first, then you can bathe," Peggy told Thea, pulling her sheets off her.

Thea flinched at the feeling of cool air against her skin. She wore an old shirt as sleepwear, trying to tuck herself into a ball to keep her warm. Her eyes were heavy, but she managed to open them enough to see Peggy in the corner of the room, digging through her case.

"Hey!" Thea shot upright, throwing a pillow at Peggy's head.

Peggy dodged it with ease, holding up Thea's blouses and trousers.

"Goodness me, we need to go shopping," Peggy tutted.

Thea let out a slightly malicious laugh.

"I refuse. You won't get me out of this room."

*

Twenty minutes later, Thea was downstairs on her second piece of scrambled egg on toast. Thomas smiled at Thea as he served her more eggs from the pan, wearing a tacky apron over his shirt. If she was in a better mood, she'd compliment Peggy on her chose of fiancé.

Peggy was sat opposite Thea, her face in her hands, elbows on the table, with a serious and calculating expression on her face.

"Who was the girl you had relations with?" she asked bluntly.

Thea froze, nearly dropping her fork in surprise at the sudden question.

Her tone was almost omniscient, and it reminded her of her mother and the conversation they'd had. The conversation that haunted her, when her mother knew her deepest secret and looked into her daughter's eyes as if she was a stranger. Peggy wasn't quite like that; she'd known about Angeline. Thea didn't feel as terrified, but her gaze did make her want to hide under the covers again, at the thought of disappointing her.

"Who was who?"

"That doesn't work on me."

"Well, your confusing question doesn't work on me."

Speaking to Peggy in that manner felt absurd. And, though Peggy's expression had not changed, Thea felt the urge to hug her and apologise.

Amongst the awkward pause, Thomas made a clanking sound as he was pottering around the kitchen, trying to make himself look busy.

"Who was the girl you slept with, how's that?"

Thea almost choked, eyes widening as she gestured furiously at Thomas.

"Oh, for goodness' sake, Dorothea. He knows you're a lesbian."

That word was destined to echo in her mind for the rest of her life. Sounding like nothing but a slur, an insult, used to describe her love for women. It didn't seem fair that the word should sound so ugly. Not when she loved so passionately. Though, strangely, the need to deny Peggy's statement was non-existent; trying to protect a damaged reputation was the last thing on Thea's mind.

"She was my friend," Thea said in confidence, looking over at Thomas and waiting for a negative reaction.

He'd stopped pottering and his eyes flickered between Peggy and Thea, whole-heartedly unoffended by their topic of conversation.

"Peggy, love, I understand you're trying to normalise this, but Dorothea seems rather uncomfortable." Thomas walked over to Peggy and pressed a passing kiss to her temple. "I'll be in the garden."

Thea met his eyes cautiously, but he just smiled and walked away.

She felt a soft hand on hers and her eyes flickered down to Peggy's hand, her manicured red nails, as she comforted Thea.

"Nobody here is against you; do you understand that?" Peggy said. "Thomas and I will protect you now. You're my family."

Thea nodded jerkily, breathing in sharply.

"Now tell me what happened."

Thea had a sip of juice before picking at the chapped skin around her nails.

"It was October. I was seeing Judy, my brother's ex, every week. Just to check up on her. She invited me out with a few of her friends, that's when I met Lizzie. She's... a raging ball of fury, to be honest with you. James, my brother, he was cheating on Judy with Lizzie at some point, and I think that was why Lizzie was so drawn to me. I reminded her of James. My mother found out, before anything had even happened, she must have just put the pieces together at last. I had to live with Lizzie and... after a while, I just had this feeling. I knew I was pushing it too far, that people were going to become suspicious of me. I wanted to protect Liz, too. So, I left."

Peggy sipped her tea from her mug, digesting the information. Her eyes were bright with curiosity.

"You didn't love her," Peggy said, matter-of-factly.

"No."

"Did she love you?"

"I don't think so."

Thea didn't believe in fate, in secret strings that tied people together and brought them back to each other after years apart. Thea didn't believe in astrology, compatibility that was written in the stars. The idea of soulmates even seemed like a stretch. But she knew one thing, and that was that she'd never love another woman the way she had loved Angeline Carter.

"I couldn't have. Even if I wanted to," Thea admitted.

Peggy didn't say anything. She must have sensed the tsunami of words gathering in Thea's mind as she buried her face in her hands and started laughing. She laughed until her lungs hurt and there were tears trickling from her palm, down her delicate wrists.

"I can't see Angeline again, Peggy, I can't, I can't," Thea wrapped her arms around herself and sobbed. "I can't bear seeing how much she's changed because I won't think of anything but all these years that we've wasted. All this time I could have married her if I was a man. But I'm not. It wasn't enough. We weren't enough."

"It's alright," Peggy came over to her, kneeling down and holding her damp face. "Just breathe, darling. I know. I know."

"But you don't, you don't know!" Thea shook her head, gripping Peggy's hands that held her face as she cried. "And you'll never know, Peg. Because you've got Thomas, and he loves you. And he *can* love you."

Tears brimmed in Peggy's own eyes and Thea almost felt guilty for making her cry.

Nobody talks about how it feels to cry in front of somebody. Nobody talks about how every movement is watched, how every hitch of breath and teardrop is monitored in the most humiliating way. Crying with an audience turns you back into a child.

"I won't force you to come to the wedding," Peggy whispered after a while, when Thea's breathing had calmed slightly. "I'm not asking you to relive 1943, I'm asking you to be my bridesmaid. As my friend, my sister."

All that pounded her head was the question as to whether facing Angeline would be worth it. Thea could picture her at the wedding. Shy and content as she ever was, doing everything in her power to please others. Undoubtedly still at her brothers' side, keeping her family together, never doing anything for her own sake.

The one thing Angeline had always been stubborn about was not marrying; at least she'd be doing one thing for herself as opposed to the wants and needs of others. At least, Thea thought darkly, selfishly, there was a possibility she'd be the only one that Angeline had loved. It must have been that tiny, hopeless idea that had Thea sitting up straight despite her body still aching from weeks in bed. She sighed, forcing a smile as she looked into Peggy's round, sympathetic eyes.

"When is the dress fitting?"

CHAPTER TWENTY-FIVE

Angeline

"Do you know how lucky you are, Miss Carter?"

"Lucky?"

The man laughed, throwing his head back in a way that exposed his wrinkled neck, wafting his strong coffee-breath in Angie's direction. She cringed.

"You are in higher education. The fact you got this opportunity is a miracle."

"Well, I am here. Sir."

Angie didn't think requesting authorised absence would be this difficult.

Plenty of people left university for personal reasons, frequently reasons weren't given, especially for the unreliable male students who didn't ever raise their hand to ask a question or to offer an interpretation.

Students like that seemed to get away with murder, Angie doubted those boys had ever been forced to sit in the attendance office that smelt like a backroom of Angie's church in London, to offer an explanation under the beady eyes of a man who looked like he'd never smiled or seen the light of day. He looked bewildered that Angie had even opened her mouth to respond to him.

"Why is it you are requesting an absence?"

"A wedding."

The man looked at her over the top of his glasses, as if she were nothing but a speck of dust.

It took some pleading for him to agree; she had to get the man to look at her spotless record and assessments which she'd excelled in throughout the past month. Despite what people thought, Angie was grateful that she could attend university. But after a conversation with Lottie, she'd agreed with her that there was no point in being eternally grateful for something that should be available as an equal opportunity for both men and woman anyway. The pair saw little point in being thankful when higher education should have been accessible regardless of gender.

Angie was glad for Lottie's presence most of the time. Sometimes she'd rather be in Lottie's company than Stanley's. It was the way they could understand one another, not that Stanley didn't try, but he wasn't exactly a woman at university himself. He was an ex-dockworker with a limited education, and Angie was intrigued by their differences.

After being granted permission, Angie took a deep breath and exited the office through the large double doors and grinned when she saw Alan sitting on a bench outside with a raised brow. Angie nodded, biting her lip to hold back a smile, a consequence of the overwhelming sense of joy she felt at the fact Alan was her friend. The joy had always been there but now, with him knowing what he knew and the way he hadn't changed, Angie was quite certain she had found herself a friend that would last for a lifetime.

"You were in there for quite a while," Alan said, standing up from the bench and brushing sandwich crumbs off his trousers.

He offered her the squished half of his sandwich, and she took it with a smile.

"He felt it was necessary to remind me that I am very lucky to be here, whilst giving me a facial expression that essentially said, 'I'm living in old times and don't think women should have an education anyway.'"

"If only Lottie was around to educate him. Or shout at him."

Angie nudged him softly, taking a bite of her sandwich.

The budding friendship between Lottie and Alan almost reminded her of Peggy or Florence bonding with her little brothers, as if Lottie was a mother-figure that Alan looked up to.

Angie swallowed her mouthful, before looking over at the fountain in the middle of the green grounds. She could almost picture Alan awkwardly perched on the side of it, trying to start a conversation with Angie when she first arrived at the university. She wandered over to it, Alan sitting next to her like they'd done on that very first day, with the sounds of students chattering and the water of the fountain trickling in the background.

"A lot has changed," Angie said, discarding her sandwich beside her. "And I like the change. I liked finding a family here: You, Lottie, and Stanley. But honestly, I think I'm scared."

The sun was beating down on her face and she was quite thankful for how strangely bright it was for March, at least Alan, with his already impaired vision, wouldn't see the tears welling in her eyes.

"What are you scared of?"

"The season changing," she spoke softly, not wanting any passers-by to hear. "Me changing. I change so much."

"That's alright."

"Alan, half of my heart is here, half of my heart is… somewhere else. I can't find it."

"What if you find it? On this trip?"

"I don't want to find it. I just wish I could give myself to this. I want Stanley to have everything he wants; I want to be a good friend to you and Lottie and I want to finish writing this chapter. But I can't finish the chapter because I'm going right back to the very beginning. I'm starting from page one if I go back home." Angie bit her bottom lip, trying to stop the hitches in her voice. "And I'll start regretting everything I've done, the choices I made to get here."

"Angeline," Alan's tone was unfamiliar; it almost didn't suit his voice. He sounded confident, entirely certain with the words he spoke. "You don't owe anything to me, Lottie, or Stanley."

Angie wrapped her arms around herself, hearing his name sent a rush of guilt through her.

She'd tried to convince herself the feeling was merely adrenaline or excitement, when, in truth, it was the overwhelming feeling that she was hiding a part of herself from somebody who trusted her. It would be easier, she thought, if there wasn't a part of her that knew she'd fall in love with Stanley, if she had not met Dorothea.

"What if I see her, Alan? What if I hear her voice again and she looks at me like she used to?"

The silence was deafening, and Angie looked around self-consciously to check nobody had heard what she'd said.

"You don't owe a thing to Stanley, if that's a concern." Alan put a shaky hand on her back. He was awkward about it, which was normal for Alan, but it made Angie consider whether he felt cautious around her after discovering the true nature of Angie's relationship with Dorothea.

"I hadn't... really... given him much thought." Angie rested her icy cheeks in her gloved hands, pressing together her chapped lips. "I have moved on, Alan. I swear by it. Dorothea won't be there anyway."

She spoke with an inconsistent tone, patches of confident words weaved with uncertain voice cracks, as if she was trying to convince herself she meant what she was saying.

Alan's hand returned to his lap, and he clicked his knuckles, pushed his glasses up his crooked nose and cleared his throat. He glanced at his watch a few times as if he was standing at a train or bus station, waiting with anticipation. Angie wondered whether it was time that he was willing to see pass, or something else.

"Are you meeting someone today? Or doing something?" Angie snapped, a little taken aback at how abrupt and demanding her voice sounded as words continued to tumble from her lips. "Or do you hate me after what I told you?"

Angie's dark-haired best friend suddenly looked up at her, his sad eyes looking directly into hers. Alan never met people's gaze. A group of students passed by, and Alan waited until their chattering could no longer be heard until he spoke. It was as if he wanted Angie to hear every single word.

"Angeline, you are my dearest friend. Nothing in the world would change that for me. I understand you. I have studied texts with characters that respond... feel... express themselves, just as you and I do."

Angie neglected to ignore the end of that sentence until she understood the meaning behind Alan's words. Her brows drew together, and she attempted to stare right back into Alan's eyes. They were now darting around nervously.

"What texts, Alan? Enlighten me because I'm lost."

"Some great poets and story-tellers."

"Shakespeare? Byron? Keats? Shelley? I can assure you; I most certainly don't relate to a scientist with a death wish."

"Like Wilde. I mean, Basil Hallward was obsessed with Gray's appearance, which couldn't have been platonic on his half. And are you telling me that Woolf writing about Clarissa and her old friend Sally Seton in *Mrs Dalloway* wasn't loaded with sexual subtext?"

Angie pressed her lips together and blushed, trying not to think of the times she'd read texts that made her whole-body light up at the hope that somebody felt like her. That was the lure of literature and language, the beauty of words. Secrets got hidden, weaved within the letters, shared without the unfair government restrictions. Most of the time.

"I thought *The Picture of Dorian Gray* was restricted after what he did?" Angie responded quietly, if anyone were to hear them discussing homoerotic literature, she'd be leaving campus for more than just a few days.

"The only thing he did was stand up for himself and try to love who he wanted. Just like you did back in '43."

Alan was uncharacteristically defensive.

Looking at her dear friend now, Angie realised something that she had been blind to. Alan's disinterest in dancing with ladies or touching Angie, never once trying to turn his friendships with girls into anything more than that.

She let out a shaky breath, a weight lifting off her shoulders. How was it, that she had found her way to him? How was it, that Angie had been lucky enough to open up to somebody who faced the exact same challenges as her? Tears filled her eyes and Alan's anxiousness seemed to disappear all of a sudden. He smiled and reached over to squeeze her hand. He knew she knew.

"There isn't anybody else in this world as brave as people like us and Wilde, Angie."

"Don't forget Virginia Woolf." Angie laughed, tears trickling down her freckled cheeks as she smiled wider than she had in months.

"Well... she was suspected."

They held hands for a while, Angie resting her head on her best friend's bony shoulder. The sound of the water droplets from the fountain behind them, the winter air that stung her cheeks and the warmth of Alan's bare hand against hers, was the equivalent of a hug from one of her brothers, a bite of Mrs

Miller's Christmas shortbread and the tickle of Dorothea placing a violet in her hair. Perhaps this was not where she belonged, but for a few moments, looking out across the vast green and castle-like structures, it definitely felt like it was.

CHAPTER TWENTY-SIX

Dorothea

It was strange to her that Peggy would want a wedding during one of the most boring months of the year. Nothing happened at the beginning of spring besides ridiculous downpours and the weather getting less icy.

The days at Peggy's merged together in a pleasant way. Thomas spent most of his days in the garden. Thea didn't know whether he genuinely had chores to do out there, or whether he was trying to give Thea some space. Either way it was greatly appreciated, because when Peggy left for work, doing something mind-numbingly boring and getting paid less than all the men around her, Thea wanted nothing more than to listen to the radio.

There seemed to be more radio stations on Peggy's chunky, brown radio, with a wider variety of songwriters, singers and musicians on to be inspired by. Thea had found a station that enthralled her, she thought of her father and found herself giggling when the presenters made radical jokes about selfish, big-headed politicians.

The first time she laughed at the radio, she was in Peggy's kitchen, chomping on an apple with her legs crossed in a way that most people would find uncomfortable. It felt like an out-of-body experience. As if she was looking down on herself, the unfamiliar sound of her own chuckles making her ears ring for a moment.

She swallowed the chunk of fruit that had got caught in her throat and, rather than biting her cheek to repress a smile, she let the corners of her lips rise slowly. Her father was dead, her brother's cruelty was exposed, she'd left Lizzie trapped in a house with her dying parents, she'd left a mother with nothing but a few farm workers and she'd lost the love of her life before she'd even become an adult. But she was smiling, and for a short while, that seemed to be all that mattered.

Peggy knocked on Thea's bedroom door one Sunday evening, holding four shopping bags filled with clothes. She raised a perfectly plucked brow when Thea opened her mouth to protest against it. Thea grumbled a few words of disapproval but opened her door to let Peggy inside.

"I could have made you come shopping with me," Peggy remarked with a smirk.

"Thank you, Peggy. I adore you. You are simply marvellous," Thea blurted out, only half-joking because she was fully prepared to flatter Peggy if it meant she didn't have to get dragged around the busy streets of London.

With her new clothes and new-found sense of peace, Thea should have anticipated a spanner in the works interrupting her beautiful false sense of security.

Thea was dancing around her room wearing a strange French hat that Peggy had bought for her, insisting that it would suit her. She'd said the same about the light pink blouse and ankle-length skirts that Thea had discarded in a crumpled pile in the corner of her room.

"I don't know what you're going to say about these clothes," Peggy said, a strange shyness to her voice as she put her hand into the last paper bag.

Thea took a seat on the edge on her crumpled bed sheets. Peggy didn't nag Thea to keep the spare room tidy whilst she was living there and, in a sort of childish way, Thea took advantage of that.

"I know you don't want to go into town, or anywhere but here," Peggy continued, "so, I got a few different sizes to try so you don't have to go and get fitted for the wedding."

Thea bit back a groan of frustration and put her head in her hands, not wanting to see the inevitably floral and feminine dress she'd have to wear to be a bridesmaid. Peggy would do anything for Thea, she was pretty confident in that fact, and yet,

Thea was getting annoyed at the fact she had to wear a dress for one day. She took a deep breath, swallowed her pride, and looked up at the item of clothing Peggy held before her...

...a clearly expensive, beautiful blouse and fitted trousers.

"But... that's not..."

"You don't like them?" Peggy frowned.

"No! I... I love them."

Peggy cracked a smile, bright eyes twinkling as she lay the items beside Thea on the bed.

"I'm sorry about the colour, I thought if you were wearing something different from the other bridesmaids the colour scheme should match, at least."

Other bridesmaids. Thea had forgotten. She ran her hand over the trousers, swallowing. The wedding was weeks away, and Thea hadn't even begun to contemplate seeing Angeline again. She'd tried to push the thought out of her mind entirely.

"Well, you can try this one on first. Here's the others if it doesn't fit," Peggy said, handing the paper bag to Thea. "The Carter boys are wearing something similar to you. William has been writing me letters, posting them himself. Can you believe that?"

Thea thought back to the light-haired, confident, eldest brother. She thought of him organising games of football and hide-and-seek with mature concentration and leadership skills.

261

"I can believe that," Thea muttered, avoiding Peggy's eyes, knowing the direction that the conversation was going, knowing what name was soon to be mentioned.

The name that would leave her breathless.

"Angeline isn't around to write for them, I suppose." Peggy cleared her throat as she made her way to the door.

It shouldn't have been hard to hold back the question. But it rose up her throat and passed her lips without a conscious thought.

"Where did she go?" Thea asked, voice shaking.

She dared to look up at Peggy where she hovered in the doorway.

There was a beat of quiet.

Peggy fiddled with her engagement ring and pressed her lips together in a tight line. Thea could have sworn that in that moment the world froze. Oceans, lakes, and rivers stopped flowing, rain stopped falling, vehicles in the road stopped, horses halted and there was nothing in the world but her heart pounding in her ears.

Until the sound of the doorbell ringing downstairs deafened her.

"You can ask her yourself."

Peggy's voice was shaking on its own accord as unwanted tears clouded Thea's sight. Thea stood up, grasping onto her blouse and breathing quick, harsh, and short breaths. Peggy didn't look remotely surprised but she took a step into the room and closed the door behind her, holding her hands up in surrender.

"This was the only way, Dorothea."

"What?!"

She stumbled over to the window, looking out across the grey, at houses and streets. There were no golden cornfields to look across, no trees and rolling hills to avert her attention.

"Isn't it better that you're here?" Peggy came up behind her, put her hands on her shoulder.

Thea had the urge to break her fingers.

"You're safe here," Peggy continued, "you can talk about anything and there's no distractions. No other wedding guests. I don't want this tension on my wedding day, can't you understand that?"

The worst part of all of this was that Thea *did* understand. In Peggy's mind, everything would be resolved in an instant and a conversation would heal all wounds.

"Where will she be staying?" Thea asked.

Demanded, would be a more appropriate word.

"A Bed and Breakfast, a short walk away."

"And she knows I'm here?"

There was a hesitant silence.

"I didn't imply that this situation was entirely well-thought out, did I?" Peggy cleared her throat.

Thea pinched the bridge of her nose.

"Pegs!" Thomas called.

Peggy cringed and felt clumsily for the doorknob behind her. Her face had paled, gone were her usual, red-tinted cheeks. Thea swallowed her guilt, kept a scowl on her face. Peggy could have warned her, Thea thought, surely it wasn't unfair to expect that of her, at least.

The worst part of knowing Angeline was downstairs was the questions. The booming voices in Thea's head that demanded every little, tiny detail about where Angeline had been, what she had seen, who she'd spoken to. What an earth made her leave her little brothers behind? But they weren't the most prevalent questions. What Thea really wanted to know was, did she still like too much sugar in her tea? Did she still sneak an extra teaspoon when nobody was looking? Was her hair still long? Had her freckles faded? Was her favourite biscuit still shortbread? Had she found somebody who made shortbread nicer than Thea's mother? Had she found somebody? A friend? A...

Peggy exited the room, saying nothing more, giving no indication as to what she was to do now. Thea pressed the heels of her hands hard against her closed eyes, laughing to herself at the absurdity of the situation.

There were muffled voices downstairs and the questions rattling around in Thea's mind seemed to quieten. All that seemed to matter was hearing that soft voice from downstairs. But it wasn't enough. The muted sounds were not enough.

Thea creeped out onto the landing, holding her breath, and biting her bottom lip as she closed her eyes, waited.

"...lovely to meet you," Angeline said.

Angeline.

Thea's heartstrings must have been tightening the crucial organ because her chest hurt. It ached. She clutched the banister at the top of the stairs and opened her eyes to peek at the shadows moving in the downstairs hallway.

A long, brown trench coat was placed on the hooks by the bottom of the stairs. Peggy looked up, met Thea's eyes from where she was at the top of the stairs and swallowed before looking away.

"You'll have to excuse the mud, I've been in the garden all day," Thea heard Thomas say to Angeline, hearing that friendly smile in his voice.

"Didn't Peggy mention we met on a farm? I'm used to a bit of mud," Angie replied with a soft laugh.

Thea heard the sounds of their footsteps fade out as they went into the kitchen. She took a step down the stairs so she could still hear the conversation. No, so she could still hear Angeline's voice. There was a little bit of awkward rattling and a long silence.

"You... want tea?" Peggy croaked.

Thea cringed at her tone and almost laughed, covering her hand to stop any noise escaping. She creeped down another step and waited again. As if she hadn't done enough of that.

"Peggy, what's going on?"

Always blunt, straight to the point. That's her girl— that's Angeline.

Peggy took a sharp intake of breath and Thea heard the kettle clank against the stove. Clearly Thomas was making the tea.

"There's something I didn't tell you in our invitation, although I'm sure you've figured it out anyway," Peggy said. "Given the fact I've invited you, of course, I've also invited…"

"Scary Mary?"

Thea couldn't help it, she laughed. She giggled. She chuckled until it hurt. Until there were tears streaming down her cheeks and she was gasping for air. And through her blurry vision she saw glossy hazel eyes, looking into hers. Angeline stood at the bottom of the stairs, her beautiful lips parted, her hand on her heart.

"…not Scary Mary," Peggy whispered, coming to stand beside Angeline at the bottom of the stairs.

"I think I'm going to be sick."

CHAPTER TWENTY-SEVEN

Angeline

She wasn't sick, in the end. But Peggy's fiancé did shove an old, tin washing-up bowl in her arms in case she did end up vomiting. He pulled a chair out for her and sat her at the kitchen table before backing away cautiously, shooting Peggy a concerned look as she shuffled into the kitchen as quiet as a mouse. Peggy had a guilty expression on her face as she went to stand beside Thomas.

They both watched Angie, who imagined that any colour had drained from her face as she rested her head on the side of the bowl, swallowing down excess saliva. She pinched her wrist under the table, willing herself to wake from this suspected dream.

When it became clear to Peggy that Angie wasn't going to be talking anytime soon, she cleared her throat.

"Well, this is all a bit dramatic, isn't it?"

"Piss off, Peggy," a voice hissed from the other side of the room.

Angie looked up slowly, spotting Dorothea in the kitchen doorway. A dark, tall, demanding presence. The same as ever.

Her blue eyes were looking anywhere but at Angie. She looked older, thinner, with prominent bags under her eyes and a frown that looked like it had become her permanent facial expression over the past few months. The off-white shirt she wore was tucked haphazardly into some old trousers, as if she'd only just gotten up and dressed. There was a strange hat upon her head. A bourrée. As if Thea could read Angie's thoughts, she took the hat off and pieces of dark hair framed her narrow face, her hollowed cheekbones, her cheeks tear-stained from laughing, crying, or both.

"I don't think *you* have the right to tell Peggy to piss off in her own home," Angie snapped, sitting upright but keeping her eyes down.

Thea breathed in sharply and Angie went back to picking at the skin of her wrist under the table.

"Sorry, Peg," Thea muttered, barely a whisper.

Months ago, Angie would have bitten back a smile at that, her capability to get Dorothea, in all her hot-headed, stubborn glory, to apologise. But she didn't laugh now, knowing Thea was in the room just made her want to throw the table at her.

The silence dragged on; Angie felt as if they'd be sat like that forever. If someone didn't speak, Angie decided she would indeed throw a table at Dorothea.

Peggy was right, Angie had been a little dramatic. Who'd be so overwhelmed by someone like Dorothea? Someone who was clearly determined to forget about Angie in the first place.

"How have you been, Angie?" Peggy asked, breaking the uncomfortable silence.

"Happy," Angie spoke without thinking. "I've found people who care."

The kettle Thomas had placed on the stove whistled, so Angie wasn't sure whether she'd imagined a hurt gasp from Thea.

"Where are you now? What are you doing?" Peggy continued, forcing the fakest smile Angie thought she'd ever seen.

Thomas started pouring a pot of tea.

"I'm living in Edinburgh. I'm studying English."

Thomas raised a brow and Peggy nodded, clearly impressed.

"Though you know I paid my way to get there," Angie added. "Wouldn't have got in on merit."

"Yes, you would," Dorothea said.

Angie glanced over at the dark figure still in the doorway. Dorothea kept her head down, shifted her weight and folded her arms. She was clearly uncomfortable, Angie felt a discreet thrill at that, it reminded her of those first few months when Angie had just met her. Dorothea hadn't seemed happy in her own skin back then, was unsure and clumsy in her movements.

269

Thomas set down the pot on the table along with two teacups, a jug of milk and some sugar. He gave Angie a little wave and turned to leave, along with Peggy, who'd already slipped passed Dorothea and into the hallway.

"Where are you going?" Angie pleaded, voice cracking.

"Nipping to the garden centre," Thomas explained as he wrapped a scarf around Peggy's neck and pressed a fleeting kiss on her forehead.

Angie heard Dorothea gulp as she tried to stay composed and act as if alarm bells were not going off in her head, at the prospect of being alone with a certain dark-haired woman.

Peggy put her coat and shoes on and left with her fiancé, without so much as a glance at Angie and Dorothea. Words of protest died on Angie's tongue and she poured tea carefully into a cup, adding too much sugar with a shaky hand. Dorothea shuffled towards the kitchen table and pulled a chair out, cringing as it scraped against the floor.

She sat down opposite Angie, pouring her own cup of tea, and drinking it black, boiling hot and with no milk or sugar. Angie winced imagining the bitter flavour, sipping her preferred milky, sugary beverage.

"I read an article in a magazine once," Dorothea began. Her voice was rough, unpractised as she ventured out into this new, unchartered territory. "It was by a woman who swore by natural remedies and all that. Would have probably been classed as a witch, back in the day. And she said that how you have your tea is like a reflection of your soul, or something?"

Angie didn't even look up as she thought, *what utter shit is Dorothea talking about.*

"I guess I'm sinister and bitter," Dorothea laughed and drank some more tea.

Angie let her hot cup burn her hands as she felt heat rising to her face before she slammed it down and let the boiling liquid splatter everywhere.

"If this is your way of some pathetic excuse, give it up," Angie spat. "You think talking about the darkness of your soul is going to change anything? You aren't a bad person, so you can't blame what you did to me on that."

Dorothea surprised Angie then, she threw her head back and laughed. Angie hated this seemingly new trait where she laughed when she was overwhelmed.

"What I *did* to you?"

"Are we playing oblivious now?"

Angie wiped up her spilt tea with the cuff of her jumper, catching Dorothea smirking like an amused teenage boy in the corner of her eye. Angie shook her head in frustration.

"God, you haven't changed a bit," Angie hissed bitterly, glaring at Dorothea until she frowned.

It was a frown that wrapped itself right around Angie's heart and squeezed. She watched Dorothea hide the frown, forcing a smile, putting on that mask she used to wear when she first met Angie and her brothers, to hide her true self behind it, her vulnerability. Angie hated it more than she hated facing her past.

"Well, you got taller. About time."

Angie shook her head and chewed on her bottom lip, pointing a finger at Dorothea in warning, "No. You don't get to do that. You don't get to wear that smirk and tease me and act like it's all fine."

Dorothea pinched the bridge of her nose.

"God, Peggy was right! What's with all the theatrics, Angeline?"

"Theatrics?! I don't know, Dorothea. Maybe it's because you stopped writing to me and I thought I did something wrong. Maybe it's because you were trying to erase everything!"

"I didn't erase a thing!" Dorothea shouted back, pushing the kitchen table into Angie as she stood up.

Angie winced in pain, tears forming behind her closed eyelids. She moved herself out from where the table had practically trapped her against the wall.

"You stopped writing."

I wouldn't have tried to move on, if you hadn't stopped writing, Angie wanted to say.

Dorothea breathed in deeply, clasping her hands at the back of her neck and looking up at the kitchen ceiling. Angie couldn't see her face for that short moment, that seemed to drag on for eternity, and she wondered whether Dorothea was holding back tears too.

"Do you know how much it hurt to get a letter from you?" Dorothea finally said, voice shaky.

Angie didn't respond.

"I couldn't move on. I stayed there, that's what you forget. I was still on the farm. I just stayed there, collecting dust. And every time I got a letter from you it was like... this ridiculous false hope, and then you just left me collecting dust. And you were everywhere, too. You left all our places behind. The piano seat, I could still see you playing if I closed my eyes, the empty left side of my bed, my rooftop, our field, our lake. You left your mark everywhere. That was enough hurt, the letters just made it worse."

Angie could laugh. Perhaps she'd picked up Dorothea's new trait of laughing at inappropriate intervals. But it was hilarious, the jealousy Angie felt coursing through her veins. It was absurd that Dorothea had all of those good memories to remember, all that happiness, when Angie had had nothing. She'd been cursed to forget, transported back to a lifeless house with an uncaring father and her brothers struggling to cope with the changed environment. And there stood Dorothea, red-faced and furious, complaining that the memories of Angie were too much for her. It was funny because those joyous memories were all Angie had to hold onto.

With a little difficulty, Angie titled her chin up, forcing herself to come face to face with Dorothea. She didn't even need to strain herself that much to be at the same height as her anymore.

Angie could smell fresh soap on her skin and tea on her warm breath that tickled her cheeks. Angie ignored Dorothea's dilated pupils, her flushed face that Angie didn't think was a result of her anger.

Angie poked Dorothea's chest and looked up at her with teary eyes.

"I was wrong about you, you have changed," Angie whispered, voice cracking as Dorothea breathed shakily. "You never used to be so fucking selfish."

"Don't swear like that."

It was as if Thea couldn't think of anything else to say, and Angie couldn't help but think she sounded like Mrs Miller. Angie stepped away from Thea, Thea following on instinct, as if she couldn't stay away even if she tried.

"Because swearing is such a major concern, right? Because God is watching my *language*, it's my language that would concern him. Not the fact we've touched—"

"Don't."

"Don't? Don't, what? Have you been trying so hard to forget? Are you scared I'll bring it all back?"

Angie drew nearer as she spoke, voice quietening and heart racing.

She was teasing and enjoying every second, because she still knew Dorothea like the back of her hand.

She knew what those wide eyes and flushed cheeks were saying, she knew exactly what she wanted. And Angie wouldn't dare give it to her.

"You say that like I haven't thought of you every day."

"Words, words, words."

Something flickered across Thea's face. Angie thought perhaps she had an idea or a suggestion, but she then registered it as a moment of hesitation. Thea's hot breath drew closer as she leaned down, mouth ghosting the skin of Angie's neck.

"Would you rather I show you?"

Angie bit her lip.

It was as if she'd been transported back to their lake, back to her years of teenage insecurity. Angie held her breath and squeezed her eyes tightly shut. The image of Dorothea's thin waist and jawline and collarbone and gorgeous, gorgeous chest and—and her.

And Angie, with her awkward movements and nervous shaking and the fear that Thea would take one look at her body and turn away. She was

275

transported back to feeling nervous, and that was what she didn't feel with Stanley. With Stanley, it was easy. There was no point in feeling insecure when Angie didn't value his opinion the way she always valued, and always would value, Dorothea's.

Angie hated herself.

She hated that she didn't feel powerful, she hated that Stanley was so perfect, she hated that he wanted her more than she wanted him.

In that moment, Angie felt she could do nothing but anchor herself to Dorothea. It was so, *so* selfish. And she hated that she loved it. Because what was the point in denying herself? Self-respect? Angie didn't think she deserved respect from anybody, certainly not herself.

And so, when Dorothea's lips touched her skin, she did not push her away.

CHAPTER TWENTY-EIGHT

Dorothea

"Please."

Thea found it humorous that Angie was the one begging, because Thea had been under the impression that Angie would never want to touch her again. She had that stubborn look in her eye that had taken her back to 1943, and yet Angie's legs gave way the moment Thea touched her.

"Not so in control now, are we?" Thea breathed.

She kissed along her jawline, then down her neck again. Thea wasn't being particularly gentle, but Angie didn't have a word to say against it. She didn't have any words to say at all. Thea took advantage of the opportunity.

Thea wanted to know who Angie had been with. She wanted to know every name, where they were from, what they were to Angie, how much they meant to her. But there wasn't time for that.

Thea placed a sturdy hand under Angie's thigh, encouraging her to wrap a leg around Thea's waist. Their shifting weight startled them both, and they stumbled into the kitchen table, Angie perched on the edge of it. She wrapped both of her legs around Thea's waist, drawing her closer.

Thea raised her head, moving back so her swollen lips were no longer travelling up and down the skin of Angie's neck. Thea tried to remember the places that made Angie tremble.

Their eyes were both wide when they met, pupils blown wide as a full moon as their instincts overtook them. Thea's hands trailed up Angie's sides, she felt more as if she was ticking a box, touching the places she'd be expected to touch if she was of sane mind, as opposed to being mindlessly overcome with desire.

Angie's fingers tangled in Thea's dark locks, lacking the gentleness her hands once had, back when it was just them and the lake. Their first and last time.

The only slow motion was them leaning in, eyes flickering down to each other's mouths. And that, frustratingly, was when Angie finally spoke.

"We can't do this."

"Fuck off."

"Don't swear like that," Angeline mocked, then her lips twisted into a frown. "I'm serious."

Thea leant in to kiss her, quicker this time so Angeline wouldn't have time to question it and speak anymore. But Angeline was faster, she tilted her head to the side and Thea's lips only managed to brush her cheek.

Thea leant back, lips parting as she looked to the ground, embarrassed. But looking down, all she could see was Angie's legs still wrapped around her waist. Angie seemed to come to terms with their position as well, and slipped out of Thea's embrace, sliding off the edge of Peggy's kitchen table. Perhaps, that was the problem. Or perhaps, that was what Thea prayed it was.

"Yeah, I agree. I can't imagine I'm in Peggy's good books right now, anyway. I suppose inappropriate activities in her kitchen wouldn't help my case."

"It's not the setting that's the problem."

Thea swallowed.

"So, it's me?"

The silence dragged on and Thea could see it in Angie's face, how desperately she wanted to get away. Perhaps an ideal scenario for Angie would be Peggy and Thomas arriving home from the garden centre. It was an unlikely situation, seeing as Thea knew Peggy well enough to know that when she was giving people space it was usually for a good few hours.

"Angeline. I... I need you. I need you. Please."

Angie met her eyes, a guilty expression on her face. She shook her head slowly.

"I can't do it, I won't cheat," Angie uttered reluctantly, picking up her teacup that was discarded on the table.

Thea's heart dropped into oblivion. She suspected that Angie and this faceless, nameless person, (whom Thea decided she already hated) were more than a coupling for convenience.

"Cheat?"

All Angie could do was nod.

Thea bit her bottom lip, nodding swiftly and praying the movement was so quick she was nothing but a blur, so Angie could not see her crying.

"Who was she?"

"He."

"Oh, god."

"Thea, I..."

Angie reached out to touch her and she pulled away.

"So, you love him?" Thea demanded, though she refused to face Angie.

"I..."

Hesitation, Thea thought, surely that meant she did. She did and she didn't want to humiliate Thea any further, didn't want to give Thea this painful reminder that their attraction had clearly been one-sided.

"It makes so much sense, actually," Thea said, mostly to herself.

"What?"

"All those times I wanted more, it felt like you hated every second of it. It seemed like you were fine with kissing and saying... how was it you put it? *Words, words, words.* But when it came down to it, pretending to actually find me attractive was too much? Was that it? Was it easy for you to pretend I was a man until I took my clothes off?"

"How *dare* you!"

"How dare *me*? You pretended... and all that time you weren't even a lesbian?"

Thea faced her now, saw tears brimming in Angie's eyes.

"I *am*," Angie cried, frustrated. "I-I was! You told me to move on! You *begged* me! You said the only thing that mattered was that I was safe!"

"I asked you to marry so nobody would know about you. I thought you were like me, I thought we were the same. I didn't think you'd fall in love, I didn't think you *could* fall in love with men."

"I didn't say I loved him! But he makes me feel... something. He makes me feel *happy* and it's easy with him. He hasn't given up on me. Is that too hard for you to hear? Is this not what you wanted? Would you prefer for me to just get with a man and live my life in misery?"

Thea didn't think she could listen to her anymore. The humiliation was coursing through her, thinking back of how she'd pined for this beautiful, beautiful girl who actually loved her back. So she'd thought. It seemed a miracle to Thea that she'd met somebody in this world who finally faced the same problems she had. Of course, there was Lizzie but that wasn't the same. Though Lizzie liked men too, it didn't faze Thea.

Thea's love for Angie consumed her. Her love for women consumed her and plagued her life. It didn't seem fair that Angie could choose both, after all they'd been through.

"You can't just... be like this and then not," Thea spat.

"I didn't realise you controlled all same-sex relations, I apologise profusely," Angie replied, voice laced with a venomous sarcasm. "I would understand you being upset that I've moved on, Dorothea, but attacking me because he's a man is just pathetic."

There she had it, Thea thought, there it was. Angie had admitted it loud and clear; she truly had moved on. Thea clenched her hands into fists and backed away, heading towards the door.

"Walking away? Is that what you do now?" Angie asked, her tone softened slightly, barely. "I remember a girl who taught me to be open-minded and learn to see the world through other people's eyes."

Don't be stupid, Thea wanted to say. It was Angie who opened *her* eyes. It was Angie who helped her see more than just a city girl, it was Angie who helped her see hope in the world, even when there was none to be found. And it seemed that, in the end, there none to be found. Because how could hope exist when Dorothea Miller and Angeline Carter had changed so much? How could hope exist when there wasn't a city girl and a farmer's daughter defying the expectations set for them? How could there be hope when Angeline Carter had moved on?

"I wanted you to come back to me," Thea blurted out.

Angie let out a laugh.

"You had a funny way of showing it."

Thea ducked her head, still hovering in the doorway. There were a few wordless moments, where they listened to the ringing of bicycle bells and cars passing on the street outside. Angie sipped her tea, avoiding looking at Thea in the doorway. Her nose would scrunch is displeasure whenever she drank. Thea knew the tea would be cold but Angie was grasping on to something to do in the awkward silence. Thea stared out the kitchen window, admiring Thomas' garden. It wasn't a flower field in Wales, but it was close enough. Thea would have walked away from the situation entirely but wasn't going to prove Angie right and be a coward.

"You live here now?" Angie asked, though her tone suggested she already knew the answer.

"Yes."

"Is Mrs Miller coming to the wedding?"

Smart, Thea thought. Angie was indirectly bringing up her mother to get the reason behind Thea leaving home. It was a clever move but Thea knew Angie all too well. Thea didn't see the point in hiding the truth.

"I'm here because my mother found out I was sleeping with a woman."

Angie choked on her tea, clumsily putting the cup down to fiddle with the cuffs of her jumper.

"I thought you said you haven't moved on."

"I haven't."

Apparently, Thea didn't need to justify what she meant. The difference between them, was that Lizzie and Thea had been on the same page. They parted as friends, and nothing more. Angie and the man who stole her away clearly meant something to each other.

"So... Mrs Miller sent you away?"

Thea thought she was holding back tears.

"It wasn't like that; I chose to move."

Angie didn't ask any other questions. Once she finished her tea, she placed it in the sink and made her way over to Thea, who was still standing awkwardly in the doorway.

"I shouldn't have let you..." Angie kept her eyes on the kitchen tiles as she searched her mind for appropriate words. "...do that. I didn't mean to give... false hope or whatever."

Thea translated those words herself: *I let you touch me on instinct, there was nothing more to it. I've moved on and you haven't. Sorry for leading you on.*

"Don't worry about it," Thea forced a smile, it faltered when Angie held out her hand to shake.

As if it was nothing but a business deal.

Thea wondered if perhaps Angie had seen her father seal deals with a handshake. Thea didn't even know what she was shaking on, but she grasped the opportunity as if it was to be the last time she would ever touch Angie. Their skin brushed and those electrical sparks still shot up Thea's forearm. They shook hands.

"Friends?" Angie asked, eyes glossy with tears.

Words couldn't form, so Thea just nodded. Angie responded with a curt nod herself, withdrawing her hand but not without letting their fingers brush, not without letting the touch linger. *Surely,* Thea thought, *surely she must feel... must have felt something. Surely this wasn't all as painfully one-sided as Thea was believing it to be.*

"I'm going for a quick walk, I need to pick something up from the B&B."

She brushed past Thea, retrieving her coat in the hallway. She fastened it slowly and Thea watched her every move. She glanced at Thea one last time, with a sympathetic expression on her face as she waved shyly and opened the porch door.

"Angeline?" Thea whispered, surprised Angie had even heard her, but she halted in the doorway. "What's his name?"

Angie pressed her lips together, looking to the side and Thea couldn't help but admire the sunlight coming in from the crack of the door. She silently praised how it framed Angie's glorious face and made her glow.

"Stanley."

Thea didn't really know what to do with that information, but Angie closed the door and left.

Thea whispered the name to herself, testing the sound. Thea was definitely disliked in society's eyes as it was, but hearing Angie say that name with a fond smile, made her think that society would hate her even more. Because Thea sort of wanted to murder him.

CHAPTER TWENTY-NINE

<u>Angeline</u>

The routine they found themselves in for the next few days was just short of a living hell. The tension was inescapable. It would have been easier if there were more people around, but Peggy was very strict on the fact she only wanted to spend time with the most important people in her life, the week leading up to her wedding.

Thomas was busy doing whatever preparation tasks Peggy sent him on and Florence was due to arrive slightly later than expected. Angie would clench her fists and internally scowl upon hearing that news, because it felt as if Peggy and Florence had planned it like that so Thea and Angie would find themselves isolated in each other's company.

Declaring to be friends was difficult enough, Angie had almost been under the impression they'd agree to it and then avoid each other. Angie was trying her best with the latter, because being in a room with Thea felt equivalent to being starved of oxygen, or so she imagined.

Angie spent as much time as possible resting at the B&B, writing letters to Lottie and Alan. She wouldn't send them because Stanley would be around to see them arrive, and Angie didn't want him to start questioning why he wasn't receiving any. It was mostly because Angie didn't know what to say, and partly because she didn't want to hear back from him.

That was the reason a stack of letters had been piling up on the windowsill.

Her days at Peggy's were spent helping in any way she could, often opening some early 'Congratulations' and late 'Happy Engagement' cards, or helping Thomas make bread in the evenings.

Thea didn't do much. She sat reading by windows for most of the day and Peggy didn't have a word to say about it. This surprised Angie, for Peggy had always encouraged Thea to speak up, but now it seemed she allowed her to sit and wallow in her own self-pity or do whatever she did when she had her nose in a book. Angie didn't say anything about it to Thea either.

She didn't say anything to her at all.

Though, one afternoon, when Thea dramatically declared she was going for a stroll, Angie rolled her eyes and turned to Peggy when she heard the front door close. They were ironing beautiful, hand-made, floral buntings for the after-party, and

Peggy kept her eyes down when Angie spoke, as if she'd been anticipating this discussion.

"What's the point in her even being here?"

Clearly, Peggy hadn't expected the harshness of Angie's words and tone. She raised a brow.

"She's a bridesmaid."

"Would've thought you'd choose someone who would actually bloody smile."

Peggy slammed her iron on the ironing board.

"You're being ever so harsh. Out of the two of you I expected you to be the mature one. What sort of manners are they teaching you at university?"

Angie frowned.

"They're teaching me to think for myself. It's helpful, actually. It's opened my eyes to the fact Dorothea acts like a stubborn child when she doesn't get her own way. It's pathetic."

For a short moment, Peggy looked like she'd start crying. It was a face Angie had seen before, the same teary eyes her mother had when Angie was fighting with her brothers. But Peggy studied Angie for a moment longer and, eventually, her expression changed, her thin lips twisting into a smile.

"If this problem continues, I shall put you in charge of the little ones. For the entirety of the wedding."

Angie felt herself scowling at the petty excuse for blackmail and was quite frustrated she had openly displayed her discontentment with Peggy's suggestion. Though, even if she'd managed to disguise it, Peggy would undoubtedly see right through her.

Peggy had known Angie hated the maternal role. It had been different on the farm, especially in the summer months, she was younger and they were all playing outside, so Angie didn't mind looking after her little brothers. But winter on the farm, with the responsibility of making sure four noisy, boisterous boys stayed away from Mrs Miller's precious plates and vases when it was too cold to be anywhere but inside when she was old enough to grow positively bored after one game of hide-and-seek, that was when Angie decided she hated babysitting.

"The tension should subside," Angie mumbled reluctantly as Peggy picked up the iron again with a familiar smirk, signalling the end of the conversation.

But Angie hadn't spoken about her brothers in a while, and she was curious now.

"How are the boys?"

"Shouldn't you be more aware than I?"

Peggy said the question passively, without any real hint of curiosity. It was as if she already knew the response to the question. And it was Peggy, Angie thought, so of course she did.

"I haven't written to them," Angie admitted, carefully folding up some of the buntings.

Peggy tutted, placing her hands on her hips.

"Honestly, Angeline, what on earth has happened to you? They're your boys. You love them."

If it was anybody but Peggy, and maybe Florence, telling her this, she would try to defend herself. But any attempt now would be futile. Anything but the truth was futile with Peggy, who turned both Dorothea and Angeline into open books.

"My mother told me, before I left, that she felt I'd stolen her role. Well, she didn't say it in so many words."

It wasn't a lie. But it was an avoidance of the truth.

"And?"

Goddamn, Peggy.

"And I thought leaving them alone would allow them to bond with mother again."

"And?"

Why did this woman have the ability to read minds?

"And I wanted to figure myself out, Peggy!" Tears filled Angie's eyes and she hated herself for it, it couldn't just be blamed on her time of the month. It was more than that. She needed to cry for herself. "Is that *so* terrible? I wanted to know who I was without them!"

It hurt. It hurt to hear the words leave her mouth because she loved Charles. And she loved seeing the world through his innocent eyes. And she loved Peter, and the way he looked up to his older brothers. And she loved Michael's cheekiness and William's premature intelligence. Then, why had it been so easy to forget them, and so difficult to forget Dorothea?

Peggy placed her hands on Angie's shoulders, guiding her to sit down at the kitchen table in her self-deprecating haze. She brushed Angie's hair off her forehead and whispered gentle encouragements.

"I think I thought... I... I had to know who I was without Dorothea... so, I just thought I might as well..."

"Push everyone away? Make yourself suffer?" She let in a deep breath, then let out a long sigh and the silence dragged. "Do you think that maybe you were punishing yourself?"

Angie chewed on her bottom lip, she didn't want to admit the truth and climb her way out of the self-punishing hole so easily. But Peggy had just tossed her the rope.

"No. I didn't want them to be around me. Dorothea was out of their lives, may as well get rid of the other lesbian too, hm?"

It was out there now. It was always about more than just 'finding herself,' it was about purging the badness out of the boys' lives. It was about freeing everyone she loved. And she'd never said it before, but, under the surface, Angie had felt like a burden since the day Thea had kissed her.

"I've never heard you speak like that before, Angeline," Peggy held her face. "And I do not want to hear you speak like that again. Nothing has tainted you. You can love women and still be the beautiful soul that you are."

Angie averted her gaze.

"Look at me, please," Peggy said.

She did, eventually.

"I like both," Angie whispered, biting her bottom lip hard. "Not so easy to understand and praise me now, is it?"

Peggy laughed softly, shaking her head. She pulled up the chair beside Angeline and folded her hands together.

"I was actually just thinking that that makes a lot of sense."

"What?"

"It makes sense that you like both, Angeline because you've got far too much love in that heart of yours to choose just one."

Angie didn't really know how to respond to that. Because that was something unexpected. That was something beautiful. That was something, Angie thought, perhaps Thea should have said to her, when she confessed where her desires lay. Surely, that was how somebody who loved her should respond?

Peggy wiped tears from Angie's cheeks with the pads of her thumbs, Angie noticed her nails. They were a light lilac, clearly done professionally, with a rounded shape that looked nothing like her usual, pointed red nails. It sort of hit Angie in the chest, like a sudden weight pressed against her rib cage.

"You are literally getting married," Angie whispered.

Peggy laughed melodically, shaking her head as a light blush tinted her smooth cheeks. She nodded slowly at first, then faster as if she couldn't quite contain her excitement. Angie glanced out of the kitchen window and saw Thomas coming up the garden path, he'd been out all day, planting new flowers 'for spring'. She turned her attention back to Peggy.

"And you are *literally* my bridesmaid. And you are here. And so is Dorothea. And Florence will be here, too. And I love you so much, I would suffer your silly arguing and even more because I love you like a sister. And I want you to talk me through my second thoughts and stop my pretty white dress from getting all muddy."

"What's this about second thoughts?" Angie could hear the smirk in Thomas' voice, as he came in through the back door, patting dried mud off his gardening gloves.

Peggy stood up, shooting Angie a glance that asked, *why didn't you point out he was coming in from the garden?* Angie pressed her lips together to stop herself from laughing and wiped her face.

Thomas pouted and Peggy stood up, making her way over to Thomas in confident strides. She picked a bit of leaf out of his dark hair, looking at him disapprovingly.

"I don't know how I'll cope with a man who *insists* on dragging mud into my kitchen," Peggy sighed.

Thomas tilted her chin up with his thumb and forefinger, pressing a chaste kiss to her red lips. When he leaned out, he flashed her a handsome grin. She pressed her thumb to the corner of his lips.

"Ah, that's how."

Angie watched the couple and felt her heart sink, like an anchor dropping to the bottom of her stomach. Angie knew how Thomas lured Peggy in after doing something she didn't like, it was his smile. Angie remembered a smile just like that, a smile that had exactly the same effect on her.

And it certainly wasn't Stanley Turner's.

CHAPTER THIRTY

<u>Dorothea</u>

Thea stumbled down the stairs sluggishly, wrapping one of Peggy's tatty old dressing gowns around her, and tying it around her waist. She hadn't slept well. Perhaps a day of walking on an empty stomach to avoid Angeline hadn't been the brightest idea she'd ever had, given the way her body ached with exhaustion and her stomach growled for food. She hadn't returned until early evening, when Angie had left for the B&B, probably writing letters to her boyfriend, Stanley.

Thea's thoughts of punching Angie's boyfriend came to a stop when she noticed how Peggy's house felt different. The air had changed. An unfamiliar pair of boots sat in the porch, a beige trench coat hanging on the banister.

"We have to go," Peggy said from the kitchen.

Her voice didn't have the softness it usually had, talking to Thomas. Thea realised somebody else was there.

"Peggy, don't be ridiculous we can't just leave." A vaguely familiar voice chirped in, amongst the sound of the kettle boiling and plates clanking behind the closed door of the kitchen.

Florence had finally arrived. She thought she'd go and greet her properly, before Angie came over and Thea would continue avoiding her like the plague. Thea glanced at herself in the mirror at the bottom of the stairs, practicing her fake smile. It faltered as the conversation in the kitchen continued. The discussion didn't sound like wedding planning, their tones were sombre and anxious, and Thea had a feeling she wouldn't have to wear an expression of false happiness.

"Florence, I think Peggy is right," Thomas said calmly, voice muffled.

Thea could see shadows under the door; somebody was pacing. Undoubtedly Florence, ever the worrier.

"Think about it, it's almost like fate. It sounds like everybody Mrs Miller still cares about is attending this wedding. It would be so easy for you to all to go and pay your respects. Peggy and I can wait."

Her heart was in her mouth at the mention of her mother. *Pay respects?* Thea edged closer to the door, with a practiced ease. She'd forever be used to sneaking around unnoticed.

"The boys will be arriving early this afternoon. That's everyone: Dorothea, you and I, Angeline and the boys. Of course, Heather isn't here but it's close enough. It's almost our little family, back together again," Peggy said.

Thea hadn't given Heather much thought, last she'd heard she'd eloped to America. In the heat of all this tension and confusion, Thea thought it was a tempting idea herself.

"Yes, back together for your *wedding*," Florence argued.

"It sounds like you're accusing Mrs Miller of deliberately being ill at such an *inconvenient* time," Peggy snapped, stubbornly biting back. It was almost childish, and Thea thought Peggy and Florence would always be like long lost sisters. "Dorothea will be heart-broken to think we'd prioritise a *wedding* over her own mother."

Thea turned the door handle, squinting at the light coming in from the kitchen. She was never normally awake this early, not anymore. But her aching body forbid her any sleep.

The overwhelming feeling of seeing Florence after two years was enough to make Thea feel faint. She looked pale, slightly withdrawn, but beautiful as ever. She gave Thea an awkward little wave. It was too early for this.

"What about my mother?" Thea croaked.

Peggy was sat at the kitchen table, Thomas had a comforting arm around her shoulders as she fiddled with the corners of an opened letter. Thea had always had good eye-sight, and she could recognise her mother's handwriting, even from standing in the doorway.

Florence opened her mouth to say something, but seemed to choke around the words. She started pacing again.

"There's been some... complications with her health," Thomas said.

Thea clenched her fists together, wondering how it was that Peggy's fiancé knew of this news before her. But then, of course, her mother undoubtably still wanted nothing to do with her. Florence had tears in her eyes, shaking her head.

"Oh, Peg, this is so unfair," Florence muttered.

"Oh shut it, Flo," Peggy snapped, eyes never leaving Thea. "Dorothea, we... we need to go back to the farm."

Thea inhaled shakily, with a nod. It made sense, really it did. Her mother was ill, of course she'd seek Peggy and Florence. Perhaps she even requested Angeline's presence before she'd ask for her own daughter. A lump lodged itself in her throat and she lowered her head, wrapping her arms around herself.

"God, Peggy, have you been feeding the poor girl?" Florence asked, clearly from her instincts because she smacked her lips together and blushed.

Peggy ignored her and Thomas started rubbing circles on her back. "I know things have happened, love, but you have to see her."

Thea frowned, lips parting. *See her?* Her mother could be on her deathbed, and Thea would be certain she'd be the last person on earth she'd want to see.

"She hates me."

299

Florence let out a pained whimper, "Oh, darling, don't be silly."

Florence came over to Thea and took her face in her hands, brushing her dark hair out of her eyes. It took Thea back, to a conversation they had out on the fields about three years ago. Florence had been the first to know, the first person who had loved Thea for who she was. Stumbling into an awkward hug was inevitable, even with Thea's restrained nature. It was a quick way of saying *I missed you*, given the fast-paced direction everything was going in, there wasn't time for proper reunions.

Thea hadn't actually had one single perfect, normal reunion since arriving in London. Peggy told her she was getting *married*. Angeline... *Well*. And now Florence was here and the wedding was getting called off and her mother was sick, and didn't hate her? *What?*

"We're calling the wedding off," Peggy declared, voice laced with finality. Nobody questioned Peggy when she spoke like that. "Florence, go and meet Angeline at the train station. We're going back to Wales."

Thea glared at Peggy. Sensing her rage, Florence tried to take her hand. Thea snatched it away. Perhaps, nobody ever disagreed with Peggy when she spoke with such authority, but perhaps it was time somebody did.

"I am not going back to that farm," Thea snapped, tilting her chin up. "You have done nothing but overwhelm me since I got here. When I tell you I'm not ready, all you do is push me. I can't see my mother, I won't."

Peggy raised a brow, standing up from where she sat at the table. She placed the opened letter in Thea's hands and Thea had no choice but to read it.

2nd March 1946

Dearest Peggy,

It has been a long time. I know that this is strange. I am afraid I'm not sure how to format this letter at all. The truth is, I have not seen Dorothea since Christmas Eve, and it has been awful. I employed a few extra men to help over the winter but the farm hasn't been the same. I don't just mean for me. The animals were getting sick, nothing seems to be growing. I can't run it like this, I need Dorothea to come home.

That leads me to the reason behind this letter. I know she is with you. I don't know how, but I have this feeling that she is safe. I know she left the village, it's a small place, so I asked somebody at the station where she got her ticket for and they said London. She has to be with you, because she wouldn't cope anywhere else. Perhaps, she's with Florence or Angeline and I got it all wrong but I have this feeling, an instinct, if you will. A mother's instinct. Because she will always be my baby girl. Peggy, I need her to come home.

They think there is something wrong with my lungs. Now, I've never been a very bright woman, but I know when someone is telling me bad news. I am taking medication, when I remember to. But I have nothing left to live for anymore, and part of me thinks the doctors got it all wrong and I'm not suffering from bad lungs, I'm suffering from a broken heart. Is that silly?

I don't think I'll get better, and I think I'm alright with that, I'll accept that. But I'm not sure I can accept dying and leaving this place, Arthur's whole life, in ruins. It's like the farm is crumbling around me, and I'm the only one left, and I'm part of the farm, so I'm crumbling with it. Dorothea and I were the foundation, and we broke, and now it's all falling down.

I am being ridiculous, I've been reading too much.

I am avoiding what I need to admit to myself, and what I need to admit is that I didn't tell Dorothea what she needed to hear. I didn't say the right things. I'm not explaining this all over writing, I won't. But then, she's possibly already told you. Maybe you don't know, maybe nobody ever really understood that girl. Maybe Arthur was the only person in the whole entire world capable of understanding Dorothea Miller. I think maybe he looked into her blue eyes when she was born, and knew everything about her. Isn't that something?

My wrist is hurting. So is my chest. I think I will take my medication, and then I will pray.

Please, help me make this right, even if Dorothea does not think I deserve it. Perhaps I do not. But I love her more than anything in this lonely world. And perhaps I'll always be waiting on our crumbling farm, for my husband, son and little girl to come back to me. Two are impossible. But there is one. My last one. Please bring her home.

Maggie Miller

CHAPTER THIRTY-ONE

<u>Angeline</u>

This part of London was unfamiliar to Angie. The whole city felt a bit unfamiliar. She and this city had only spent a few months apart but it didn't feel like home anymore. Perhaps it never really did, or perhaps it would feel like home if she'd gone to visit her family, like a good daughter would. There was too much happening. Seeing her brothers wasn't something she looked forward to. Angie hadn't been lying with what she'd said to Peggy, sometimes she thought they'd be better off without her.

Her mother was a different story, one she neglected to think about. She wanted Angie to live the life she couldn't have, to avoid getting trapped. She hoped that she'd forgive her for the lack of communication, as contacting her mother meant contacting her father, and contracting her father meant a risk of being trapped in a life she did not want.

Angie realised she wasn't very good at communication anymore; not with Peggy, her family, Dorothea, her friends or Stanley. She visibly flinched at the thought of him, and an old white man with a neat moustache who she strolled passed, gave her a judgemental glance. The walk to the train station was not as long as she'd hoped it would be. They'd be back at Peggy's house in no time. And that meant facing Dorothea, again. It was becoming more of a painful occurrence, as opposed to a nuisance. Thea looked so small, which was ridiculous, because she still towered over Angie. But her frame was unhealthy, her cheeks were gaunt and her skin was white as snow. Was she punishing herself for something, just like Angie did? Or was that how she coped with jealousy?

Angie knew Thea was envious of Stanley. She'd seen the scowl when she'd told her his name. It was misplaced, because the only thrill Angie seemed to be getting out of that man anymore was the fact he made Thea jealous. He made Thea possessive. And that sent an shock through Angie's body. It sort of lit her up on the inside, and made her want to grab the back of Thea's neck, pull her in and kiss her, open-mouthed.

Angie wasn't sure where these feelings were coming from, because they'd never felt this... electric, before. Perhaps it was the new-found confidence, perhaps it was because Angie was too angry at the time they'd lost to worry about her appearance like she had in her youth. Angie just wanted Thea.

Thea wouldn't understand that even if she tried to explain it. Angie recalled her words,

All those times I wanted more, it felt like you hated every second of it. It seemed like you were fine with kissing and saying... how was it? Words, words, words.

304

But when it came down to it, pretending to actually find me attractive was too much? Was that it? Was it easy for you to pretend I was a man until I took my clothes off?

Angie wanted to scream at her. Because she had it all right, and yet she had it so wrong. Angie had dreaded it, because Thea was so *beautiful*. And sure, beauty doesn't determine everything: beauty doesn't equate to goodness, purity, or morality. But Angie was just a girl, in love with another girl.

So, Thea was right, because it wasn't easy to pretend she was a man when she took her clothes off, because she was so magnificently female.

And yet, none of that mattered now, because Angie had kissed Stanley Turner and she was pretty sure he was in love with her. But it was so tempting, it would be so easy to forget that fact.

A whistle averted her attention, then the train that chugged closer made her lose her breath.

"Angeline," a woman's voice called from behind her. Angie turned around to meet the motherly smile of Florence. "I still think it's such a pretty name."

Angie ignored the opening doors of the train and flung herself at Florence, squeezing her tightly and shaking her head.

"You're here, you're here," Angie cried. "Oh, Flo, I've needed you so much. It's been so hard. I should've written to you."

"Flo's not the only person you should have written to," mumbled a voice sounded far too deep.

Angie leant away from the ex-land girl and closed her eyes tightly, turning around to face the voice. When she opened her eyes, she saw her brothers.

They stood in a line, tallest to shortest, with unreadable expressions. They clung to their luggage and, being dressed in their best clothes, she was reminded of the day they were evacuated. Angie could have sworn Charles was the same height William had been when she'd left home. Tears trickled down her cheeks and she brought a hand up to her mouth, shaking her head.

"You got the train here on your own?" She croaked.

Charles nodded, with a proud smirk.

"It was only twenty minutes," Michael said, bursting his little brother's bubble.

"Twenty minutes really isn't very long," Peter said. "Somebody could write and post a letter in twenty minutes."

Angie didn't really know what to say to that. She ducked her head, suspecting she'd have to add her brothers to the growing list of people who disliked her at the moment.

However, much to her surprise, her brothers drew nearer and wrapped their arms around their older sister, one-by-one, until they were just a mush of arms and legs, damp cheeks and occasional sobs.

"Don't do that again, Angie," William ordered.

"I won't, I won't," Angie repeated over and over again.

Florence stood behind them, smiling down like the proud mother she would never be.

Angie hadn't explained the situation to Florence, Florence had only just arrived. And yet, it seemed that Florence understood Angie, that she understood why she'd avoided the boys. Florence was always on her side, even when she was wrong, it seemed. Perhaps Peggy had told her, but perhaps she'd known Angie was suffering with too much self-hatred, too much change, too much of everything, to be a good sister. Angie thought she'd probably spend the rest of her life trying to make it up to them.

"Look at you, hm?" she said, breaking the silence and leaning out to hold Michael's face in her hands. "You've got all big. Who let you get all big?"

She chose him, because she knew he'd roll his eyes and wiggle his way out of her touch. She couldn't help but seek that familiarity, and let herself feel like a sister who actually knew her brothers, and hadn't ignored their existence for months.

"You sound like an old lady," Michael mumbled after shoving her away and folding his arms.

Florence laughed softly from behind them, and the boys charged at her all at once, as if they had just noticed her. They hugged Florence just as they had hugged their sister.

"Oh, I can't wait," Charles squealed excitedly. "We'll see Dorothea, and we'll see Peggy and—"

"About that..." Florence cut him off.

"What about it?" Angie frowned.

"Mrs Miller… is… unwell."

"Oh."

Florence ushered the children aside, after listening to the many grunts and sighs of people passing their stationary position on the train platform. Angie followed, eyes never leaving Florence as she spoke hesitantly.

"The wedding is being postponed."

"But— but—" Charles began.

"—we just got here," Peter folded his arms. "I don't want to go back home again."

Angie made a mental note to ask him why later.

"Mrs Miller's condition is serious," Florence continued, looking frustrated at the interruptions.

"I don't want to catch anything," Michael remarked.

"Shut it, Michael," Angie snapped, her anger rising too, because *what on Earth was going on?*

"We're returning to Wales, all of us," Florence concluded, straightening her back and speaking with a tone of finality. "We will fund it all, and if your parents are concerned with it they can—"

"—shut up," William finished, tilting his chin up in that self-assured manner. "Mrs Miller cared for us and let us stay on the farm when we were evacuated. We could have been split up. We were so lucky."

"She did a wonderful job and she deserves this. Peggy wouldn't postpone her wedding unless she really thought this was serious."

Florence's grin was contagious and Angie couldn't help but squeeze William's hand, feeling that overwhelming sense of pride that she was related to him.

"Well then," Florence let out a little laugh. "I hope you boys packed your wellington boots, and aren't too tired, because the tickets are booked for later today. Pegs and Dorothea are meeting us here."

The boys beamed and Angie gripped the stair rail behind her as she felt overwhelmingly faint.

They were returning to the farm.

She repeated the phrase in her head, until she could think of nothing else. And when she closed her eyes to take a deep breath, she could see Thea. She was an image of beauty, standing with her elbows resting on a fence, her face in her hands. She wore her dungarees, the left side unfastened. Her hair wind-blown and her cheeks so gorgeously red. Angie noticed that her skin was tainted with specks of mud, as she reached out a beckoning hand. She smiled and said, in that low and melodic voice:

Come home to me.

CHAPTER THIRTY-TWO

<u>Dorothea</u>

The time was set and the tickets were booked. In no time at all, they were making their way to the station. Thea didn't know why but she hadn't expected Thomas to come to Wales with them. Perhaps Thea wasn't used to couples and she didn't understand their conventional relationship, where they could so openly follow the other everywhere and love so freely. Well, of course she didn't understand it. The closest she'd got to it was Angie.

Florence was sat on a bench with the boys. They'd somehow all managed to fit on it and were eating ice cream from tubs. Florence was subtly giggling at Charles, who appeared to have managed to get more of the treat on his face than in his actual mouth. Thea was knocked breathless for a short moment, when she'd seen how much the boys had grown. But her attention was diverted when she spotted Angie, pacing up and down the platform. Thea glanced at Peggy, who raised a brow expectantly before nodding to Angie. Thomas walked ahead to meet the boys.

"She doesn't want to talk to me," Thea said under her breath, getting déjà vu.

It felt as if she was reliving 1943.

"No, she does. *You* don't want to talk to *her.*"

Thea couldn't exactly disagree with that, when she'd made it a personal mission to avoid the younger woman. Without another glance at Peggy, she let her feet carry her to Angie, who didn't see her approaching.

Angie was counting quietly as she paced up and down the platform, too close to the edge for Thea's liking.

"Why are you counting?"

Angie's hazel eyes snapped up and she furrowed her brow, clearly displeased. She took a step back.

"Because."

"That was a pointless response."

"I don't owe you a valuable one," Angie snapped back.

She unclenched her fists but her shoulders remained tensed.

"I'm trying to breathe," Angie explained reluctantly. "I work myself up sometimes, and then I get breathless. Then I get worried about being breathless."

Thea didn't bite back her smile and Angie's eyes lingered on her mouth for a brief moment. Thea's chest swelled with excitement and familiarity. Lizzie had once mentioned how Thea's smile lured people in, Thea hoped it had the same effect on Angie. Perhaps it once did.

"Sounds like something Florence would teach you." Thea didn't stop smiling, and she thought that was what made Angie clench her fists again.

"It was Stanley, actually."

The name knocked any happiness out of Thea. She couldn't tell whether Angie was actually being truthful, or whether she'd said it to make Thea hesitate.

"Right."

A silence, that was coming to be rather familiar, lingered between them. Then a wave of realisation flashed across Angie's face, and her expression turned to something more sympathetic.

"I'm sorry to hear your mother is unwell," Angie said, so formally that Thea audibly scoffed.

"She hates me now." Thea shrugged absentmindedly, she was growing accustomed to saying that phrase.

"I don't imagine that is true."

"She doesn't understand who I love," Thea met Angie's eyes.

It shocked her when Angie stared right back.

"You don't understand who I love, does that mean you hate me?" Angie asked innocently, voice laced with curiosity.

But Thea *did* understand it. Loving two genders had never been a concept that confused her. When Lizzie told her of her preferences, she hadn't second-guessed her truthfulness, and she certainly understood her. It didn't bother Thea if it was *Lizzie* liking both sexes. But the thought of Angie with a man, made Thea

312

feel all kinds of rage. It was the fear, mostly. The fear that Angie would realise how much easier it would be to settle down and marry Stanley and give up a fight that she didn't *have* to participate in.

In Thea's mind, the thought of Angie being with anybody but her was like forcing two puzzle pieces together that belonged to different sets.

Thea spoke as their train arrived at the platform, rattling against the tracks and muting any voice but her own.

"I don't understand who you love, if the person you love isn't me," Thea said, with her chin jutted out and her eyes never leaving Angie's.

Thea still thought it a miracle that Angie held her gaze.

The wheels of the train screeched and Thea, for the first time in her life, wasn't even contemplating the travel sickness for the journey ahead. The only thing that seemed to matter was Angie's words.

"Is it the hope of home that brings you back to me?" Angie whispered, barely audible.

The people boarding the train wouldn't know what she'd said, but Thea had traced and kissed that mouth. She could read what her lips were saying, without much thought at all. Thea shook her head slowly and could feel her heart beating rapidly in her chest.

"Is it your jealousy?" Angie guessed again.

The platform was clearing, and almost everyone had got on the train already. It baffled Thea that the boys hadn't been eager to see her. Though, perhaps Peggy told them to keep their distance whilst she spoke to Angie.

Peggy lingered in the carriage doorway now, waiting for them to board. Thea held her hand up dismissively, giving Peggy a glance that said: *Give me a moment.* The older woman rolled her eyes and turned away to join the others.

"No," Thea said, as they made their way onto the train just as the whistle was blown.

The carriage door closed.

The train was sectioned off into carriages and, standing in the narrow hallway, the pair were unseen by other passengers. Thea breathed in shakily upon realising this. She let her fingertips skim the delicate skin of Angie's wrist, just under the cuff of her coat. Angie grabbed the right side of Thea's collar, pulling her so close that their noses bumped and they were breathing each other's air.

"Tell me what brings you back to me, then," Angie demanded.

Under that heated gaze, Thea suspected that her lack of travel sickness was because Angie made time stop. She made the entire world slow down. And perhaps that was all in Thea's head, but it felt like an opportunity. Angie and her marvellous mind and turbulent thoughts had slowed down for a moment, allowing her to be so demanding. To respond in an unfavoured way would be a waste of such a privilege.

"I will *always* come back to you."

Angie closed her eyes, dark lashes kissing her freckled cheeks. Thea's thumb traced circles on the inside of Angie's wrist as they breathed shaky breaths in unison. It was as if their bodies remembered the way they had once blended together so effortlessly, like the smudging of oil pastels; one a fiery red, and one metallic and golden.

"I haven't written a letter to Stanley since I returned to London," Angie whispered, like a sinning Catholic at confession.

"Good."

It was all Thea could say.

"That doesn't mean he's gone anywhere," Angie continued, keeping her eyes closed.

"End it."

"What?" Angie laughed, raking her eyes back up the Thea's face.

Angie hadn't let go of her collar, but had loosened her grip.

"End it. Come back to me. You would have written to him if you loved him."

A lifetime seemed to flash before Angie's eyes. Perhaps, she was imagining all the loses she'd face if she were to choose Thea: No children, no marriage and a life of people growing suspicious and eventually disgusted. Thea was scanning her mind for something to convince her, but what could a Welsh farmer's daughter offer somebody like Angie?

"Think about what it would be like to fall in love with me again," Thea tried, with a desperate smile.

It was a heart-breaking, painful, ridiculous smile, paired with an equally ridiculous idea. Thea didn't know if she'd suggested it with any scrap of hope that Angie would agree, or whether she'd suggested it knowing Angie would decline, and she just wanted the comforting knowledge that at least she'd tried, one last time.

"No," Angie said.

She released her grip on Thea's shirt. Thea closed her eyes so hard she saw funny shapes. It must have looked strange, but it was better than Angie see her eyes well up with tears.

"Why?"

Thea waited for Angie to say 'Stanley'.

"Because you'll only hurt me."

Thea opened her eyes to see Angie turning away.

"Don't pretend it's because I hurt you when I stopped writing. That isn't why you're running," Thea said, stopping her.

"It's not because of Stanley, Thea, so don't even think of saying that."

"No." Thea nodded, mostly to herself. "It's because you deserve better. The world is unfolding before you and there's a train waiting for you that goes so much further than London to Wales. The whole world is at your feet and I can't even last a day in a busy city. You love people and all I want to do is hide away. That's the biggest problem. You are too compassionate to live your life hiding how you truly feel. I can do it, because I

316

keep everything inside anyway, but you... you need to—
"

Thea must have closed her eyes again at some point, because she hadn't realised that Angie had come close again. It was Angie's little hand, cupping her cheek, that made Thea feel like she'd been woken for the first time in months.

Angie was crying; Thea watched a tear trickle down her button nose to settle in the corner of her mouth. She wanted to kiss it, and taste the salt and sweet of Angeline Carter once again.

"—you need to walk down an aisle, in some big poufy dress, holding some flowers that bring out your eyes," Thea teased, recalling something Peggy had said.

It got a laugh out of Angie, followed by more tears.

"You need to stand on some tall building and announce your love to the world. You need to travel to another country for a honeymoon and stay in some fancy hotel and roll around in rose petals on your wedding night. You need to dance in the street, with the person you love holding you," Thea croaked, shaking her head. "And I... I *can't* be that. And I'm so, so sorry."

Angie pressed her forehead to Thea's, and the world seemed to let out a sigh of relief at the touch.

"I never wanted that," Angie whispered. "I just wanted *you*."

They were in a bubble, like the one they formed in 1943. And it was reckless, because anybody could have stepped into the hallway and seen them. But that didn't seem to matter, because Angie raised her chin up and pressed her lips to Thea's.

It was a delicate kiss; a fragile moment. One that should be cradled like a baby bird. It tasted like tears. And they were shaking, together.

Thea leant away.

"What would you do, if I told you that made me fall in love with you all over again?"

Angie brought her free hand up to cup Thea's other cheek.

"What would you do, if I told you I never stopped?"

CHAPTER THIRTY-THREE

Alan Hallwood

Snow in March wasn't uncommon in Scotland. Lottie had told him when he complained about layering a shirt, jumper, blazer and coat just to go for a walk. He spent far more time with Lottie since Angie had left for London. Stanley was a little more attached to his sister now too. So, in less than a week, the three of them became a trio. It wasn't that they hadn't been close when Angie was there, but Stanley and Angie seemed to prefer each other's company to the company of a small group.

Alan liked this change. There was an absence of subconscious competitiveness without Angie. Her smiles and moments of laughter were so few and far between, that both Alan and Stanley wanted to be the prime reason she was happy. Stanley, as a romantic partner, and Alan as a friend. A best friend. Lottie sort of floated above it all; a superior presence, in Alan's eyes. Her awareness of music, culture and *everything* was so admirable that Alan saw her as greater than human. He thought Stanley believed the same. And thus, Alan came to a personal conclusion that he and Stanley were not as different as he had once suspected.

"I do have a confession," Stanley announced one Thursday evening, when classes were over and they lounged in the light of the pub's roaring fire.

Thursday walks to Lottie's favourite bookshop, followed by a pint at *The Red Lion*, were to become a tradition. Stanley only worked in the mornings, perfectly content with his little job at the Greengrocers, and lectures finished early on Thursdays. Plus, it was 'Student Night' and the town was buzzing, and the drinks were cheaper. Thursday outings really were ideal.

"Do tell, brother," Lottie said with a raised brow and a grin.

Alan could always feel the comfortable air between the two, even when they were bickering. It made him wish he hadn't been an only child who'd done nothing but disappoint his father. Growing up, he'd been certain he had no ability to love or be loved. But, it didn't seem to matter when he taught himself to live vicariously, by watching love flow between others, and by escaping to fictional universes through prose and poetry.

"I hate going to your bloody bookshop. I only go out with you two for a free pint," Stanley admitted.

Alan snorted, looking at Lottie who joined in laughing. Stanley pouted, raising his hands in question.

"That's not exactly a secret," Alan explained. "We all know you'd rather watch paint dry than read a book."

"Hey! I read that one Angie gave me," Stanley protested.

"*The Wonderful Wizard of Oz* is a children's book," Lottie laughed.

"With a deep, alleg... al..."

"Allegorical meaning?" Alan supplied, eyes sparkling with interest as he searched Stanley's eyes for an answer. "Do tell."

Stanley ducked his head sheepishly.

It was no secret that Stanley was a ridiculously handsome man, with his dark, curly hair and low voice and his adorable confused face whenever Lottie went off on a tangent. It didn't hurt Alan, being attracted to men. He was growing used to it, and just basking in Stanley's company, positivity and general radiance was enough.

"It's about American politics at the time, I believe," Lottie filled in Stanley's absent knowledge. "Although I read that one critic argued that The Scarecrow represented agriculture and..."

As Lottie went on, Stanley's oblivious expression appeared. Alan smiled uncontrollably in his tipsy state, fumbling his pint to have a sip of his beer. Some sloshed over the side and Alan cursed under his breath, grabbing Stanley's attention. Their eyes met and Stanley smiled.

At first, Alan felt a little guilty for fancying Stanley. But, it wasn't like it would lead anywhere, and Angie didn't love Stanley or anything.

Lottie's ramble about American 'democracy' came to an end after a while. She must have sensed that nobody was really interested. A silence settled between the three and Stanley was staring at a spot on the table, zoned out. Alan looked at Lottie, eyes asking: *What's wrong with him?* Lottie, miraculously, understood what the look meant, and shrugged.

Finally, Stanley broke the silence.

"Do you think Angie will come back?"

Alan swallowed, he'd been dreading any mention of his best friend. He wasn't the type to get argumentative and feared Lottie and Stanley would be rude about Angie's decision. They must have realised that Angie had been withdrawn since her departure. Her lack of letters revealed this. Alan feared he'd say too much if he had to defend Angie. Stanley was clearly already suspecting her motives for leaving.

"She's left a lot behind," Alan began.

Lottie pressed her lips together in contemplation, reading Alan's every move. Stanley just stared at Alan obliviously.

"She never really settled here, did she?" Alan shrugged, trying to act casually as he had another swig of beer.

"Did she say she wouldn't come back? Can she just leave Uni like that? I thought education was what mattered to her most," Stanley said, baffled.

"She didn't explicitly say anything." Alan saw Lottie place a comforting hand on her brother's forearm. "This was a fantasy, for her. You *know* that, Stanley."

"But... but... she..."

"It was harsh of her to lead Stan on," Lottie said. "She's treated him like something disposable. What, did she just feel sorry for him? Was that it?"

Her chest was rising and falling rapidly as she grew more frustrated. Though, Alan acknowledged, she looked more upset than Stanley did. His face was blank. He patted Lottie's shoulder, nodding to himself.

"I know you both think I'm stupid, but I think I figured her out a while ago," Stanley said.

"We don't think that—"

"Lott, it's fine," Stanley laughed and, judging by his bright eyes and wide grin, it really *was* fine. "She's a wonderful person, we all know that. But clearly this wasn't her first choice. She made do with what she had, being forced into a situation she didn't want to be in. I don't know where she'd rather be, but she seemed so absent, all the time. I don't think that's our fault, and I think we should be honoured that we got to know her. Even for a few months. *We* made her life more bearable, *we* got to make her smile. All we can hope now, is that she finds what she was missing."

Alan had been holding his breath for the duration of Stanley's speech. He didn't think he'd ever heard him say so much in one go. But, both he and Lottie were positively breathless.

They left the pub after a few more drinks; Alan and Lottie on the beer, but Stanley quite content with lemonade after his first pint. Stanley's mood had altered. He was less reserved, as if his little speech about Angie had given him some well-deserved self-worth and confidence to speak freely. Or perhaps, he'd just laid out the truth in front of his own eyes, and it calmed him to accept the reality that he'd have to let Angie go.

They stumbled up the cobbled streets of Edinburgh, heading back to Stanley's flat. Lottie was giggling at anything anyone said, and had her arms around her brother and Alan's shoulders. They walked like that, helping each other when they tripped or skidded on the icy, uneven ground, and smiling and laughing so hard that their cheeks hurt. They spoke about nothing important, until Lottie posed a question, one that must have been playing on her mind. Perhaps it had been playing on Stanley's, too.

"Did Angie leave a lover behind? Is that what was missing?" Lottie asked.

Alan looked towards Stanley as Lottie asked the question, wondering how he'd respond. He looked at Alan with a curious expression, though he appeared absent of any jealousy.

"No," Alan admitted. "I think she left a part of her soul, maybe."

Lottie's eyes widened a little and they all slowed down as they reached Stanley's apartment. There was a moment where the only sound was the snow as it crunched under their boots. Both Lottie and Alan waited for Stanley to say something. Lottie unlinked them and Stanley turned to face his sister and Alan, eyes flickering between the two.

"We better get searching, too, hm? Find the other halves of our souls," Stanley smiled.

Alan took a step forward and placed a hand on his friend's shoulder.

"I think some people are born with only *small* parts of their soul missing. I don't think those people need a soulmate to fill the gap. I think they just need good company, a hatred for reading, beer, a wonderful sister who loves them endlessly and a smile that seems to brighten everyone's day."

Stanley put his hand on top of Alan's, glancing at his sister. And, in a tipsy and clumsy and ridiculous manner, the three of them hugged.

Snowflakes landed in their hair and their clothes were probably getting all creased, Stanley's landlady could see them all through the window and was looking at them strangely. But none of that seemed to matter, because Alan was finally getting a taste of what it felt like to be loved.

CHAPTER THIRTY-FOUR

<u>Angeline</u>

Following their kiss, Thea and Angie found their seats and sat opposite each other. Thea squeezed in beside the boys and Angie sat beside Florence, with Peggy and Thomas next to her. The position made it difficult for Angie to look at anybody but Thea, though she doubted anything could avert her attention anyway, not when her lips were still tingling and her heart rate had yet to slow down.

Seeing Thea reunite with her younger brothers brought her nothing but regret for the time she'd let slip through her fingers. It made her question everything. Conversation between Angie and her brothers did not flow as easily as the conversation between Thea and the boys. She wondered whether they would ever truly forgive Angie for leaving home and failing to communicate with them, in any way, for months. She was starting to question whether university had been worth it.

"How was Edinburgh, Angeline?" Florence asked, as if reading her thoughts.

Thea looked up, for the first time since she'd sat down. Her cheeks were flushed red with excitement and it seemed as though she'd been utterly consumed by talking to the boys. Angie hated that she felt a little jealous, had Thea missed *her* that much?

"It was pleasant."

Peggy leant forward, resting an elbow on the table in front of her, to rest her chin in her hand and listen. But Angie didn't have much more to say.

Learning had always been something Angie honoured, specifically seeing her mother longing for the freedom that higher education often provided. And yet, she lacked the passion for it now. It was as if the farm and Thea had opened her eyes to the life she wanted, and it was too late to turn back and choose something else. University had been wonderful, but she would never settle. It was like trying to read a book that one rated as average, after reading the best book in existence.

"You talk about it as if the experience is over," Thea remarked.

Her tone was curious and questioning, and Angie felt a little frustrated, because it felt as if Thea was asking her whether she was planning to leave university. It felt as if Thea was awaiting a definitive answer right in that moment. Angie didn't see herself going back, but she could hear her father's voice in the back of her mind, telling her it was a waste of such a valuable experience.

Kissing Thea had sent her heart racing fast enough for one day and Angie thought it would be wise if any other major decision-making was avoided.

Evidently, Florence didn't share this thought, as she was leaning forward and listening with a keen interest.

Peggy didn't lift her head up from Thomas' shoulder. Thomas was humming a song, clearly uninterested and just happy to have the window seat. Angie wondered what it would be like to be in a relationship so carefree and relaxed. Nothing seemed to faze them. Their conversation never seemed to be heated, and they were constantly at peace. Of course, Angie hadn't been there to witness the entirety of their relationship, but she didn't think Thea and her had gone more than a few hours without a row, in their entire time together. Was Peggy and Thomas' relationship everything that love should be? Could happiness be found for a couple who were as strikingly different as Thea and Angie? The complication that Thea and Angie were both women, only seemed to be the start of their problems.

Angie internally scorned herself for letting her thoughts get carried away. But one thing was blatantly obvious: she was considering what the future would look like for her and Thea. She'd never so much as considered it with Stanley. Angie didn't think she'd care if she and Thea spent their entire lives screaming at each other, red-faced, with tears streaming down their faces. She didn't think she'd care if Thea frustrated her so much she got daily headaches. If it was Thea causing her pain, it didn't seem matter. Because Angie would sell her soul for a future with Dorothea Miller, no matter what it looked like. And that, she believed, was what provoked her to say,

"I don't think I shall return to Edinburgh."

Her brothers looked to her with a sudden interest and surprise. If Angie had a mirror, she reckoned she herself would be wearing a similar expression.

"What?" Thea asked, sitting up straight and uncrossing her arms.

Thea had had her arms around her stomach since she'd sat down, and she looked a little pale. Angie smiled to herself, deciding to put a little colour in her cheeks as she leant forward slightly. She was closer to Thea than anybody had ever seen her be. She felt Florence stiffen beside her, and she could hear Peggy gasp subconsciously and she could sense her brothers' wide eyes. She reached across the carriage and took Thea's hand, bringing it to rest on the table. She laced their fingers together and met her grey-blue eyes.

"I go where you go," Angie declared.

Thea's eyes didn't leave hers either, even when Charles perked up and said to his sister,

"Father was silly to try and set you up with George Clark. Everybody knows you love Dorothea."

Angie let out a little laugh. She felt her cheeks warming and ducked her head.

She wondered when the fear of discovery had faded away. Perhaps it was only in that moment, when she had decided that nothing else really mattered. She'd disobeyed her father before and it was thrilling. She'd only be doing the same again.

They were going home, Thea was going to fix whatever had been broken with her mother, and Angie was surrounded by a love that was not forced, as it had been in Edinburgh. It was a love born of an unfortunate circumstance, that turned into something eternal. It turned into family. And, looking around at her brothers' adorable wide-eyes, Peggy cuddled up to Thomas and Florence smiling proudly, Angie realised she had nothing to be afraid of in their presence.

The journey felt shorter than it had on their first trip to Wales. It only struck Angie in that moment that she'd only ever been in this position once before, a lifetime ago, when Michael had been notoriously cheeky. Peter wouldn't eat his lunch because he'd eaten too much chocolate, and Charles had pressed his face up against the mucky window when William had tried to be sensible. The memory hadn't been recalled in such a long time that it actually left Angie feeling a little disorientated at how long it had been since the war.

She still held Thea's hand; an anchor to reality. Though, Thea looked a little troubled herself.

Angie tuned into the conversation when Florence nudged her gently. Angie tilted her head to look up at the woman. She'd aged beautifully, and the ring on her left hand hadn't gone unnoticed.

"Why haven't you brought your partner?" she asked.

"He's a doctor, therefore, a very very busy man," Florence explained.

William sat up excitedly. "*I* want to be a doctor," he declared.

Angie hid her surprise, and Thea smiled at him fondly, as if she already knew this information.

It was striking how distanced Angie had become from her brothers, and it scared her a little.

"You'd be a wonderful doctor," Florence said, turning to Thea. She looked directly at Thea, as opposed to their joined hands. It was obvious how comfortable Florence was with them, and Angie wanted to thank her. "Do you remember when I told you about my cousin?"

Thea nodded, and the boys continued with a conversation amongst themselves, about who would get to sit by the window on the train home. It was strange that Angie didn't see herself going with them.

"John is my cousin," Florence explained to an oblivious Angie. "He's a homosexual. I had to tell Thea about him so that she'd understand that I would respect her, in the same way I respect him. Anyway, he's found himself a partner. They're living together, and they're happy."

Angie looked at Thea with wide, hopeful eyes, praying that she, too, saw this as confirmation that they had a chance together. But Thea lowered her head, clearing her throat before dropping Angie's hand.

"Good for them," Thea said bluntly.

Florence pressed her lips into a thin line, Peggy stirring from where she rested on Thomas' shoulder.

"So, there's hope for you two," Florence elaborated. "Times are changing. The expectations for women are changing."

"What would *you* know about changing times?" Thea snapped, silencing everyone in the carriage.

Florence laughed weakly, shaking her head and looking Thea directly in the eye.

"I suppose you're right. What would an infertile woman know about the changing expectations for women?"

Thea stiffened and began to stutter out an apology.

"You don't need to be so pessimistic all the time," Angie interrupted her.

Peggy closed her mouth and smiled softly.

"Well, that's exactly what I was going to say," Peggy said.

Thea rubbed her upper arm.

"I'm sorry. I know it's no excuse but I... I just don't want to think about stuff like this. The future, I mean. Of course, I want you in it Angie." Thea looked up, squeezing her hand under the table. She was shaking a little and Angie wondered if she was anxious or felt a little travel sick. "I just don't want to let her down. I don't want her to think badly of me if she's going to..."

The word 'die', ironically, died on her tongue. Angie opened her mouth to ask who 'her' was but Peggy interrupted.

"Mrs Miller."

Angie watched Thea shiver again, and she squeezed her hand back, still under the table, rubbing little circles on her palm. Perhaps, Thea was not yet comfortable enough to display affection.

Angie had seen Mrs Miller at different highs and lows throughout her evacuation, but it seemed that she was always acting in her daughters interest. Even when she tried to keep the death of James and Arthur a secret, it was to protect a deadly turmoil of emotions. Of course, it was not a well-thought out decision, but Mrs Miller had done it with a good heart. It was difficult for Angie to picture Mrs Miller ever turning her daughter away.

"We'll be okay," Angie promised in a low voice.

Thea squeezed her hand.

"If not, come and live with us." Thomas perked up.

"Or come home," Michael suggested to Angie.

"Father wouldn't tolerate you," William said, unafraid of speaking the truth. "If you leave Edinburgh, and you aren't getting married…"

"He's right," Peter said. "We're pretty pissed at you for abandoning us but we don't want you cast out of our lives for good."

"Language," Florence scorned.

Angie was too busy trying to calm her racing heart to tell him off. Because Peter was confirming that the boys *did* still love their sister.

"Well, Peggy and I will always welcome you," Thomas continued.

"Enough," Thea snapped, looking a little green. "Please."

Thomas blushed and the boys lowered their heads guiltily. There was a moment of awkward silence, and Thea fumbling for a paper bag indicated that it was a mix of both anxiety and travel sickness that was bothering her.

"Can we talk about the wedding?"

CHAPTER THIRTY-FIVE

Dorothea

They arrived in Wales in the late evening. The days were drawing out, so there was still a little bit of light left. Thomas and William were carrying everyone's bags, in a very gentlemanly manner. Peggy and Florence insisted that Thea had to see her mother first, alone. Thea thought it was ridiculous, given the time. They were all exhausted from their day of travel and needed sleep. Plus, though Thea had tried to hide it, she hadn't quite recovered from her travel-sickness. Such tiredness warned her that a reunion with her mother, alone, wouldn't be ideal.

"Well, we can't all just show up. It's too much pressure to put on Mrs Miller in one day," Peggy insisted.

"We don't exactly have any other choice," Michael groaned, frustrated. "Please. I am so tired."

"What about a B&B?" William suggested, face red from the exhaustion of carrying bags.

Angie came forward to take a few, he opened his mouth to protest but her ruffling his hair silenced him.

The bond between Angie and her brothers seemed to be repairing itself gradually. Perhaps, in the Welsh air, they'd recall all their memories on the farm, and they'd realise the simplicity and peaceful life that they had left behind. Perhaps then, they'd stay. Thea could only hope, no matter how outlandish the idea was.

They settled on finding a B&B in the end. It was the largest one in the village, white with black beams. The woman at the desk seemed disapproving upon her declaration that they needed rooms to house nine people for the night.

"Eight," Peggy interrupted.

Thea paled, glaring daggers at her.

When they went upstairs to the rooms; a double for Peggy and Thomas, and a single for Florence and a five-person for Angie and her brothers, Thea pulled Peggy aside.

"You can't expect me to go home, seriously Peggy," Thea said, pinching the bridge of her nose, still feeling greatly nauseous.

Peggy wasn't listening.

"Dorothea, we're all exhausted. I'm not arguing with you now."

"I can't go on my own."

Peggy let out a frustrated sigh, slouching on the stairs. Thea sat down beside her, hearing doors close behind them as everybody found their rooms. Thea glanced behind her, at the three doors along the corridor. She spotted Angie, lingering in the hallway.

The shift between them was undeniable. Angie, unexpectedly, was pouring her whole heart into their relationship now. She'd been brave enough to stop hiding in front of her family. *Their* family. Thea couldn't help distancing herself a little, fearing it was only a temporary hope, and she'd soon leave. It happened last time. But then: *I go where you go.*

"Come with me," Thea breathed out, barely audible.

Angie read her lips and nodded in agreement.

"I'll go with you."

Peggy glanced behind her, a smile pulling at the corner of her lips. She stood, and walked away to her room without another word. Their walk through the village was more or less silent, too. Occasionally, Angie would let out a breathless laugh and mumble something about how strange it was to be back in Wales. Thea remained reserved, internally counting her breaths like Angie had been on the train platform. It did little to settle her distress.

Angie didn't push her to speak, as she once had. Thea could almost hear Angie's mind racing. Thea did not have enough energy to comfort her with words, so she took her hand. Angie didn't open her mouth to protest. It was quiet, the streets mostly empty and only lit by some old gas lamps. Despite the end of the war, it seemed everyone was still too afraid to produce light that would attract attention.

It was strange. How much an outside source, such as a war, affected relationships. It was as if, during war years, a layer of restraint had been ripped away from everyone. Everything was passionate and open, as there was no time to hide any feelings, when the fear of death was looming over everyone. Though, dynamics between people changed with many factors. Time, place, other people. Thea and Angie had faced all and yet there they were, holding hands, on their way to confess the truth to Thea's mother. Even after all this time, and after everything that had happened. They were just flesh and bone and, despite the hatred of other people's beliefs, they'd found their way back to each other. As if they were linked, as if they had *always* been linked. To express such a thing in words would be futile.

"We are infinite, Angie," was all Thea could whisper.

Angie didn't look at her, though Thea's eyes never left Angie. She watched her brow, her lips, her eyes and any feature that would show her what Angie was thinking. Thea didn't think Angie would respond to such a thing. Her expression remained neutral, and Thea gave up searching. She was too busy watching the way the stars reflected in Angie's eyes. After a long while, the silence was broken. And it felt as if the whole sky and all the planets, stars and galaxies lit up as bright as the sun.

"Yes. Yes we are."

*

Thea didn't knock, when she reached the front of the place she grew up. The ivy crawling up the wall was now tickling the borders of the door frame. As if the cottage was soon to be submerged amongst the weeds.

338

Thea dropped Angie's hand, but gave her a reassuring look. That didn't seem to be enough for Angie, as she leant in close and pressed her forehead to Thea's. It felt like a kiss.

Thea bent down and found the spare key, still in the empty plant pot. She opened the door as quietly as possible, and watched the lamp in the porch, that occasionally flickered, brighten the ugly floral paper in the hallway. She entered the house, Angie close behind, and traced the faded colours, marks and scratches. The radio could be heard in the kitchen, as well as the distinctive sound of her mother washing dishes that undoubtably did not need to be washed, in search of something to pass the time. Thea could feel her palms growing sweaty and her breaths came faster. Angie hung back as Thea turned the kitchen doorknob.

There was a glass of red wine on the table, next to a half-empty bottle. Beside it, knitting needles, tangled wool, and a pathetic excuse for a blue scarf. Her mother turned upon the sound of the door creaking and she dropped the plate she washed in the sink. The smashing sound echoed around them, as Thea's mother wept. Tears trickled down Thea's own cheeks and nothing else seemed to matter.

Suddenly, she was a little girl again. She was a little girl who had ruined her best dress, and it had upset her mother. At first, it didn't seem to matter, and being so naughty made a child feel like she could rule the world. But, eventually, daughters come to the conclusion that the only thing that seems to matter is knowing that they have their mother's trust, love and attention. There was nothing a daughter longed for more, than a mother who was on her side.

They found themselves in an embrace, clinging to each other like ivy clings to oak.

"I'm sorry, Mum." Thea could feel how frail her mother was as she sobbed. "I'm sorry. I'm sorry. But I can't change, I can't. And I don't want to. It's just me. It's just who I am, who I have always been. And I wanted to change, for so long. But I'm just… I'm just *me.*"

"Dorothea," her mother whispered. She had frozen at Thea's words, and leant out with her bottom lip trembling. "You are my daughter. You are everything. You are the only thing that matters."

Thea was lost for words.

"Mother, will you not hear me? Will you not hear what I have told you? I *will not* change."

Her mother brought a cold hand up to Thea's cheek, wiping a tear away with the pad of her thumb, as she had done when she was a little girl, stubbornly trying not to cry when she scuffed her knee.

"And do you know where you get that from?"

Thea cried a little more.

"You get that from you father."

"I thought you hated me." Thea put her hand on top of her mother's, closing her eyes.

It was hard to see her mother looking so unwell, knowing that she'd left her to suffer all alone.

"I feared *for* you," her mother clarified.

"You don't have to do that anymore."

340

"I know that now," she sobbed, bringing her other hand up to cup Thea's face. "How is it you look so grown up now? Hm?"

Thea pressed her lips together, ducking her head.

"It's because I know so much now. I know that I have nothing to fear anymore. And I know that no matter what, I refuse to change. Also... that I bloody hate London."

Her mother laughed softly and seemed unable to stop studying her daughter's face. She wanted to tell her mother more than that, she wanted to tell her that she knew exactly what she wanted in life, and that she would never be complete without Angie. But that seemed to be too much, all at once, and Thea still feared letting herself acknowledge these inescapable desires, fearing the pressure it would put on Angie.

"And, how is Lizzie?" Her mother raised a brow, curious, though not judgemental.

"It was never Lizzie," Thea managed, too tired to blush or shy away.

Angie appeared in the doorway. Even after a day of travel, she was the image of beauty. Like a figure in a stained glass window. Was it immoral for Thea to compare her to a holy, angelic being?

A flash of realisation crossed her mother's face, and her lips parted. She had to sit down, and stifle a laugh.

"How could I have been so oblivious?" Mrs Miller said. "Is this why you went to London?"

"No, I stayed with Peggy," Thea said. " I didn't think I would see Angeline again. But, Peggy is getting married, everyone was gathering together."

"Married?" Her mother's eyes lit up, then she slanted her mouth. "I wasn't invited?"

"Well, I... asked her not to invite you," Thea explained guiltily.

"Ah. So, why are you here?"

"We're all here," Angie said. "When we got the letter expressing you had fallen ill, well, Peggy postponed the wedding. And here we are."

Her mother looked a little overwhelmed, a little bewildered, and a little over-the-moon.

"All of you?"

"All but Heather and Scary Mary," Thea answered.

"Scary Mary," her mother chuckled.

"Well, she wasn't as accepting as you have been," Angie explained.

"She knew?"

"Yes."

"Oh goodness."

"She threatened us." Angie looked at Thea and, God, Thea wanted to hold her hand.

But perhaps that was too much, too soon. And she didn't want to get carried away with Angie, and lure herself into a false sense of security that they had a future.

"Girls." Thea's mother glanced between the two, standing up to hug Angie. Thea glanced at them affectionately, her heart aching as she wished this could be the start of something new. The start of something eternal, everlasting... *infinite*. "I wish you'd told me."

Thea didn't put herself through the trouble of explaining why she had not.

The evening passed by. It started with Thea's mother offering tea, and ended with them sharing a bottle of wine. It slipped away as fast as 1943 and 1944 had. Thea's mother seemed open and interested in most things, even despite her clear exhaustion. Though, she didn't ask many questions about Thea and Angie, and their relationship. A part of Thea was thankful, because she undoubtably wouldn't be able to answer most of them without feeling overwhelmed. Plus, it was understandable that she'd need time to adjust. God knew Thea and Angie had yet to adjust themselves.

They spoke about the wedding, about the boys, about Angie's experience in Edinburgh, and how Lizzie had been there for Thea in a time when nobody else had. Angie didn't seem too jealous, as Thea wasn't when she spoke of Stanley and her friends in Edinburgh. It was only a mere episode of their lives, that shaped them as people. Thea avoided any mention of all she and learnt about her brother, James. They discussed Thea's mother's illness, though Thea suspected she was hiding the severity of her condition. Thea let her have her secret, as she hid what she had learnt of James. It seemed fair, in a world where she and her mother had faced so much unkindness and lost so much.

Seeing her mother beside Angie and being home again, in the place where she'd read her favourite books for the first time, where she'd heard Angie play piano, where she'd last danced with her father... Thea knew *exactly* where she belonged.

CHAPTER THIRTY-SIX

Angeline

It was past midnight when Mrs Miller finally went to bed. Angie stayed in the kitchen, watching Thea link arms with her mother and help her up the stairs. It was disturbing how pale Mrs Miller was, and her occasional wheezing and coughs that interrupted the flow of conversation, had been an uncomfortable reminder of why they were there. Thea had been acting strangely, but little else could be expected given the situation. The fact did nothing to stop Angie's concern that Thea was having second thoughts about: *I go where you go.*

Mrs Miller's response to their past relationship had been ideal. There was no room to complain. Angie just wasn't comfortable with how Thea spoke about it as if it had been just that: A *past* relationship. Was it nervousness? Was it the fear of admitting her true feelings in front of her mother? Or was Thea just being cautious? Had she reconsidered whether she still loved Angie? Reality seemed to be setting in now, as conversations about the future were yet to be had.

Thea was gone for a while. Her cheeks were tear-stained and red when she entered the kitchen once more, but her slight smile seemed to juxtapose her whole expression. Angie didn't ask what they spent so long talking about, and she never really found out.

Thea glanced over at the clock on the kitchen wall, her smile turning into a frown.

"We were gone for a while."

Angie looked to the clock, too. Angie had barely realised that an hour had passed.

"Yes, you were."

"What did you do whilst I was gone?" Thea asked awkwardly.

She was clearly just in search of making conversation, avoiding the things that really needed to be discussed.

"I did what I always do when you're gone." Angie stood up from the kitchen table, taking the last swig from her wine glass. "I waited for you to come back."

Angie looked at the cracked tiles of the kitchen floor, unsure if Thea was looking at her as she placed her glass back on the table. Thea was undoubtedly still hunting for the right words, if such even existed.

Angie thought it was most likely that Thea would open up in the quiet of the night. It had always been when the rest of the world was asleep, that Angie and Thea were most awake. It seemed unfair that their relationship had always been bound to the protective blanket of the night, but it became special for them, and

Angie found herself thinking of Thea, even more so, when night fell.

To the ticking of the clock, Thea stepped towards Angie, like a silent dance. When Thea was close enough that it become indetectable whose shaky breaths were whose, Angie looked up at her. Thea had her eyes on the ground.

"I want to go outside. For a walk."

"Alright," Angie said, incapable of doing anything but agreeing to all that she said, for fear that Thea would distance herself until she felt like a stranger

"I want you to come with me."

I go where you go died on Angie's lips.

"I'll come with you."

Thea nodded once, then made her way to the front porch.

"Borrow some of my walking boots. It's cold and your toes will fall off if you wear your pumps."

Angie didn't protest.

*

A lifetime ago, midnight walks were the thing Angie longed for most. At night, when loneliness consumed her as it so often did, she'd recalled their steps on each pathway, each bridge, each field. The world had once felt so vast, especially at night. It felt as if the entire universe had possibilities laid out for the both of them. But now, the world felt so small, and so insignificant.

Angie had explored corners of the country and had planted seeds in new places. And yet she had no intention to let them grow and flourish, because her

347

routes were buried deep beneath the soil of Wales. It seemed to her that, so long as Dorothea Miller walked this earth, they always would be.

They walked a route that Angie was familiar with. She knew exactly where they were heading from the first left turn. Angie lagged behind, uncomfortable in Thea's boots. Thea didn't seem to care, and had no intention of waiting for her to catch up.

"Thea, please," Angie panted. "Slow down, what's the rush?"

Thea didn't slow down, and Angie thought she heard her let out a laugh, but she couldn't tell because there was a grumble of thunder. Angie was beginning to wonder whether Thea was taking her all this way to talk about her mother's illness. Angie wasn't sure whether her own mind was *too* consumed by Thea, feeling that their relationship was still a priority when Mrs Miller was so ill. She felt a little guilty about the whole thing. But Thea had been the one to change Angie's mind on that train platform, it seemed unfair for her to put their relationship on hold now.

Angie wrapped her coat tighter around herself, and stumbled behind Thea as she led her through the woods. They came to their clearing, and the lake made Angie's breath hitch in her throat. There were mostly buds in their flower field, it always looked best mid-spring, not at the end of winter. Angie recalled a distant memory of Thea telling her that violets most commonly bloomed in April.

Thea walked through the field, keeping her back to Angie as she came to a halt. She looked up at the sky, acknowledging the grey rain clouds that hid the stars.

"I want to be here when the violets bloom," Angie declared.

"Well, that's only a few weeks," Thea said, turning to face her. Her eyes remained on the ground. "You might still be here."

Angie clenched her fists in frustration, and the thunder rumbled once again. Angie spoke above it.

"I want to be here when the violets bloom next month. And I want to be here when they bloom in a month and a *year*. And I want to be here when they bloom in a month and *fifty* years."

They were too far apart to touch, facing one another like opposing chess pieces. Angie was certain Thea didn't know what move to make next.

"We'll spend all the days that we can together," Thea said.

Angie suspected she was refraining from saying 'until you return to London'. That thought alone made a cry escape Angie's throat. Rain started pounding and Angie thought she'd drown in it. It wasn't long before her wet hair was sticking to her face and her cotton coat was soaking right through. Angie tugged it off and threw it aside, uncaring. She was not fighting with Thea in a wet coat that she couldn't move in. Thea watched her movements, turning away when Angie stormed closer.

"I'd do anything for you, *anything*," Angie cried, chest burning with every hurried breath. "Is it Lizzie? Do you love her?"

Thea laughed into the rain. She combed back the wet curls that stuck to her forehead and then tugged on her locks in frustration.

"It's not Lizzie, Angie! It's *never* been her! Just like it's never been Stanley!"

When Thea raised her voice, Angie could have sworn her heart was beating just as hard as the pouring rain.

"Then what? Why won't you talk to me? Why won't you think about me staying? We'd be like Peggy and Thomas, Thea. Sure, we'd argue more. But that's just us. And I love it. And I want us to live together. I want us to be like a real family. "

"We're never going to *be* that, Angie! Don't you get it? I want to give you everything, but I can't."

Angie sobbed, shaking her head.

"Don't say that, don't *say* that! I'd take anything you gave me! Haven't I shown you that I don't want anything else but *you*?"

The rain was becoming more relentless. It was ridiculous that they were even out in such weather, they were bound to catch colds. But nothing else in the world mattered for Angie, and she'd been taught stubbornness by the very best.

"*You* were the one that came back to me, Thea," Angie cried. "*You* spoke to me on the train platform and you changed my mind. *You* made me realise that I don't want life if you aren't in it."

Thea let out a sob herself. Her distress was only confusing Angie further.

"You're just confirming my point, Angie."

"What point?"

"That I've already asked so much of you. I'm selfish. The most selfish person alive. And the worst part is that I can't stop. I'm going to ask for more. And it's ridiculous and unfair and dangerous, but that's all we've ever had to face. They haven't let us love each other any other way. So, I'm going to be selfish, because after what the world has taken from me, I deserve this."

Thea edged closer and Angie could see rain droplets clinging to the ends of her long, dark eye lashes. Her pupils were wide and she brought a hand up to Angie's neck, shaking from the cold or fear, Angie wasn't sure.

"What are you saying?" Angie whispered.

"I'm saying that I don't want to hold myself back, and I don't want to hold you back," Thea said, raising her hand up to cup Angie's cold cheek.

The sentence only reminded Angie painfully of what Thea had said before she made Angie swear to get married upon returning to London.

"I don't want to hear it," Angie hissed, walking away from her touch.

She stopped just at the edge of the lake, unafraid to hold back her cries. She didn't stop, even when she felt Thea came up behind her. She didn't stop, even when Thea's warm breath tickled her ears, and she wrapped her arms around Angie. Angie could do little else but relax into the touch, her head falling back against Thea's shoulder as a sob escaped her lips.

"I want to marry you."

Angie held her breath.

"I know it's not really possible, but I also don't really care. I don't care if everybody thinks it's pointless or fake. It would be real to me. I want you, every time the violets bloom, for the rest of our lives. And it's selfish. And I don't care. Because you're the only permanent thing left. When my mother passes I want no one but you. And it's not that I couldn't get by on my own, because I could, I shut everyone out and did it before. But I don't want to get by on my own anymore. I want you with me, forever. I want you to go where I go. Because I love you and it's *always* been you."

Angie couldn't move. She turned up to meet Thea's grey-blue eyes and her loving smirk. The smirk that had lured her in in the first place. She could do little else but lean in and press their wet lips together and laugh and cry and kiss until she felt dizzy.

It was then, that Angie opened her eyes and smiled tiredly, nodding with the little energy she could muster.

"You mad, mad woman."

And so they stood there, in the middle of the night, rain pounding on them. Angie's best coat was discarded on the muddy grass, as if she was throwing away her past life and immersing herself into a life with Thea.

It suddenly became so real. Never again would Angie have to experience the torturous pain of the possibility that Thea may only exist in her memories. She was real now, clear, bright and in colour.

Angie wasn't sure what marriage meant for them. But she could close her eyes and see the violets blooming and reaching up to the sun. They felt warm, even in the rain.

And, as they held each other, the time they had lost, the lives they had left behind, didn't matter. Not anymore.

someone, I tell you,
will remember us,
even in another time.

–sappho fr. 147

THE END.

ACKNOWLEDGMENTS

If someone asked me to express the true extent of my gratitude, I would need far more than a page...

Angeline and Dorothea are figments of a sixteen year old's imagination; one desperate for representation and a voice. And I have been heard.

I am eternally grateful for the support I have received from my Dad, Mum, Nanny, the Brathertons, Auntie Deb and my work family, my English teachers, my Godparents, Uncle Craig, Auntie Sarah, Scarlett, Eliza, Emily, Josh, Chris, Danny, Joe, Hannah, Ruby, James and Jude (to name a few!). It's easy to forget that many members of the LGBT+ community don't receive this support. So, yes, *The Lives We Left Behind* and *The Lives We Found* are partly for me and my family, but they are entirely dedicated to young people who don't have a voice yet, and for those beautiful souls that we have lost, who never had one.

Angeline and Dorothea are for you, and they will always be for you.

Printed in Great Britain
by Amazon